# Of
# Eagles
## and
# Ravens

The Eagle Wings Series

# Of
# Eagles
# and
# Ravens

Linda Rae Rao

Fleming H. Revell
A Division of Baker Book House Co
Grand Rapids, Michigan 49516

Published by Fleming H. Revell
a division of Baker Book House Company
P.O. Box 6287, Grand Rapids, MI 49516-6287

Printed in the United States of America

**Library of Congress Cataloging-in-Publication Data**

Rao, Linda Rae, 1943–
    Of eagles and ravens / Linda Rae Rao.
        p.   cm.— (Eagle wings series)
    ISBN 0-8007-5580-4 (paper)
      1. United States—History—War of 1812—Fiction. I. Title. II. Series:
Rao, Linda Rae, 1943– Eagle wings series.
PS3568.A595703    1996
813'.54—dc20                      95-43684

To Jeff and Jennifer,
our beautiful children

# Acknowledgments

In selecting the time period for the story of Christiana, Mac and Jessica Macklin's daughter, I settled on the years during the War of 1812. This very brief period in American history is often overlooked because many view it as a mere comedy of errors. While the country did suffer one humiliation after another, it was, however, during this time that many military traditions were established, the young republic was at last recognized as a truly independent nation, and the unique American character began to emerge with a feeling of greater national unity.

Since the true historic events of that time were as exciting as any a writer could ever invent, I chose to involve our characters more directly than in Books 1 and 2. This required more detailed research.

For their help in this research, I must thank my daughter, Jennifer, her high school history teacher, Doug Anderson, and the librarian at Willis High School, Gail Dillard. When needing specific information about the U.S. House of Representatives during the War of 1812, who better to call than my friend Kathy O'Brien who is staff assistant for U.S. Representative Jack Fields in his Conroe, Texas, office. Kathy kindly put me in touch with Ken Kato at the National Archives in Washington, D.C. Mr. Kato was very helpful, not only with basic facts, but also with insight into the mind-set of Americans during that time period.

I must also thank Anna Fishel and Sharon Van Houten for their wonderful editorial expertise in helping transform this story from manuscript to publication. Also, to the rest of the Revell staff for their part in the production of this book, my many thanks. It is a pleasure to work with such a great publishing company.

One can never underestimate the importance of a loving, supportive family. Without the continued encouragement and support of my husband, Buzzy, our children, Jeff and Jennifer, the rest of the family, and dear friend and agent, Helen Hosier, I might never have written this book.

Ultimately, my deepest gratitude must be to our heavenly Father for allowing all of this to happen. To him must go all honor and glory.

I hope you enjoy reading this book as much as I have enjoyed writing it.

# Prologue

An icy wind sweeping down from Lake Erie penetrated the deep forests along its southern shores. Moving inland through the woods, its gale was diminished to gusts swirling about a small clearing on the edge of the American frontier protected by Fort Stanford. Nestled in the clearing was a log hut with snow drifted high against its rough-hewn walls. The sighing of the wind through snow-shrouded fir trees was the only sound to be heard except for the occasional snuffling of the stocky draft horse hitched to the sleigh in front of the cabin. His little puffs of steamy breath clouded the crisp air as the horse stamped impatiently waiting for his passengers.

The fire burning brightly on the hearth inside the hut had little effect against the penetrating, late January cold that seeped in through the chinks in the mud plaster between the logs. Three men sat stoically watching two men across the table. Chenault, the bearded one in buckskins and a lynx-skin hat, was speaking to them in their Shawnee tongue while the other, his employer Axel Harrod, huddled in a fine woolen greatcoat and listened with a patronizing smile.

"Your friend has delivered the blankets for your people as promised," he said. "We know that your great leader,

Tecumseh, will be very happy that you go to join him and the British father, General Proctor, in the great struggle against the American intruders. After this, you will understand that some Americans are also allies of the English father across the water and trust his word."

The three Indians pulled their blankets closer about themselves and stood, prepared to leave. The man in the greatcoat hastily motioned to the bearded interpreter who then addressed one of the three, asking him to stay a moment longer.

Chenault frowned slightly at Harrod. He would relay the proposition, but he didn't have to agree with it. He had worked for the Canadians and the British as an interpreter and trapper for many years and, although this American businessman-soldier appeared to be sympathetic to the British-Canadian side of the border conflict, it never did sit well with Chenault for someone to profit from the misery of others, especially when it was done under the guise of loyalty to a cause. He had nearly had his fill of the foolishness of this war and was considering heading back to the wilderness, far away from the conflict.

The blue-eyed Shawnee waited. Nearly six feet tall, he had broad shoulders, indicating a powerful frame beneath the blanket held in place against the cold. The stern set of the jaw and the cold look in the young man's eyes convinced Chenault that he had been right to warn his pompous American employer not to take this Indian lightly or underestimate his cunning. If Harrod thought that because this man dressed in Shawnee garb was White he'd be more likely to take care of this special job, Harrod had better think again. Physically the young man was White, but mentally he was as Shawnee as old Tecumseh himself. However, unlike Tecumseh, who was a man of integrity, this one was treacherous. Chenault had heard stories about this one approaching the camps of White trappers using his Caucasian appearance to put them at ease. Then, when their guard was down, he would signal his small war party to attack.

The American became impatient with Chenault. He wanted to hurry back to his warm quarters at Fort Stanford and the hot meal that would be waiting for him. He normally left these meetings to his aide, who also appreciated the material benefits of this business on the side more than the meager compensation from the Army. However, this meeting was too important to leave to a subordinate.

Harrod was glad to discover the young Shawnee spoke English. He somehow never trusted interpreters to say exactly what he wanted them to say. Briefly he explained that there would be a group of American government officials coming to the fort the first week in February to inspect conditions there. If they found out that he had been selling provisions meant for American soldiers to the Indians, he would be taken away and the Indians would have to do without the supplies he had been channelling their way.

Harrod told the Indian it would be most advantageous to the Shawnee people and himself if the congressman leading the group should fall victim to a brief attack along the wilderness road between Fort Stanford and Erie, Pennsylvania. It must be a very controlled attack, however, with several of the party escaping to carry the news. The young Indian should come to the trading post at the fort on the specified day and Harrod, a quartermaster at the fort, would direct him as to who should survive and who should not.

Although the Shawnee refused to shake hands, Harrod had no doubt that he would carry out the plan. They understood each other. Like two jackals, they could work together to accomplish something of mutual benefit but would never dare turn their back one upon the other.

After the young Indian and his friends had left, Chenault and Harrod climbed into the sleigh. A smug, satisfied smile on his face, the American soldier settled under a heavy lap robe as the trapper grumbled about getting back to the high country to the west where one knew who was the enemy and who was not. A grizzly never made any pretense about being a friend while sharpening its claws. Chenault had no doubt that Harrod would welcome the congressman and his companions with open arms and warm hospitality then send them off with a smile and wave right into the trap he had just set for them.

If this was the civilized world of 1813, give Chenault the wilderness.

# 1

"Christiana! Christa, darling, it's a letter from your father," Jessica Macklin called up the stairs. An attractive woman in her early fifties, she still cut a trim figure in her travel ensemble of heather green linen and the matching bonnet that covered her chestnut brown hair, which was now generously streaked with gray.

"I'll be right down, Mother," came the reply from the second floor of the comfortable frame house.

The front door opened and a young man in his mid-twenties with curly sandy-colored hair and blue eyes entered. "Your trunk is all set, Mother. We'd better be on our way if we're to reach Lynchburg this evening."

"Thank you, Robert dear. We have a moment. This letter from your father just arrived."

In a flurry of muslin skirts, Christiana came rushing down the stairs. She looked very much like a younger version of her mother except her hair was much darker, and her eyes a bit bluer than the gray-green of her mother's eyes. Her constant companion, a big golden retriever named Copper, followed her closely. A fifteenth birthday present from her Uncle Rob two years before, the dog was seldom far from her side.

"When is he coming home?" Christiana asked.

"He's not sure." Jessica held up the letter as she read.

June 12, 1813

We've called an extended session here in Washington to try to pass the new military appropriation. If we can't get it through, we'll have redcoats marching the length of the country just like thirty years ago.

Tell Christiana I had dinner with the Burkes last night. Rachel sends her best wishes and is anxious for Christiana to return to Washington.

James came to town yesterday. He is fine but said to pray for Alex who is aboard the *Sea Sprite* making for Santo Domingo.

I miss you both. I was in hopes of getting home before you leave for the mission, but it looks impossible now. Thank Robert for escorting you over there and give my love to Ram, Marianne, and the children. If all goes well, I'll be able to come after you myself by the time our newest grandchild is born and Marianne is back on her feet . . .

Jessica stopped reading and smiled wistfully, "The rest is just a little note to me."

Christiana watched her mother's face as she silently read the last bit of the letter. She knew the words expressed her father's deep affection for her mother. She only hoped that someday she would find a young man who would put a sparkle in her eyes just like the thought of her father kindled a spark in her mother's.

Serving as a representative from Virginia, Andrew, or Mac as Jessica had always called him, was now in Washington in the midst of the turmoil surrounding "Mr. Madison's War" with England. The couple had been married for thirty-two years and still delighted in each other's presence. While seldom apart, Mac and Jessica now found themselves going in opposite directions.

The birth of Jessica and Mac's third grandchild was expected at any time. Their eldest son, Roger Aloysius Macklin (Ram for short), and his wife, Marianne, were living with their two children, Luke and Amy, at Mercy Ridge, the mission to the Cherokee Indians in the mountains just west of Lynchburg where they were carrying on the work started by Mac's grandparents many years before. Because Marianne's mother, Ada, had died when she was very young, she had asked Jessica to come to be with her at this time.

"Mother, we really must be going now," Robert reminded her gently.

"Yes, dear, of course." Jessica pulled on her gloves as she gave her daughter last-minute instructions. "Try to get Gran Barton to rest. I'm so afraid she'll overdo."

"Now, Mother, you know Gran. She'll just frown as sternly as she can manage and say, 'There's no glory in rust or dust!'"

Jessica and Christiana laughed together. The widowed mother of Franklin Barton, Mac's boyhood friend, Gran had come to stay with the Macklins many years ago to help Jessica take care of her newborn twin boys, Alexander and James, Christiana's older brothers. Christiana had been born three years later, and Gran was still there. Still energetic at nearly eighty, she had no intention of slowing down. Jessica couldn't imagine their home without her.

Just at that moment, Gran scurried into the entry hall carrying a basket covered with a white cloth. "Now, here's some chicken for your lunch, and I put in the rest of the blackberry pie from dinner last night."

"Thank you, Gran. You're a dear." Jessica smiled as she handed the basket to Robert.

After hugging Gran, Jessica then embraced Christiana tightly and kissed her cheek. "If all goes well with Marianne, I'll be back in three weeks."

Copper whined and nuzzled her hand. "You take good care of Christiana, Copper," Jessica said, bending down to stroke the broad golden-red head.

"Mother!" Her second son was anxious to be on the way. He lightly kissed Christiana's cheek and patted Copper's head then opened the door.

"Yes, dear," Jessica said as she and Robert hurried out to the carriage.

As they pulled away from the house, Jessica waved to Christiana and Gran who were standing on the porch of the house that had been their home for the past thirty-two years. She marveled at the sight of her youngest child, Christiana. When had she grown to be nearly a head taller than Gran? She'd always been a pretty child, but now she was becoming a beautiful young woman. Tears blurred Jessica's eyes with the realization that in all likelihood some young man would soon come along and Christiana would marry and establish a home of her own just like her four older brothers.

Glancing over at Robert, Jessica saw the reflection of her own brother, Robbie. Of the four boys, Robert was the one who had inherited her family's Scottish features as well as her brother's temperament. While Jess's brother, Robbie, had always tried not to be partial, it hadn't been easy when the nephew named after him had always taken a special interest in his horses at Cherry Hills Farms. When young Robert accepted the offer to move his new bride, Suzanne, to Cherry Hills to help manage the large thoroughbred operation, Robbie had been delighted. The horse farm located fifteen miles north of Dunston was well-known for the quality of breeding and training of their animals.

Robert looked at his mother. "Chris will be fine. Don't worry, now."

"I know," Jessica sighed. "I guess I was just thinking about how quickly you all have grown up. Reading your father's letter referring to the Revolution brought all those memories back. For the life of me, I can't imagine it happened so long ago. It seems like only yesterday that your father and I made that perilous trip to Charleston together when we first met.

"I can hardly wait for him to come to Mercy Ridge," she went on. "He needs to be away from Washington for awhile. He sounded very tired in his letter."

Robert laughed. "How could you tell that? Maybe he was worried about Alex going to sea with the British roving so close!"

"Of course, he's tired," Jessica interrupted. "I don't think he's rested very well since President Madison declared war last June. Everyone knows that the British troops haven't launched an all-out attack on us, because they're busy fighting Napoleon.

"Just look at what happened two months ago when they sailed right up the Rhappahanock River and captured the *U.S.S. Dolphin*. Our sailors have embarrassed the British best on the high seas and bruised their pride in the process. With the blockade tightening down, it's probably the worst time yet for either of the twins to be going to sea!"

Robert would like to have disputed his mother's words and comforted her, but he knew it would be foolish to try. She was right. The young United States of America was in a very precarious position these days. And now, June 1813, his younger twin brothers, James and Alexander, seemed to be in the thick of things with their shipping business in Boston. One of the biggest reasons for this war was the British practice of blatantly taking young American sailors off captured American ships and forcing them to serve in the King's navy. For this reason alone, Alex was obviously taking a very dangerous chance on the *Sea Sprite* trying to break out of the blockade.

His mother's voice drew Robert's attention back once more. "You do think Dunston is far enough away from the coast that we won't have to worry about Christiana and Gran, don't you?"

"Of course," he replied, "especially with the militia setting up headquarters just outside of town. They'll be quite safe."

# 2

Dunston was a quiet little village in the Piedmont district of Virginia. The Macklin family home and silversmith shop had been established here when Mac and Jessica were married. All five Macklin children had been born in this house, and Gran was convinced that she used to be able to hear the house sigh with relief at the end of each day when the children were all tucked in bed.

Gran sighed deeply now and turned to go back into the house. Christiana remained on the porch watching the carriage disappear down the lane and wishing she was going with her mother. Mercy Ridge was one of her favorite places in all the world.

But Christiana knew she had to stay home this time. Father would be back from Washington soon. He had been serving as a district representative in Congress for six years now, trying to balance the silversmith shop and his congressional duties. In the past two years, Christiana had taken over the bookkeeping duties for the shop as well as helping her mother manage the house and cook for her father's two apprentices who were living with them.

The two apprentices, Eric Lowe and Stephan Page, were able to handle the minor orders of repair or reproducing patterns developed by Macklin over the years and therefore helped keep the shop open when her father was away. Eric only had two more years of his seven-year apprenticeship to serve and was very adept in his work. Page was a newcomer, and while Christiana had her doubts, her father said he showed promise.

A short time after her mother and Robert left, Christiana sat in the study making a few notations. The house seemed so quiet it made Christiana uneasy. She found herself longing for the days when all four of her brothers were still at home.

It had been a lively household, full of love and laughter. She could remember the last two years before the twins had gone off to Harvard in 1808. They had found great delight in teasing her, and she had more than once chased them through the house declaring she could hardly wait until they were gone to school so she could have some peace. Now it was too peaceful. She missed them all terribly. Although she was thankful Robert lived close by, she especially missed the twins.

Christiana tried to shake the melancholy mood that had settled upon her. Somehow Copper sensed her feelings and leaned against her, nudging her hand with his wet nose. She reached down and scratched behind his ear. "Come on, boy, we could both use a little fresh air. Nothing helps cheer me like tending the flower garden."

From the study, she could hear the tapping of the shaping mallet in the shop as one of the young men, Eric she guessed, was shaping a blank sheet of soft silver into a new piece, probably the tankard ordered by Mrs. Abbot for her husband.

Eric Lowe had been a great help to her father since beginning his apprenticeship five years ago. He had a good eye for form and style. A local boy two years older than Christiana, he was third born of eight children. His father was a veteran of the Revolutionary War as was her father. Since the Macklin home was no longer as crowded as the Lowe house, the new apprentice had moved in with them. A bit irresponsible at times, Eric had nevertheless proven a good student and Christiana's father had begun to allow him to work on some of the more important pieces they were producing.

Then there was Stephan Page. He'd only been in their house for three months and while he seemed responsible, there was something about him that bothered Christiana. She had been a bit surprised by her father's lack of caution about the young stranger. When she had expressed her concern, her father had only smiled and assured her she needn't worry for Copper had taken to him and the dog had always been a pretty good judge of character.

Strangely enough, it was true. Copper was not especially fond of Eric, but he had made friends quickly with Stephan. Yet, this fact had not swayed her lack of trust. To Christiana, Stephan was not what he appeared to be. The fact she had caught him watching her father carefully, as if to measure what sort of man he was, possibly to find a point of vulnerability, did not help matters at all.

Andrew Macklin was a man of integrity and well respected. However, Christiana realized that whenever a man is willing to stand up for what he thinks is right and is asked to be a leader in the community, there is always the chance of making enemies with those who do not have the public good at heart. Over the years, she had watched her father stand up to local bullies and rowdies. He was never one to look for trouble, but he had never stepped back from it either, if it was unavoidable. Such men tend to be envied and sometimes even hated by lesser men.

Mac's daughter had been especially concerned about her father's safety since the assassination attempt during an inspection trip this past winter at Fort Stanford. Her father had been slightly wounded; the man standing next to him had been killed. If the government officials had not received an anonymous warning and been accompanied by additional guards, the entire party might have been wiped out.

Upon his return home, Christiana's father had said little about the incident. She had learned the disturbing details from their old family friend, Harold Smythe, who had been with the inspection party. Smythe had known Mac and Jessica since before they were married; as an attorney, he had administered the estate Jessica inherited during the Revolutionary War. Now a U.S. District Judge, Smythe had been appointed by the President to travel with the party as an observer.

An escort of ten soldiers accompanied Mac and Nathaniel Burke (both members of the House Military Affairs Committee), Smythe, and two congressional aides. They travelled on horseback with Smythe riding in a cabriolet.

The commander of the fort was Colonel Edward S. Sloane, one of Mac's officers during the Revolutionary War. An able officer fighting the war, he was now in his late seventies and relied heavily upon his staff to carry on the operation of the fort. Unfortunately, the quartermaster, Axel Harrod, had tremendous influence on the colonel. It had disturbed Mac greatly to see that his old commander's abilities had diminished and that he was relying on someone Mac knew to be of questionable character. Reluctant to make any accusations against Harrod without solid evidence, Mac was aware that such a scandal would reflect badly on Colonel Sloane. He also must move with caution for there were those who might suspect Mac was causing trouble for Axel Harrod because his father, Rupert, was a competitor of the twins in the shipping business out of Boston. Rupert was also one of the most vocal advocates of the New England states withdrawing from the United States, a position Macklin had denounced vigorously.

They had hoped to gather the necessary evidence from the young lieutenant who had requested the inquiry into the affairs at the fort. Unfortunately, the young man died of pneumonia shortly before the inspection party arrived. Everything appeared to be in order and the only concern they were able to present to the colonel was urging caution in allowing the small group of Indians to come and go as they pleased from the trading post in the fort. The colonel assured them that the handful of Shawnees did not follow Tecumseh and were quite docile.

The morning that they were to leave the fort, Mac received an anonymous message warning of an ambush on the wilderness road east of the fort. The message warned that Mac was the real target of the ambush. As a precaution, four additional guards started out with the party on the road east toward Erie. The ambush did come as warned and Smythe saw his old friend, Macklin, pulling a wounded soldier to cover when one powerful young Indian jumped him from behind and knocked him to the ground. Smythe told Christiana that the young Indian pounced on her father and swung his tomahawk down, narrowly missing Macklin's head, burying the blade of the weapon in the snow-covered ground. Thankfully another patrol returning to the fort from Erie appeared before the Indian had a chance to swing the weapon again. Smythe had caught a glimpse of the powerfully built warrior's face as he scrambled to his feet to escape; he was surprised to see blue eyes.

Their friend Smythe's parting remark kept nagging at Christiana: "Be very wary of strangers, Christiana. These are perilous times." Somehow she could not shake the feeling that a dark cloud was descending about them—a cloud that meant more danger for her father.

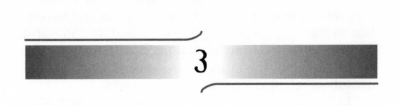

# 3

Having finished her work in the study, Christiana was enjoying the early morning sun as it filtered through the overhead canopy of the huge oak tree splattering light across the small garden. A fresh breeze rocked the branches sending the light dancing in a lacy pattern across Christiana as she knelt beside the flower bed at the foot of the garden wall. Deeply absorbed in digging in the warm moist earth, she softly hummed to herself as she carefully placed tiny marigold seeds in neat little rows. Her dark hair was pulled back with a ribbon, a few curls escaping to frame her face. At the moment, though, her face was smudged with dirt and she looked even younger than her seventeen years.

The young woman stopped suddenly and straightened up. The light breeze was carrying the obnoxious scent of skunk. Very slowly she turned to discover just how close the black and white creature might be. The sight before her eyes made her want to laugh and cry at the same time.

"Copper! Oh no, you didn't!"

Her large dog lay behind her with his ears drooping miserably, the very epitome of humiliation and discomfort. His deep brown eyes with golden flecks flickered at his mistress then looked away in embarrassment.

"Well, I bet that's the last time you chase that little black and white kitty," Christiana grimaced, pinching her nose.

Copper let out a pitiful whine.

"Poor boy. Oh dear, we must do something for you." She quickly got to her feet and wiped the dirt from her hands onto the long apron covering her light muslin skirt. "You just stay here. I'll be right back."

"Gran! Gran!" she called as she hurried to the back door of the house.

"What is it, child?"

"It's Copper, Gran. He tangled with a skunk. What can we do?"

"Oh land! I knew he'd be a nuisance the minute your Uncle Robbie brought him here."

"Gran, you always say that, but you know we wouldn't know what to do without him." Christiana protested teasingly. "What can we do?"

"Well, go on down to the spring house and bring up the jug of vinegar. I'll get the soap." The little elderly woman shook her head at the forlorn dog in the garden then hurried off to get the lye soap from the pantry.

Christiana hurried out to the small stone building constructed around a spring that bubbled up cold and clear water from deep in the granite bed under the rich Virginia soil. It was cool inside, a perfect place to store vegetables from the garden. Constructed several years before the newlywed Macklins bought the place, the spring house was about eight by six feet with a low roof that allowed enough room to stand in. A deep stone basin had been built to hold about three or four gallons of water at a time with an overflow pipe running out through the side wall and into a narrow brook that ran through the backyard.

A heavy wooden door had been placed on the entrance to guard vegetables and venison quarters from the wolves and bears that lived in the adjoining forest. Bears had not been seen for years now, but occasionally the wolves would still roam nearby.

Christiana located the vinegar jug and filled a bucket with water. Within minutes she had filled the oaken wash tub beside the spring house with water and been joined by Gran. "If I were you," Gran suggested as she handed her the soap, "I'd have Stephan come out here and help me get Copper in the tub."

"I don't need Stephan to help me," she replied adamantly. "He has work enough in the shop finishing the tea service for Mrs. Caskell. Besides, I'd ask Eric if I needed help."

"I really can't understand what you have against Stephan," Gran mused. "He may be quiet, but he seems nice. Is it you're a wee bit jealous because Copper likes him so much?"

Christiana frowned. "Gran, that's nonsense." Then, brushing a dark curl out of her eyes, she added firmly, "But it is strange that Copper likes him so much yet doesn't take to Eric. He's usually an excellent judge of character.

"It's just I don't trust this Stephan Page."

"Why not?" Gran was helping Christiana stir some of the vinegar into the water in the tub now. "He seems a fine Christian boy. He works hard and appears responsible. Which reminds me, Judge Albee sent word that Eric still hasn't delivered the silver brooch he ordered for his wife's birthday."

Christiana quickly assured Gran she'd speak to Eric about it.

"You still haven't given a good reason for not trusting Stephan," Gran persisted.

"Well, for one thing we're not really sure where he came from." Christiana stood up and wiped her hands with a cloth. "I just don't believe he's what he presents himself to be, a farmer's son come east to learn a trade."

"Why?"

"He's supposedly a farm boy but he's never once expressed the slightest interest in the garden! And he moves more like an Indian than a White farmer. I've seen him some evenings walk out to the garden wall and look into the forest. Father has that same look in his eyes when he's just come back from Washington or Baltimore and needs to breathe the cool, quiet forest air."

"What's so bad about that?" Gran tightened her white apron as they talked. "Your Grandmother Macklin was Delaware, and some of your best friends are Cherokee, not to mention Ram's wife."

"Oh, Gran, you know what I mean." Chris looked straight at Gran. "There's nothing wrong with acting like an Indian if you're an Indian. Stephan obviously isn't with those blue eyes and light brown hair. But he's not a farm boy either."

She stopped short of admitting she suspected that Stephan might be a spy. Gran had not heard Harold Smythe's warning to be wary of strangers, and Christiana was sure Gran would not take her fear seriously.

"Robert has light brown hair and blue eyes like your mother—"

"Gran, really!" Christiana threw up her hands in exasperation. "Why are we standing here discussing Mr. Stephan Page while poor Copper is lying over there so miserable?" Chris eyed the dog. "Will that vinegar really kill this wretched odor?"

"It'll help. Then he must be bathed with this soap." Gran patted the girl's arm. "I'll leave you to your task and go prepare lunch."

Christiana watched Gran returning to the house. She couldn't help smiling. She loved the little lady as dearly as if she had truly been her grandmother. She had never known her own grandmothers since they had both passed away before she was born.

The thought of her grandparents brought her mother to mind. Christiana wondered how she and her brother were faring on their trip to Mercy Ridge. Robert, the brother who'd always come to her rescue when the twins were tormenting her, would be returning right away, but her mother would be gone for at least three weeks. Chris had always felt a bit uneasy when her family members were scattered in different directions, and the tension from the war situation only made it worse.

A short bark brought her attention to the present as Copper reminded her of his plight. Christiana called him to come. Unhappily he submitted to being doused with the pungent vinegar. However, when she was ready to put him in the tub of water to shampoo him, the dog resisted. Since Copper weighed at least ninety pounds, there was little she could do.

"Come on, Copper boy. It's alright," she coaxed gently.

It was no use. Although the dog was devoted to Christiana and was normally obedient, the traumatic experience had been too much. To be asked to climb into the tub was more than he could bear.

The girl stiffened her resolve. Picking up the animal's front half, she reached around the dog's chest just behind his front legs. In the process she was almost overcome by the strong fumes of vinegar. Just as she was about to submerge Copper's forepaws in the tub of water, the powerful animal whined, then twisted and struggled out of her arms. The move threw her off balance. With a splash she found herself in the middle of the tub!

Spluttering and thrashing to regain her balance, Christiana heard the sound of laughter. Her father's two young apprentices stood nearby laughing. Realizing how utterly ridiculous she must look, she gritted her teeth and said, "If one of you gentlemen will kindly give me a hand—"

"Gran Barton said you might need a helping hand, but we didn't think it would be for this!" Eric grinned as he pulled her up out of the tub.

Regaining her footing, the young woman glanced down at herself. Her clothes were soaked, and wet hair hung stringily down in her face. When she looked up, her eyes met Stephan's, crinkled with merriment. Suddenly she too was struck with the humor of the moment. Try as she might, she could not resist laughing.

Stephan reached over to touch her cheek and wipe a smudge of dirt away. His touch was electric and for a split second, their eyes met again. He stepped back.

Eric continued to chuckle. "I don't know why you make such a fuss over that mutt. Look, he's already hightailed it to the creek to take his own bath."

A short time later after changing, Christiana came down to the dining room for lunch. Slightly perplexed by her reaction to Stephan's touch, she found herself relieved when Gran told her that he had already eaten and had gone to deliver the silver brooch to Judge Albee.

"Didn't your father say Eric should make that delivery?" Gran asked as she sliced a piece of fresh-baked bread.

"Yes, but maybe he was busy with something else," Christiana suggested.

"Busy avoiding the judge, if you want to know the truth," Gran muttered.

"What do you mean?"

"Seems Miss Millicent Albee has been expecting a proposal from our Eric, who certainly is not ready to settle down. When her father, the good judge, saw Eric sitting with the eldest Shaw girl on her front porch, he had a talk with Eric's father."

Christiana poured two glasses of lemonade and giggled, "How do you know all of that?"

"Now, dearie, I know gossipin' is a tool of the devil, and I haven't said a word of this to another soul, and won't either, but Eric's mother was by here yesterday afternoon and told your mother and me all about it. She would love to have Eric marry into such a nice family as the Albees, but fears he'll never settle down to the responsibility of a family of his own."

"I'm sure one of the girls in the village will settle him down someday," Christiana grinned.

"Unless he changes, I pity the poor girl who tries. It would be like tryin' to hold water in a bucket with holes in it. I'm so glad you've had the good sense not to fall for his handsome face and sweet talk."

Smiling at Gran's observations, Christiana was about to admit that she used to be very attracted to Eric, but was interrupted by a knock at the door.

A messenger waiting on the porch presented her with an envelope closed with the impressive seal of Caskell House, Hampton. She broke the seal and opened it.

Dear Andrew,

I beg your forbearance in the matter of the tea service ordered last month. As you know, Clara was most anxious to have the service ready in time for the dinner party she is giving for our governor. Due to the tumultuous events of this ill-begotten war, we have been warned to evacuate Hampton and move to the summer house at Roanoke as soon as possible. However, Clara is determined to have the dinner party first as the house at Roanoke will not accommodate as many guests.

I would be forever in your debt if you could possibly deliver the tea service by the twenty-third day of this month, June.

Please convey my respects to your lovely wife and daughter.

Sincerely yours,
Chauncey Caskell, Esq.

Addressing the messenger, Christiana said, "It'll take a few minutes for me to prepare a reply. Come in. You must be thirsty and tired after your long ride. Gran Barton has some cold lemonade in the dining room."

"Thank you, miss, that would be very kind."

After leading him into the dining room, Christiana walked out to the silversmith shop adjoining the house.

She knew her father had finished the elaborate pieces for the Caskells before leaving for Washington but had left the stamping of the insignia and final polishing to his apprentices. This had been an especially important commission as there were several silversmiths in Williamsburg and Richmond closer to Hampton, but Chauncey Caskell, an influential attorney, had been acquainted with her father since Mac had served in the state legislature as a representative from Dunston County. Mr. Caskell had given the order to her father with the possibility of others from Caskell's many friends.

Christiana knew that, quite frankly, they needed the business. "Mr. Madison's War" had caused many economic hardships and with her father in Washington so much lately, the business had suffered. For this reason, Christiana didn't even consider not delivering the tea service to the Caskells even though Hampton was located on the Virginia coast and close to the British raids.

Looking at the gleaming pieces on the work table, she glowed with pride. Her father was a fine artisan, and this set was probably the best he had ever produced.

"I'm not sure Stephan finished stamping them," Eric said in response to her question about the set. "He hurried out of here to deliver the brooch to the judge so fast I didn't have time to ask. I think he was in a hurry to see Millicent Albee."

"Millicent?" Christiana asked absently as she carefully checked each piece of silver for its creator's touch, her

31

father's signature—A.M. "I thought Millicent was your sweetheart."

"Mine! Oh no. She's pretty alright but too flighty for me. I prefer a pretty girl with a good head on her shoulders."

Eric patted Christiana's shoulder as he spoke. She looked up at him quizzically and cleared her throat a bit nervously, remembering Gran's observations a few minutes before.

Turning back to her task, she said, "I'm a little surprised Stephan would be attracted to Millicent; he's so serious. You know, I think today was the first time I've seen him laugh or even smile since he came here three months ago."

"He's a grim fella, alright," Eric agreed a little too heartily. "I, on the other hand, dear Christiana, am a very jolly fella who enjoys making pretty young ladies smile. What can I do to bring a smile to your very pretty but very serious face?"

Christiana had thought many times about being the object of Eric Lowe's attention. They had grown up in the same village together. He had always been a handsome boy and was considered a prize catch among the young ladies of Dunston. Eric's father had arranged for his apprenticeship when he was fourteen, and now nearly five years of his seven-year term were gone. Yet, in those five years, Eric had hardly seemed to notice Christiana, that is, until today. He had always treated her as a little sister before now. Today, there was not one hint of a big brotherly tone in his voice.

Christiana smiled. "I was just thinking about delivering this service," she replied. "Father was going to do it himself but next week will be too late."

"It's been a long time since I was last in Hampton," Eric began. "There's a tiny pub down along the waterfront on Victoria Avenue near Blackbeard's Point. They have the best fish chowder you can imagine. If we leave early in the morning, we can spend the night at Shelton's Inn at Hanover and be in Hampton before dark the next day."

"We?" she asked turning to face him.

"Well, yes, of course. You don't think I could let you go all that way by yourself carrying such a valuable cargo, do you? There are bandits on the roads, you know. It'd be very dangerous." He didn't add that he would like to spend some time with her away from the shop. Until that morning in the garden, he hadn't noticed what a pretty young lady she had become. Perhaps it was the way that Stephan looked at her that made him suddenly realize that she was no longer a little girl. He could only marvel at how he could have been so blind not to see it before.

"I forgot for the moment that neither Robert nor the twins are here to go with me. I suppose you're right."

"Two guards would be better than one."

Christiana and Eric were startled by the voice from the doorway.

"I think I can handle the job without help, Page," Eric said sternly.

"Miss Macklin should agree there is safety in numbers."

"Have you been standing out there eavesdropping?" Christiana was suspicious.

Unperturbed by Christiana's accusation, Stephan answered, "I've just been talking with the messenger from Caskell House."

"Oh." She didn't apologize.

"Actually, with things like they are along the coast, you ought to leave the delivery up to Eric and me," Stephan added.

"The problems with the British have been along the northern bay coastline," Christiana challenged. "No one this far south has even seen an Englishman. This order is so important it needs personal attention. I'm going, and that's that."

Stephan frowned. "If you're so determined, I'll have the carriage out front in the morning at dawn." He turned to go then added, "Oh, by the way, I saw Copper sitting out on the back doorstep. He could certainly use a bath now. He's covered with mud. I'll lend a hand if you'd like."

"Thank you, I think I can manage by myself," she answered with frosty confidence.

"Suit yourself." Stephan shrugged and left the shop.

"I thought you didn't trust him," Eric commented.

Christiana responded with a curious glance. "Don't you remember?" he asked when he saw her expression. "I was in the study when you spoke to your father about him."

"Well, I don't trust him, but if he's with us, we'll at least know where he is and what he's doing."

"Well, I've wondered what he's up to myself. I didn't want to worry you, but perhaps there's something you should know."

A very serious expression clouded Eric's dark eyes.

"What is it?" Her pulse quickened with the thought that her suspicions about Page were not unfounded. She had begun to think everyone else was right, and she was being foolish.

"Well," Eric almost whispered, "about a month after he arrived, I saw him behind the spring house where the trees meet the backyard. He was talking to a stranger. Although I couldn't see who it was, he was a big fella standing way back in the shadows. They seemed to be arguing. Then the stranger just slipped away. I could have sworn he looked like an Indian, but I didn't get a good look."

"Did you tell Father?" she asked quickly.

"Yes, but he didn't seem to think there was anything to it. Said it was probably someone asking for directions. But I noticed that Page was even more surly than usual for days after that."

This news didn't give her any sense of satisfaction. Her first suspicions that he might be a spy were rekindled. For this reason, she had never felt Stephan was a danger to her. Since it was her father she was concerned about, she would rather have Stephan with her and Eric if he returned while she was away.

"Are you alright?" Eric asked.

"Oh yes," she replied, although her thoughts still seemed miles away. "Eric, will you please finish the crate so we can pack these pieces this evening."

"Where are you going? Why don't you stay and visit with me while I finish building the crate."

She smiled, flattered by his attention, but shook her head no. "You heard what Stephan said. Copper is in desperate need of a bath. We can't have his muddy feet in the carriage."

"You're not thinking of taking the dog, are you?" Eric questioned.

"Of course. He goes where I go. Besides, he's probably the best guard of all. You two just got off on the wrong foot.

"Oh dear, I nearly forgot, I must write a reply to Mr. Caskell. I'll be back later to help with the packing."

Christiana quickly penned a reply promising delivery on the twenty-third. Once the messenger was on his way, she turned her attention to Copper. This time, he meekly submitted to his bath.

Later that evening after supper, Christiana was seated at her father's desk in the study preparing the paperwork for the Caskells' tea service. Figures had always come easily for her. When none of her four brothers wanted to follow in the silversmithing trade, she felt obliged to take an interest in it. It was practically unheard of for a young lady in America to apprentice as a silversmith. Christiana actually found making finely detailed pen and ink drawings of the pieces created by her father more to her liking than the mechanics of working with the metal itself. Taking care of the bookkeeping had been a great help to her father, and her drawings had proven to be valuable in presenting a selection of patterns to prospective customers.

She was just finishing the paperwork when Gran knocked at the door and entered carrying a tray with a glass of milk.

"Thank you, Gran. This is very sweet. You've always spoiled me so. You really need to start taking it a bit easier."

"Take my ease? Pshaw! As I always say, dearie, there's no glory in rust. It's better to wear out than rust out! You know I like to keep busy."

The expression on Gran's face grew serious. "Now, Christiana, you must promise that you'll be very careful on this trip. I would never forgive myself for allowing you to go if anything happened to you."

Christiana hugged the little lady and smiled to reassure her. "You mustn't worry, Gran. I'll be just fine."

Gran wasn't so sure. "But what if the British decide to attack? Since they captured the *Dolphin* and have been stealing chickens up and down the coast, who knows where they might strike next?"

Christiana laughed at Gran's remark regarding the British forces as chicken thieves. As her father conceded, all armies have their "chicken thief" element from general to foot soldier. However, the British forces as a whole were noted for their courageous determination and discipline.

"Gran, I'm no military genius, but I do know there are other places far more important than Hampton. I'm sure Norfolk or Portsmouth would be a much greater prize. My goodness, Mrs. Caskell wouldn't be planning her big dinner party if they thought there was any real danger!"

"All the same, I wish your mother and father were here. Perhaps you ought to send word to your Uncle Robbie. He could surely spare someone for a day or two to make the delivery."

"I'll be fine, Gran."

She kissed the older woman's cheek and walked her to the door. Watching Gran make her way down the hall to her room, Christiana smiled to herself. Gran had been born in England and brought to America as a young girl. She had been particularly fond of the English tradition of afternoon tea. However, when the Revolutionary War came along, a staunch patriot to her new country, Gran had refused to buy any tea that had passed through British hands. She had learned to dry herbs such as mint and camomile and roots such as sassafras to brew as refreshing teas, some even with medicinal properties. When the present British blockade had begun to cause shortages and high prices of imported products, Gran had merely clucked her tongue and said, "Well, now maybe this country will begin producing its own goods instead of running all over the world for what we can make right here."

Gran's words had been prophetic. When prices soared, sending tea to four dollars a pound and flour to twelve dollars a barrel, American production was encouraged and began to thrive in a way that might have taken years longer without the adversity of the blockade.

Having completed the necessary paper work for the Caskells' order, Christiana left the study with Copper following as always. Entering the shop, she was surprised to see Stephan carefully wrapping the last piece in batting and placing it in the crate.

"I thought Eric was going to pack that," she commented dryly.

"He went to pick up his new suit of clothes from the tailor before he closes." With the last piece nestled in the crate, Stephan turned to study her solemnly. "Have you reconsidered your plans to go to Hampton? It's really not a good idea to take a trip right now. Your father probably wouldn't approve, especially with the British so bold about running the Chesapeake Bay now. Like I said before, Eric and I can deliver it."

Christiana picked up the wooden lid to the crate and handed it to him. "Nothing against you and Eric, but the Caskells' order could be very important to Father's future business. As I said before, it needs the Macklin's personal attention. Since I'm the only Macklin here, there's not much choice. Besides, have you ever been to Hampton?"

He shook his head no in response, and she continued. "Hampton is a quiet little fishing village for the most part. There's little there that the British would be interested in. The militia is never far away, so I'm sure it'll be quite safe."

What neither one of them knew was that British Admiral George Cockburn and British Colonel Thomas Beckwith were preparing to attack Norfolk, the major American naval port across the bay from Hampton. It was, indeed, not a good time to be planning a trip to the coast.

# 4

The group was ready to leave early the next morning. Taking the barouche, Stephan sat in the driver's box. Eric was seated comfortably across from Christiana with Copper poised regally next to her as if he were another person.

A perturbed Eric smoothed his new suit coat and sniffed irritably, "He still smells like skunk."

"Oh, the odor's almost all gone," she corrected with slight impatience as she stroked the silky coat of golden red. Watching Eric now as he regained his composure and smiled warmly at her, she told herself she should be delighted that he was at last showing her some attention. He was handsome with snapping dark eyes and dark hair reflecting his French heritage. He was witty and most charming, a little too sure of himself; but then, he had every reason to be, for all the young ladies vied for his attention. While his elders considered him slightly irresponsible, the ladies considered him a challenging free spirit they longed to tame. If it was not for the way he reacted to Copper, she might feel the same. Somehow, his attraction had diminished slightly with his aversion to such a wonderful animal.

"What a great morning! I have a feeling this is going to be a wonderful trip." The apprentice smiled then called with a slight affectation, "Let's be off, Stephan."

Sitting in the driver's box, Stephan picked up the buggy whip halfway up the shaft. Turning slightly, he caught Eric's top hat with the handle and knocked it slightly askew.

"Hey, watch what you're doing there!" Eric grumbled.

Christiana thought she detected a smile at the corner of Stephan's mouth before he faced forward. "Yes," she thought, "it might prove to be an interesting trip. Perhaps I'll have a chance to find out a little more about this man."

The first day of travel went so smoothly no one would ever have guessed that just to the southeast, less than a hundred miles away, the British were attacking Craney Island in an attempt to reach the major American naval base at Norfolk. Thanks to the stout defenses and lack of knowledge of the lay of the land, the British were not having much success. British land troops had disembarked and were trying to attack the island from the rear while their boats prepared for a frontal attack. However, due to deep unfordable creeks, the land force wasn't able to reach its objective and the boats ran aground in unfamiliar waters. These factors made it easy for the seven hundred American troops on Craney Island to repel the attack and prevent the British forces from entering the Elizabeth River, thus saving the city of Norfolk as well as the American frigate *Constellation* berthed there.

News of the successful defense of Norfolk traveled fast. As the three young people reached Shelton's Inn at Hanover, there was little talk of anything else. The mood was jubilant as the story was repeated for each newcomer.

As the home of Patrick Henry's wife, the inn was naturally a gathering place for many of the veterans of the Revolution. By the time Christiana, Eric, and Stephan were served supper, the ale was beginning to flow freely.

"It'll be impossible to sleep tonight with this rowdy bunch celebrating," Eric complained. "To hear them, you'd think the war was over."

"The way things have been going, any victory is cause for celebration," Christiana commented wearily before turning to Stephan. "You're very quiet. Aren't you pleased with the news?"

"No. With the British so close, we should turn back tomorrow. But I have a feeling you intend to go ahead to Hampton."

"I really see no reason to turn back," she answered. "Do you, Eric?"

"Well . . . I . . . I don't suppose. Although Hampton is sitting right there on the peninsula. It might be considered a strategic point to command the James and the York Rivers."

"But there's really nothing of military significance there," she insisted. "Surely, if they wanted it badly enough, they would have attacked it long ago, don't you think?"

"This has been a crazy, unpredictable war from the beginning," Stephan replied dryly. "Your father would want you to turn back."

"You seem awfully anxious to turn back," she challenged. "Is it because you know something we don't? Or maybe you don't want to interrupt your courtship of Millicent Albee?"

Christiana was almost as surprised by her own words as Stephan seemed to be. After a moment, he replied without emotion, "The only thing I know is that common sense would suggest returning home. If you'll excuse me, I'll take these meat scraps out to Copper."

Christiana nodded silently as he left the table. She could feel her ears turning red. She was angry with Stephan for ignoring her challenge and at the same time completely chagrined with herself for the comment about Millicent. Whatever in the world possessed her to say such a thing?

Taking a deep breath, Christiana asked, "Do you think we should return home?"

Eric had turned his attention back to his meal. He set his tankard down after a long sip of ale and smiled, waving a careless hand toward the merrymakers in the pub.

"It would appear the fine militia of the Virginia Tidewater is doing an admirable job of protecting our coast." Eric's words were slurred. "If you wish to continue, I say, let's do so. If Page is afraid to go on, let him stay here and wait for us, or go back by himself. We can manage quite nicely by ourselves." He patted her hand. "Shall I go tell him your decision?"

"Perhaps you'd better go on to your room and get to bed. We'll want to be off early in the morning," she directed. "I'll tell Stephan what we've decided."

"My apologies, Christiana. The ale is a little stronger than I thought. I think I'll take your advice."

The apprentice excused himself and walked unsteadily toward the stairs leading to their accommodations. He and Page were sharing a small room next to Christiana's tiny alcove room.

As he disappeared up the stairs, Christiana realized that one of the revelers was looking at her. She left the table to go outside and find Stephan. With difficulty, she made her way through the boisterous crowd.

As she reached for the door latch, a big rough hand suddenly clasped her wrist. Looking up, she found herself face-to-face with the man who had been watching her.

He was a thickset fellow only a little taller than she. From the look of his homespun clothes, she figured he was probably a hired hand from one of the tobacco plantations nearby. He had obviously been celebrating for some time.

42

"You can't leave the party so soon, little lady." The burly man slurred his words. "Come sit with me so's I can tell you all 'bout how we're gonna' twist them redcoat tails and send 'em back to where they come from."

"Please let go," Christiana insisted more calmly than she felt. Her hand was already beginning to go numb from the tight grasp around her wrist. The sour stench of ale and stale tobacco was nauseating.

"Oh, come on—"

Suddenly a hand appeared on the man's shoulder, stopping him in mid-sentence. "The little lady might listen to your story some other time when you're sober. Right now, she's weary from her long journey." It was Stephan's voice.

The grasp on her wrist suddenly slackened. Although a head taller, Stephan was outweighed by the stranger by sixty or seventy pounds. Surprisingly his grip seemed to paralyze the stout arm.

Amazingly the man let go and mumbled an apology. With a nervous glance out of the corner of his eye, he moved back to his table without another word.

Taking a deep breath, she looked at her rescuer. His steel blue eyes met hers. "Thank you, Stephan. I'm sure he meant no harm, but I really didn't want to hear his story."

"I'm sure you're right, but it might be a good idea to go on up to your room. It may get a little rough down here."

Raising her chin a bit, she replied assertively, "I'll go check on Copper first. I think it's ridiculous that they won't allow him in here. He's obviously better behaved than the majority of these patrons."

Outside, she took a deep breath of the fresh air and hurried to the carriage where Copper waited. The dog greeted her with his wide tongue lapping her hand, and happily wagging his bushy tail.

"I'm sorry, dear old fella," she told him. "They say you have to spend the night out here. You'll probably be better off though. It's awfully stuffy and noisy in there."

She scratched him behind the ears and hugged her beloved furry lion with his thick golden-red coat. With that, she went back inside and upstairs to bed.

In the meantime, Stephan sat at a table in the corner, a cup of coffee in his hand. Amid all the noise, it was not easy to hear the conversation of the two men at the next table. If they hadn't been drinking, they would surely have been more careful about their British accents. He strained to hear more.

"These cocky colonials had better enjoy this while they can. If Admiral Cockburn acts true to form, he'll have 'is retribution for the fiasco at Norfolk."

"Aye," the second man agreed. "Just before I made my getaway, I heard that he's got 'is eye on some place called Hampton. There's a store of weapons there."

"Well, I'd 'ate to be there if Admiral Cockburn takes a notion to go after it. From what I hear, Colonel Beckwith's a good man, but he may not be able to keep that crew of French prisoners in line."

"Aye, they're a surly bunch, and why not? Bein' taken prisoner of war and forced to fight your enemy's battles can spoil a body's good humor." The sailor took a long swallow of ale.

"All I know is we need to be long gone from here. After seein' the way Cockburn convinced those colonials along the waterfront there in Yorktown to supply what they needed to repair that captured schooner, I'd say we won't be safe till we're far from the coast and takin' up a new kind of job."

"Aye, if I never see the ocean again, 'twill be too soon for me! I wonder if our young mate, Twigs, has made 'is escape yet."

The other man shrugged, then spotting Stephan, motioned to his companion to leave.

Stephan frowned as he watched the two British deserters work their way through the crowd. Even if he told

Christiana what he had overheard, he knew she would pay little attention to his warnings.

Christiana had a difficult time going to sleep, but once she did, she slept remarkably well and woke to the bright rays of first light breaking through a crack in the shutters. Sitting up, she was instantly aware of a movement at the foot of her bed. She grinned as a large furry creature jumped up on the bed and began licking her hand.

"Good morning, Copper," she smiled sleepily. "How are you this morning? . . . Wait a minute. How'd you get in here?"

The dog jumped down and playfully bounded over to the door and back again. Puzzled by his appearance in her room, she dressed quickly. On her way out, she knocked on the door next to hers but there was no response. Copper followed her downstairs, where she found Eric sitting at a table drinking a cup of tea.

Eric looked up and winced slightly from the painful reminder of last night's indulgence in ale. His head throbbed with the slightest sound, but he forced a smile at Christiana, hoping she wouldn't notice his discomfort.

"Good morning, Christiana. How did you manage to sneak the dog in?"

"You know nothing about it then?" she asked.

As he slowly shook his head no, a young girl carrying a large tray with a cup and a large steaming pot of tea approached the table.

"Morning, miss. Did you sleep well?"

"Yes, thank you," Christiana answered.

"Lovely dog you have there. Haven't seen any like him before. My uncle said it was arranged for him to stay. That's surprising, considering my uncle. Would you like some breakfast?"

"Yes, but perhaps I'd better take Copper outside first."

The girl nodded and left for the kitchen.

"Where's Stephan?" Christiana asked.

"Out hitching up the team. He's already had his breakfast, I think."

Outside, Copper bounded up to greet Stephan who was working with the harnesses, getting the team in their traces.

Christiana walked over. "Good morning—" she began rather haltingly.

"Morning," he replied briefly with a slight nod.

"How did you manage to arrange for Copper to spend the night in my room?" She decided to be blunt.

"What?"

Taking his response as purposely evasive, she persisted. "You somehow arranged for Copper to stay in my room last night, didn't you?"

Stephan continued to buckle the leather straps of the harness without looking at her, then he gave the horses a gentle pat on their shoulders.

"The innkeeper agreed it was more sensible for Copper to stand guard in your room than for the innkeeper himself to spend the night on duty outside your door."

"And why would he have thought about standing guard outside my room?" she asked curiously.

Straightening the reins, he answered casually, "The rowdy crowd last night worried him. He didn't want to take a chance that word might get around that his place wasn't safe for decent people, especially a congressman's daughter. Bad for business."

The longer she was around this man, the more confused Christiana became. His intervention the night before when he protected her from that unpleasant drunken man had only reinforced this confusion. Yet, she was unable to deny the deep-seated uneasiness that continued to raise a warning flag within her that there was something terribly wrong.

Stephan was obviously capable of being very considerate, yet he had established an impenetrable wall around himself. In the three months he had been with her family, he had rarely talked about himself or shared his feelings about anything. In fact, he'd spoken more to her in the past two days than anytime since he first arrived. While he had clearly influenced the innkeeper about Copper, he had made it sound as if it had been the innkeeper's idea. Why?

This part of his character only intrigued her more. Perhaps she was giving him more credit than he deserved. Maybe even the nice things he did had some sinister motive behind them. Christiana quickly excused herself and turned back toward Shelton's Inn.

"Miss Macklin—"

She stopped as Stephan caught up with her. "I really think you ought to stay here while Eric and I deliver this order. There are rumors that Hampton could be the next target of an attack."

"Rumors?" she asked, brushing the dust off her long skirt. "Did you hear those rumors last night? Now really, how reliable do you think such rumors could be when spawned out of a drunken mob? I'm sure after their defeat at Norfolk, the British won't be in a hurry to attack anyone now.

"But if you're afraid to go, you can wait here until Eric and I return tomorrow."

With that, she turned on her heels, squared her shoulders, and marched purposefully back to the inn.

Perplexed by her stubbornness, Stephan was unable to deny a measure of admiration for her spunk. He wished he could have convinced her but then he knew that no matter what he would have said, Christiana would have disagreed with him just like she had with nearly everything since he had first arrived in Dunston.

# 5

Bright and warm, the morning air was fragrant from the colorful profusion of wild flowers blanketing the countryside. Leaving Hanover, the Dunston young people found the road to Hampton well traveled. Several times they had to slow down for lumbering wagons heavily laden with produce or tobacco headed for the port cities. Even though the war was playing havoc with the American economy, plantation owners were still taking their products to those ships willing to attempt to break the blockade. They reached Hampton just before dusk that evening just as the western sky began to blush pink with the sun settling behind the trees along the river bank.

Although not actually in the town of Hampton proper, the Caskell estate was not difficult to locate. It was a large, two-story home in the middle of several acres of rolling lawns and manicured gardens along the edge of a bluff overlooking the James River. The long, stone-paved drive ended in a graceful curve in front of a wide portico with four white Corinthian columns guarding the front entrance. It had been a long day, and everyone sighed with relief as the carriage finally rolled to a stop.

After Eric gave her a hand down, Christiana directed Copper to stay put. Then Stephan removed the crate of silver pieces from the luggage straps and followed the others up the wide steps.

While she had visited many fine homes such as this with her parents, she could tell by Eric's obvious amazement and Stephan's quiet curiosity that this was probably the first time either had been to such a grand estate. The butler directed them into a cavernous library where they were soon joined by Mr. Caskell.

"Miss Macklin? Christiana? Surely not—" Mr. Caskell entered the room and reached for Christiana's hand. A rotund little man with thick silver hair, Christiana remembered him from a reception she had attended with her parents three years before.

"Yes, sir," she smiled. "It's very nice to see you again."

"The last time I saw you was at the Governor's reception in Richmond. You were a pretty little thing then, but you've grown into a beautiful young woman. Ahh, and who have we here, your brothers?" He turned to Eric and Stephan.

"No, sir. Meet Stephan Page and Eric Lowe, my father's apprentices. Father would have come himself, but his committee called an emergency session."

"Yes, yes. I've heard. I suppose you've heard the good news about Norfolk."

The three young people nodded.

Mr. Caskell continued. "The governor's dinner party may well be an occasion to celebrate a turn in this blasted war."

"We can only pray it will," Christiana agreed. "How is Mrs. Caskell?"

"Near exhaustion from preparing for this dinner. Has retired to her chamber already. But believe me, she'll be elated over having the new silver for the party."

"I hope she'll be pleased with it. I think it's perhaps my father's finest work yet."

"Wonderful, wonderful." Mr. Caskell smiled and rubbed his hands together in anticipation. "Let's have a look."

Stephan set the crate on a large desk. After prying it open he carefully removed the gleaming pieces.

Mrs. Caskell had expressly ordered the designs to follow the Empire style. The rather squat shape with a round base or ball feet was currently very popular on both sides of the Atlantic. Christiana's father had created an elegant design of broad fluting rising around the bowl from a round base. With graceful scrolls arching on the sides for the handles, the design reminded her of an elegant swan rising out of a lotus blossom.

Picking up the gleaming sugar bowl and the cream pot, Mr. Caskell examined the pieces closely. "Exquisite. Simply exquisite. You're right, my dear. This is the most exemplary work I've seen in a long time. Mrs. Caskell will be delighted.

"Now, can I offer you some refreshment after your long journey?"

Christiana declined. "Thank you, no. It's getting late, and we need to find accommodations for the night."

"Accommodations? Goodness, no, you must stay here. I couldn't think of allowing my good friend's daughter to stay in Hampton's poor excuse for an inn. Wharf rats and that sort, you understand."

"That's very kind of you, sir, but I have my dog along as well," she added.

"Well, bring the little thing in. It will be fine, I'm sure."

Christiana had to smile at Mr. Caskell's assumption she had a small lap dog. "Copper's not exactly a little thing," she told him.

"Oh? Well, he can stay in the guest house with the two young fellows here. You may stay in the guest chamber upstairs."

Obviously the gentleman was accustomed to having his own way. Their accommodations were settled.

Mr. Caskell was clearly pleased to have company. After dining on a sumptuous meal of Cornish hen with mushroom and wild rice dressing, asparagus in a rich wine sauce, fresh melon, and a rich caramel creme for dessert, Stephan and Eric joined him for brandy and cigars in the library. Christiana excused herself to take a walk with Copper in the garden before turning in for the night.

A soft breeze sighed through the slender branches of a willow tree growing beside a magnificent fish pond. Sitting on a stone bench beside the pond, the young woman watched the reflection of the three-quarter moon rising in a cloudless sky of deep lavender blue. A sweet fragrance of honeysuckle and wisteria mingled with the salty sea air. Copper sat quietly beside her as she gently stroked his silky head.

The atmosphere seemed almost enchanted, and Christiana was overcome by a strangely wistful mood. She could imagine herself being whisked off to some magical kingdom, a princess waiting in the castle garden for her knight in shining armor to come by and rescue her from the evil duke.

"This is quite a place, isn't it?"

She jumped at the sound of Stephan's voice behind her. Copper turned and immediately wagged his tail, waiting for his customary scratch behind the ear.

"You startled me. It really is a bit annoying the way you move so quietly and sneak up on a person," she grumbled, secretly embarrassed at having been caught dreaming a childish dream.

"Sorry," he apologized, giving Copper his scratch. "I wasn't sneaking. The grass is just very thick here."

Crickets and tree frogs began their nightly serenade.

"I thought you were going to have brandy and cigars with Mr. Caskell."

"I've never developed the taste for either. It's not a common thing where I come from. Besides, I needed a bit of fresh air myself."

"Where do you come from, Stephan Page?" Her question was abrupt but now seemed the right time.

The man gazed across the rolling lawn as he spoke. "West. I think I told you that my parents had a little farm along the frontier in Kentucky.

"There were fields of corn and several cows. The valley stretched as far as you could see, with hills rising all around like blue-green palisades of protection. My father used to take me fishing down along the river—"

For a moment Christiana's suspicions seemed to evaporate in the magical atmosphere surrounding them.

Stephan stopped and sighed. "Then the Creeks came and destroyed it all."

"I'm sorry," she said sincerely.

Looking down at her upturned face, Stephan was slightly taken aback by the soft look of empathy reflected in her eyes. This expression of compassionate understanding rattled him. Swallowing hard, he stepped back, forcing his voice back to a matter-of-fact tone.

"It's getting late. I think we should start back first thing in the morning. Eric has a notion about fish chowder at some place on the waterfront, but I think we should leave as soon as possible."

"Why such urgency? You both have worked hard the last three months. What harm would it be to take a little time to see the waterfront and let Eric have his fish chowder?"

Tempted to mention the conversation he had overheard, he doubted if she would give any more credence now than before to something overheard in a pub filled with men who had been drinking too much. Stephan answered simply, "The British might be discouraged by their defeat at Norfolk, but then again they might want to get even and strike back at a less protected area. Out here on this peninsula, Hampton is like a duck sitting alone on a pond. Besides, your father is due home any day and we need to get back to work."

The mention of her father and the insistence upon returning home as quickly as possible suddenly reminded her of her suspicions regarding Stephan and her father's safety. Christiana searched the man's face for some clue to the truth.

"With the emergency session, he probably won't be home before next week," she replied.

"With this trouble at Norfolk, the legislature may take care of its business quicker than expected," he countered.

The lights dancing on the water vanished, and the shadows deepened about them. Dark clouds were beginning to gather, skirting the bright moon. As the shadows deepened, suddenly so did all of the suspicion and doubt she had been harboring these past months. In exasperation, she blurted out, "Who *are* you, Stephan Page?"

The young man stared at her in stony silence.

Unable to wrestle with her fears any longer, she declared, "You're not what you pretend to be, I just know it. I have this dreadful feeling that you mean to harm my father!"

She fought to regain control of the emotion in her voice and spoke her next words barely above a whisper. "But I'll do anything to prevent that. Do you understand me? If you're a spy, you'll be caught and hung. I promise you that."

Trembling, she backed away. Sudden tears threatened.

He stepped forward. "You think I'm a spy?" he asked incredulously, catching her arm and holding her fast. "No wonder you've rarely spoken a civil word to me." His laugh was not a humorous laugh. "A spy—" Overwhelmed by the true nature of his purpose for coming to Dunston, he frowned and sighed, "If only it were that simple."

The clouds had drifted away, washing the garden in silver light again. Christiana's heart was pounding because

53

of Stephan's nearness and the strength in his grasp. Strangely, she wasn't afraid for herself for he wasn't hurting her. Yet there it was in his eyes, something dark and dangerous.

An emotion-packed silence engulfed them as the two people stared into each other's eyes. Christiana thought she detected a slight flicker in the turmoil that darkened his gaze. For a breathless moment she was sure he was going to tell her the truth. However, stoic reserve veiled his eyes once more, and the apprentice relaxed his grip.

"I'm not going to harm your father or anyone else in your family," he said calmly. "We need to get back. It's dangerous here, and there could be danger for your father at home—a danger he's not prepared for."

"Danger? What kind of danger? Please, Stephan—" she implored.

"You must trust that I mean you no harm, Christiana," was all he replied. The sincerity in his eyes and the tone of his voice as he spoke her name for the first time jolted her. Had she just been allowed a glimpse of the real Stephan Page?

The intense moment was interrupted by the sound of Eric's voice. "Christiana!" Stephan released her arm and stepped back but the feeling of their highly charged contact held a moment longer.

"There you are! I was just—Oh, it's you too, Page. Is something wrong?"

Christiana quickly brushed aside the tears that had defied her efforts to hold them back. Clearing her throat, she said, "Nothing's wrong. We were just discussing getting an early start in the morning."

Glancing curiously at them both, Eric questioned, "But what about the chowder and a stroll along the wharf?"

"I agree with Stephan," she managed as she turned to face him.

"I find that odd," Eric declared suspiciously. "You two haven't agreed on anything since Stephan came to Dunston."

Stephan stepped forward and intervened. "That being the case, it must be the right thing to do. I'm afraid you'll have to wait for your fish chowder."

"I am sorry, Eric." Christiana had finally regained her composure. "We really should go." The thought of a casual stroll along the waterfront with Stephan now posed to be awkward indeed.

"Whatever you say," the apprentice sighed, "but Mr. Caskell wants us to have breakfast with them in the morning before we leave."

"That will be fine," Christiana agreed. "See you in the morning." Stooping to pat Copper, she said softly, "Copper boy, stay with Stephan." With that she hurried toward the terrace doors.

"Stay here, boy," Stephan commanded, laying a hand on the dog's head when he started to follow her.

"Did you say something to scare her?" Eric demanded.

"I don't think she scares easily," Stephan replied as he watched Christiana through the terrace door speaking with Mr. Caskell. "Didn't Caskell say the guest house is over here? Come on, Copper."

Eric scowled as Page and Copper walked away. For just a moment he thought he had sensed something happening between Stephan and Christiana, but recalling Christiana's distrust of the young stranger, Eric quickly dismissed such an idea. Glancing up at the moon he regretted missing the opportunity of walking in the moonlit garden with Christiana himself. He wasn't happy about missing out on the planned excursion to the fishing wharf either. His mouth had been all set for that chowder. Now, to make matters worse, he was having to share his quarters with that dog.

# 6

Christiana's chamber was beautifully decorated in the tradition of the many elegant estates along the banks of the James River. Rich paneling of oak and walnut had been used in the guest chamber as well as throughout the house. Fine paintings and rich tapestries graced the walls. Exquisite brocades and damasks had been used for draperies and upholstery. The bed in her room was probably the most comfortable she had ever been in; however, Christiana couldn't sleep. Her mind kept replaying the scene in the garden. As the moonlight traced the delicate patterns of the leafy boughs outside her window, she clutched the coverlet under her chin.

What was happening to her? Three months ago, she was a poised, polite, happy young woman. Listening to the fiery speeches of the young War Hawks had inspired in her a deep national pride and that indomitable optimism of youth that, come what may, her young country could rise to the challenge. Despite the slight adjustment at having her brothers away from home, she had been enjoying her new responsibility of helping her father. Everything had seemed comfortable and predictable.

But somehow all of this had changed that rainy spring day she had opened the door to find Stephan Page standing on the doorstep. With eyes the color of dark blue steel, the tanned young face at the door was set in stern square lines. He was soaked from the spring shower. She had quickly invited him in. From that moment, she had not been quite the same.

The stranger had asked for her father, introducing himself as Stephan Page. He said that their old family friend, Brother Adams at the Moravian Mission near Fort Stanford, had sent him. She knew that her father had received a letter from the old missionary and seemed satisfied with the young stranger's story.

At first Christiana had been disturbed by the way this man watched her father. He seemed to have a cold calculating manner as if he were sizing Macklin up. She imagined a cat circling a bird cage searching for a way to retrieve a feathered dinner.

Then Christiana remembered overhearing a conversation that had left her even more uneasy. The new apprentice and her father were talking one afternoon in the shop. Stephan had asked, "When a man has given an oath sealed with his blood to repay a debt, do you agree that he can do nothing less than what is asked of him, even if it means taking a man's—an enemy's—life?"

After a long moment, her father's reply was cryptic. "A man must do what his conscience tells him, but he must be certain who his enemy really is."

Their new apprentice pored over the newspapers they received every two or three weeks. He constantly asked Macklin questions about the war and his part, as well as her brothers', in it. Christiana began to suspect he was a spy.

To Christiana, this stranger moved as quickly and silently as an Indian through the forest. It was unsettling to turn and discover him suddenly in the room beside her. Never talkative, he seemed so moody at times. Occasionally he would be warm, almost congenial. Then suddenly, as if reminded of something unpleasant, he would grow distant.

She had become irritated with his poised self-confidence too. Her own poise seemed to vanish in his presence. She began dropping things, like a bookend she was dusting when he came into the study to ask for a drawing for her father or the bushel of apples she had spilled all over the kitchen floor when he came in for a cup of tea. Once a whole cake slipped off the plate and onto her lap as she began to slice the pieces for everyone's dessert. And then, of course, was the most recent—falling in Copper's tub of bathwater.

Copper was another matter she could not understand. Stephan was the first stranger Copper had ever taken to so quickly. Every other one had always been given a reserved appraisal as the dog politely guarded Christiana, ready to give a warning growl if any false moves were made. Perhaps Gran Barton was right. Maybe she was a little jealous of the fact that Copper was so fond of Mr. Page.

Christiana lay in bed and looked back over the past three months. She had changed from poised to pathetically clumsy, from considerate and tolerant to suspicious and downright rude. She had become increasingly miserable and uneasy.

And it had all unexpectedly reached the boiling point that evening in the garden. She, who had endured lizards on her pillow, mice in her shoes, and any number of other brotherly torments without batting an eye, had been reduced to a total loss of control and babbling accusations.

Why? Why should she even care? She shouldn't care at all, she told herself, especially when he might very well be her father's enemy, or even her country's enemy! But was he? What could he have meant when he said that being a spy would have been a simple problem? He asked for her trust, and something inside her wanted to give it.

Something struggled to believe this man was not what he appeared. Somehow she had to find out the truth.

At last, the soft rose-tinted rays of dawn began to steal into the quiet corners of her room. The circus of thoughts still tumbled in her mind. Rising, she went out to the balcony overlooking the gardens and the river. The morning was clear. A cool salty breeze refreshingly swept away some of the weariness from her sleepless night. The sun breaking over the horizon sent fiery sparks dancing across the silver slate of the distant bay. She could just see the billowing sails of ships miles away gliding over the glistening surface, silhouetted against the brilliance of the new day. Too distant to identify, the ships reminded her of her brother, Alex, sailing on the *Sea Sprite*. She prayed for him and the other U.S. sailors defying the world's most powerful navy.

Suddenly the young woman's reveling in the glorious scene before her was interrupted by a knock at the door. A maid entered to announce that breakfast would be served shortly on the south terrace.

Christiana dressed slowly. She donned her favorite empire-waist gown of fine light blue linen, the short puffed sleeves edged with a ruffle of delicate lace and having a shallow scooped neckline. She had always heard that looking one's best somehow helped maintain confidence to face difficult situations. Wondering how Page would react to her this morning, she quickly brushed through her dark curls and patted cold water on her face to restore the color in her cheeks, pale from weariness.

The terrace was on the south side of the house overlooking the spot where the James River merged with the Chesapeake Bay. The mid-June sun was already warm, but the large terrace sprawled in the cool shade of two huge tulip poplars standing at the edge of the lawn that gently sloped away from them toward the bluff.

Mr. Caskell and Stephan stood as the young lady joined them at the table.

"Good morning, Christiana," Mr. Caskell smiled. "You look especially lovely this morning. You rested well, I trust."

"Yes, thank you," she said, not wanting to admit that she had not slept at all.

"Morning, Miss Macklin," Stephan nodded.

He couldn't help but notice how the blue of her dress accentuated the blue of her eyes. He also detected the look of concern in her eyes. Was she as worried about their encounter this morning as he was? He had slept very little last night, mulling over their discussion in the garden. For such a lovely evening, it had been a disturbing confrontation. At least he now knew why she had been so wary and disagreeable around him. Disturbed deeply by the fear in her eyes as she confessed her suspicions, he'd come very close to telling her the truth. However, hearing the truth, he was sure, would turn the fear in her eyes to hatred and he wasn't prepared for that.

Christiana acknowledged Stephan's brief greeting. "How did Copper do last night?" she quickly asked as they all sat down.

"He paced a bit, wondering about you I think, but he settled down. He's having his breakfast now in the kitchen," he replied cordially.

Christiana could detect nothing in his voice to indicate he was angry with her. Surprisingly relieved, she couldn't help but feel uneasy about how he really felt beneath that passive exterior.

As a servant poured a cup of strong hot coffee, Mr. Caskell announced, "Clara will be with us shortly. She was admiring the tea service, last I saw of her."

"Is she pleased?" Christiana asked.

Her answer came from the doorway as an attractive woman in an elegant morning dress of shimmering yellow silk entered. "Why, I'm delighted! Simply delighted. Chauncey tells me you insisted on making the trip yourself, Miss Macklin. How very kind of you."

Mrs. Caskell joined them at the table. Just as she was being seated, Eric came through the doors.

After introductions were completed, Christiana turned to their hostess. "I know Father will be very glad to hear that you're pleased with the tea service. He would have made the trip himself, except for an emergency committee session that was called."

"It is a shame he couldn't come. He is such a charming and handsome man." Mrs. Caskell smiled and fluttered a delicate lace fan.

Christiana remembered how she had monopolized her father's attention at the governor's reception and smiled back. "Yes, Mother and I think so, too."

"And how is your mother?" The woman's tone sounded hollow.

"Fine, thank you. She's at the Cherokee mission at Mercy Ridge helping my brother and his wife with their new baby."

"Indian mission? Oh my."

"Yes, my great-grandparents established it nearly seventy years ago at Iron Mountain in South Carolina but moved it to Mercy Ridge. My brother, Ram, is now supervising it."

"How interesting. Oh, before I forget," Mrs. Caskell abruptly changed the subject. "Chauncey dear, please do make certain the gardener knows we will need ten baskets of flowers for the centerpieces. I've decided to add one more table. We must separate the Addisons and the McKees. They do manage to be so unpleasant with each other."

Christiana felt a twinge of irritation. She had always been proud of the fact that her Grandmother Macklin had been a Delaware Indian and her grandfather had been the son of Scottish missionaries to the Indians.

She had never been to Iron Mountain, the site of the first mission. Nestled in a valley at the southern end of the Appalachian chain, the Iron Mountain Mission had played an important part in her father's youth. His stories of time spent there had always fascinated her. The White settlement that had been allowed to share the valley had eventually grown so large that the Cherokee had been forced to seek another place. A high plateau in the mountains west of Lynchburg had been chosen for the new site just before Christiana was born. Sheltered from punishing north winds by a long ridge of granite along the northern edge, the plateau known as Mercy Ridge had a commanding and breathtaking view of Virginia. While she was growing up, Christiana had spent a great deal of time there, and she had many dear Cherokee friends.

She wished she were there now instead of listening to this pretentious prattle. She had learned long ago that many people had preconceived notions about Indians as either murderous savages wreaking havoc along the frontier or great noble spirits stalking the wilderness. The plain truth—that they were simply human beings, good and bad, living in a different culture—was apparently unacceptable. She had learned, for the most part, to overlook such ignorance. However every once in a while, a little comment or attitude such as Mrs. Caskell's would catch her off guard and strike a spark of temper.

Stephan watched the fire that sprang into Christiana's eyes in response to Mrs. Caskell's reaction. When first becoming acquainted with the Macklins he had been somewhat surprised that Christiana didn't try to hide the fact she had Delaware Indian ancestors. On the contrary, she seemed proud of it. He had quickly learned, however, that Christiana Macklin had a mind of her own and was not necessarily impressed with the popular opinion.

Christiana took a deep breath and sipped her coffee as if to swallow any comment she might be tempted to make. Lowering her cup, she glanced across the table and noticed Stephan watching her. Was she mistaken or had there been a hint of sympathetic understanding? She wondered if he somehow knew her inner reaction.

The rest of breakfast was spent listening to Mrs. Caskell's elaborate plans for the governor's reception. In discussing the impressive guest list, she expressed her disappointment that Christiana's parents had been unable to accept their invitation due to other commitments. Christiana soon found her attention wandering to a dozen other matters as their hostess chattered on and on.

Suddenly the chattering stopped. She glanced over to see Mrs. Caskell waiting expectantly for a response. She had no idea what the woman had just said. Thinking quickly, she replied, "I'm sure your dinner will be a great success, Mrs. Caskell. I do hope the British won't spoil it for you."

"Not to worry, my dear," Mrs. Caskell smiled confidently. "For the right price, they'll keep a respectable distance. After all, my brother Rupert Harrod tells me Admiral Warren is a gentleman of high repute and is even an officer in the Halifax Bible Society. In fact, Rupert deplores the fact that we're even involved in this silly little war. It's been such a burden on his shipping company since some of his captains refuse to sail vessels carrying any cargo bound for Canada or England."

The woman seemed oblivious to the choking spasm Christiana suddenly suffered as she apparently swallowed wrong. Aware of Christiana's strong opinion about Americans paying off British troops to protect their property and those New Englanders who continued to trade with them, Eric quickly chimed in, "My goodness, it is getting late! If you'll please excuse us, we must be on our way."

Mr. Caskell touched Christiana's arm. "Are you alright, my dear?"

Taking a deep breath, she nodded. "Yes, excuse me, something caught in my throat."

Eric watched her anxiously, wondering what she might say. His relief was noticeable when she replied, "I'm afraid Eric is right. We really must be going. It was very kind of you to allow us to stay the night."

Mr. Caskell left the table with the three young people to complete the transaction for the silver and see them on their way. It was nearly ten o'clock by the time their carriage rolled out through the gate.

The sun was shining fiercely through the early summer haze. It was going to be a long, hot ride back to Hanover, where they would again spend the night. Only the breeze from the river kept them from becoming miserably uncomfortable.

Copper was perched on the seat next to Christiana, panting from the heat but enjoying being on the go again. Eric sat across from them with a rather satisfied smile.

"You seem quite pleased with yourself, Eric," she noted. "I'm glad you're not too disappointed about returning home so quickly."

"No, of course not. Don't you think the Caskells are fine people?"

She could tell by his smile that he was nearly bursting to tell her something. Having been taught to say little or nothing about someone if you couldn't say something nice, she answered, "Yes, Mr. Caskell seems quite nice."

"You know, Christiana, he was really impressed with the tea service."

"That's good. I'm sure Father will be happy to hear that."

"Yes, it was a fortunate day for me when my father arranged for my apprenticeship with Andrew Macklin." Eric mused pleasantly about the conversation he and Mr. Caskell had the evening before. "With this single order, your father's reputation will grow that much more; and that means my credentials will be very well received when I move out to establish my own shop. Mr. Caskell said as much. He even went so far as to offer his own personal backing if I should decide to settle in Roanoke where they have their summer house."

"That sounds like quite an opportunity for you, Eric," she admitted. "Somehow, I thought you might be staying on with Father, even after your apprenticeship is completed."

The young man leaned forward to take her hand in his. He smiled his most charming smile, a smile that had made many a heart flutter around Dunston. A year, even six months ago, she might have felt giddy herself. However, helping with the shop and spending more time around him, she had come to realize they had little in common. His charming veneer wore a little thin especially when he fussed about Copper. His new attention now made her feel slightly awkward.

Eric noticed her reserve. He was not accustomed to cool reception of his attention. Undaunted, he continued, "Just think, Christiana, my own shop! You're absolutely right; it is a great opportunity. Why, a young man could even begin thinking about starting his own home and family."

"That would be very nice," she replied absently as she watched the back of Stephan's head. Was it her imagination or was he driving at a quicker pace than on their journey over. Seeing the tenseness in his straightened shoulders only increased her own uneasiness. What was he really thinking?

"Copper!"

Eric was scolding the dog, who was laying his head across Christiana's lap and drooling on his hand. He took out his handkerchief and grumbled, "Christiana, have you heard a word I've been saying?"

"I'm sorry, Eric, I . . . I was just noticing Stephan seems to be in quite a hurry."

Eric noticed their speed of travel. "You're right. At this pace, we'll be in Williamsburg by noon."

He tapped on Stephan's back. "Page, do you think you should be traveling this road so fast? You could break a wheel. What's the rush?"

"I have a feeling that the quicker we get away from the coast, the better," he called over his shoulder.

They traveled at a rapid, steady pace for another hour and a half, stopping only to allow their team a breather. During these brief stops, Eric dominated the conversation with a lengthy commentary on the wonderful Caskells and their lavish lifestyle. Christiana tried to appear interested.

By encouraging Eric's narrative, she was really avoiding the awkward, silent exchanges passing between her and Stephan. Although she regretted her emotional outburst the previous night, she felt that she was nearer to learning the truth. At least now there was no pretense between them. He knew her suspicions. It was now up to him either to prove or disprove them.

Their travel pace remained brisk and, true to Eric's estimation, shortly before noon they spotted the brick chimneys of Williamsburg.

Just then, a team and wagon bolted in front of them from a side lane obscured by a tall hedge. Stephan had little time to react. He jerked the lines hard to the left. The team swerved and closely missed colliding with the other team.

Suddenly, their left front wheel dropped into a rut at the edge of the road, jerking out of control. In a blinding split second, amid a shattering of wood and panicked whinnies, the carriage careened wildly tossing its occupants like rag dolls.

# 7

Christiana felt a wetness on her face. Gradually she became aware of a bright light, hurrying footsteps, and voices. As she tried to gather her senses, she realized that Copper was licking her. At the same moment, she heard Eric's voice far away angrily yelling, "Get that mutt away from her. Page, if she's badly hurt, I'll never forgive you."

Strong hands gently lifted her slightly. Tender strokes gingerly brushed the dirt and grass from her face. Then she heard a deep voice say quietly, "I'll never forgive myself, if . . . Christa? Christiana?" Someone was calling her name.

As her senses cleared, she opened her eyes to look up into Stephan's face, taut with apprehension. His blue eyes were filled with concern as he gently pushed her dark hair back from the large knot swelling on her forehead.

"Stephan," she whispered weakly. "What happened?"

"Rest a minute, Miss Macklin," he replied, again assuming his more formal demeanor. "The carriage overturned. You were knocked unconscious."

"You're hurt!" she said, touching his face just below a cut across his right cheekbone.

Surprised that he hadn't noticed it before, he touched it himself. Dismissing it, he turned his attention back to her.

"What about Eric?" she asked.

"I think my arm is broken," Eric replied as he knelt beside her. "Are you badly hurt? Get back, Copper!"

Eric's command was met with a deep growl, and Christiana could see the flash of white teeth as the dog curled his lip in warning.

"Copper," she spoke softly, reaching for the animal. "It's alright."

"Do you think anything is broken?" Stephan asked her.

It was only then that Christiana realized he was cradling her in his arms. Tempted to rest there a moment longer, she said, "If you'll help me up, I think I'm alright."

Both young men helped her to her feet and although she stood unsteadily, she knew she had suffered no broken bones. Looking down at her light blue linen dress, she discovered the white of her petticoats showing through a long tear across her skirt.

"I think the only thing damaged is my favorite dress," she added.

She started to take a step but swooned slightly and leaned back against Stephan's arm for support.

"Just take it slowly," he admonished her.

"I'm alright, really," she assured him as she turned to see their carriage upside down with one broken wheel still spinning slowly in a crooked circle. "Much better than the carriage, I think."

A young boy about fifteen was standing by anxiously wringing a battered felt hat in his hands.

"Miss, I . . . I'm powerful sorry. My pa will hang my hide in the barn for sure. It was just . . . me and Jasper were havin' this little race, and . . . and I was in the lead. I didn't even see you. He'll have my head for sure. Jasper ran back to tell them at our place."

"You—" Eric almost exploded when Stephan interjected, "We were both driving too fast. Can you take us into Williamsburg to the doctor and to get a new wheel?"

"Oh yes, sir. Yes, sir!" the lad gulped with relief. "I'll drive careful as can be."

Stephan pulled their bags from the luggage straps and put them in the farm boy's wagon as Christiana fashioned a splint from a broken wagon rung for Eric's broken arm. Using a blue silk kerchief from her bag, she tied a sling to stabilize the arm.

"You were too easy on him," Eric grumbled at Stephan as they climbed up into the wagon.

"The damage was done, and from the look on his face, I doubt he'll be racing again any time soon."

As they traveled the last two miles to town, Christiana untied the ribbons of her capote bonnet hanging limply down her back. Once stylish, the bonnet with tiny blue flowers was now crushed and soiled beyond repair. She frowned.

"I guess I'll have to buy you a new bonnet," Stephan remarked as he reached over to pick some dry grass from her dark hair.

"You're lucky it was just the hat that was ruined, Page," Eric scowled. "You should be horsewhipped for driving so carelessly. We might have all been killed."

"But we weren't," Christiana said firmly as she patted Copper, who was sitting next to her. She could see by the remorse in Stephan's eyes that he agreed with Eric. "It was an unavoidable accident." With that, she pulled a hanky from her reticule and gently dabbed at the cut on Stephan's face. "Hold that there until the bleeding stops," she directed.

"I'm sorry about your arm, Eric, but we all agreed we ought to hurry on home and away from the coast."

"I didn't agree," Eric fumed. "What were we running from anyway, some imaginary British invasion?"

"It wasn't imaginary," Stephan finally snapped with impatience at Eric's continued complaining. "When we stopped in Hanover, I overheard two men talking. They were deserters who had just escaped from the Royal Navy. They were talking about how foolish it was to let the navy decide where to deploy the land forces when it knew so little about the countryside. They said Beckwith is a good man and soldier, but Admiral Cockburn is a scoundrel and he'll likely be out for some retribution after their failure at Norfolk."

"What makes you think that they'll choose the shore along the James or York?" Eric scoffed with a certain interest.

"They mentioned that Cockburn knew Hampton was sitting like a ripe plum. He also knew about the small battery of arms there."

"Rabble talk," Eric declared, cradling his broken arm carefully.

"If you'd been standing on the Caskells' terrace this morning at dawn you would have been able to see for yourself."

Met by questioning gazes, Stephan went on. "I caught a glimpse of at least nine tall masts moving northwest. Mr. Caskell took little heed of it, but—"

"That doesn't prove a thing," Eric interrupted. But he realized that three or four ships sailing together in the bay under the present circumstances could only mean a British maneuver afoot. With their influence, perhaps the Caskells had nothing to worry about. However, more than one young American fellow had been pressed into the British navy as a prisoner of war. Eric decided to say nothing more.

Christiana said nothing, for she remembered seeing the ships as well. The thought that they were British sent a chill up her spine.

Upon arriving in Williamsburg, the boy named Lemuel escorted them to a doctor's house then went over to the wheelwright's to find a replacement for the broken wheel.

Eric's left arm was broken, and the doctor set it. He then tended the cut on Stephan's face and recommended that Christiana rest at the Windham House Inn on Duke of Gloucester, Williamsburg's main street. He wanted to be certain the blow to her head was not more serious than it appeared.

Before long, Lemuel returned from taking their bags to the inn and stopping at the wheelwright shop. A wheel would be ready in the morning, and the boy promised to return to take Stephan back to replace the broken one. He then offered to return to the accident scene to see to the horses and carriage.

As they walked to the Windham House, Eric remained perturbed about the reckless Lemuel. "I hope he doesn't take to racing our horses," he said a little too loudly.

"The boy's doing all he can, Eric, to help make up for his mistake. I've seen others who wouldn't take such responsibility as seriously as this young lad."

Christiana glanced over at Stephan with curiosity when he said this. Had their confrontation in the garden the previous night jolted something in her that was now allowing her to see him more clearly? Had her suspicions so blinded her that she hadn't seen this facet of compassion he seemed to possess? Or was it that, knowing she was alert to his deception, he was playing a role to throw her off track?

Her thoughts were interrupted by their arrival at the inn, a large two-story building. Its first floor was divided into a dining room on one side and an ale room on the other. Upstairs were eight small but clean guest rooms. Cleanliness not being a virtue shared by many inns throughout the country, it was a welcome feature.

Arrangements were made with the innkeeper to permit Copper to stay with Christiana. After a late lunch of cheese and hot fresh bread Christiana went to her room. A quick sponge bath with cold water from the pitcher in the basin helped refresh her. Exhausted, she changed into her nightgown and tossed the tattered remains of her dress and bonnet on a nearby chair.

A smile crossed her lips as she thought of Stephan's statement about buying her a new bonnet. Her mind quickly drew sober, however, by telling herself it would take more than a new bonnet to allay her suspicions. It would take knowing the truth.

Although this bed was not nearly as comfortable as the Caskell bed, the soft pillow and sheets invited her to drift into sleep. The lack of rest the night before and the events of the day had left her exhausted. In that elusive realm between wakefulness and sleep Christiana could almost feel Stephan's touch on her face and see the anxious look of concern in his eyes. The thought that this concern had been genuine and the echo of his calling her name yet not meaning for her to hear, slowly washed like an eroding tide against the wall of suspicion she had constructed against him in her mind.

A knock sounded at the door, and she woke to Eric's voice. "Christiana, are you alright? It's past noon! You've nearly slept the clock around."

Sitting up quickly, Christiana's head throbbed as she blinked her eyes. "I'll be out soon," she replied, her stiffened muscles protesting each movement.

A short while later, she joined Eric in the dining room downstairs. She asked about Stephan.

"He went with Lemuel to repair the carriage," Eric responded. "He said to tell you Copper's with him because he was scratching at your door wanting out. They should be back any time now. How are you feeling?"

"Other than a slight headache and a few stiff muscles, I'm fine. What about you? How's your arm?"

"Gave me fits last night. Guess I'm just glad that it's my left instead of my right. I'll still be able to do a little work."

Christiana noticed that her friend seemed distracted. "Is something wrong, Eric? You seem troubled."

Before he could answer, a young kitchen maid came to their table. She had been crying and was still very upset.

Eric ordered tea and fresh muffins, and the girl scurried away. He then gazed out the window, to avoid looking at Christiana. She followed his gaze and noticed tight groups of people hovering together in the street.

"Why was she crying, Eric? Why are those people out there? What's going on?"

Reluctantly he began. "Page was right. The British attacked Hampton at dawn this morning. Soldiers disembarked ten miles this side of the village while part of the British naval force closed in from the bay. The militia retreated, leaving the village to the mercy of Cockburn's cutthroats. The men that pillaged were promised booty and beauty. They didn't burn the village, only ransacked it, but the women . . . Colonel Beckwith had little control.

"Apparently the majority of these black-hearted villains were French prisoners-of-war who'd been pressed into the British navy."

Color drained from Christiana's face and a tight knot doubled in her stomach. "Oh dear," she finally breathed. "I wonder if the Caskells are alright. Should we go back and see?"

"We must get home." Eric clutched Christiana's hand. "I never would have forgiven myself if we had stayed and been caught . . . They must have landed their troops only an hour or two after we left the Caskells'."

"We'll not think about it," she instantly declared.

"All I know is that I'd hate to be a Frenchman in these parts right now. As it is, I'm ashamed to admit that even a drop of French blood flows within these veins."

A small clatter at the table next to them diverted their attention. Christiana glanced over to see a man with a woolen scarf around his neck retrieve his fork from his plate. Christiana thought it odd that on a summer day in June someone would wear an article of clothing that covered half of his face.

"That's foolish talk, Eric," she replied, turning back. "You can't deny your heritage because of some horrible men who happen to be French."

When the maid finally brought their food, Christiana discovered she had lost her appetite. She only sipped some tea.

"Oh, by the way, Miss Macklin," the maid turned back to her. "The doctor stopped by earlier to check on you. He asked me to remind you to see him before you leave today."

"Thank you, I will," she replied.

"There's Page with the carriage." Eric spotted the other apprentice through the window. "I'll go up and get our bags while you finish your tea."

Stephan pulled the carriage to a stop outside. The sight of Copper sitting regally on the passenger's seat as if he were being chauffeured made Christiana smile.

Then without warning, a hand gripped her arm. The man in the wool scarf whispered hoarsely, "Mademoiselle Macklin?"

# 8

Coming into the inn, Stephan removed his hat. Wiping the perspiration from his brow, he paused a moment to let his eyes adjust to the dimly lit room after the brightness of the outside sun. He turned toward the stairs as he heard Eric call his name.

"Are we all ready to go now, Page?"

Nodding yes, he asked, "Where's Miss Macklin?"

"Over there . . . Well, she was over there finishing her tea a few minutes ago," Eric answered, looking about the empty room.

"Miss?" He addressed the kitchen maid who was gathering the dishes from a table. "Do you know where Miss Macklin went?"

"Why, yes, sir. She left."

"Left?" Both young men echoed simultaneously.

"Yes, with the man in the scarf. They went out the back through the garden."

Eric and Stephan exchanged quick, puzzled glances and hurried to the back door. Just as they reached the back step, they caught a glimpse of Christiana's billowing pink skirt disappearing around a corner.

"What in the world—" Eric exclaimed. "Why would she leave with someone she talked to for no more than ten minutes?"

"We'd better hurry or we'll lose her," Stephan directed, beginning to run before he finished the words.

Bolting down the footpath between the back gardens of the houses and shops, the two men reached the corner where Christiana had disappeared. No one was in sight. Stopping to catch their breath, they quickly surveyed a walkway that emptied onto a side street. Several small buildings were situated along the side. Quickly they dashed to the end and looked down the street both ways.

"They can't have disappeared that quickly," Eric panted, clutching his arm.

"Maybe back along the path—" Stephan was out of breath too.

Retracing their steps, they searched the shadows and doorways of the buildings along the alleyway. Then, from inside a small garden shed, they heard a muffled voice. "No! No! Please!"

Instantly, Stephan lunged against the wooden door, smashing it open. In the dim light, he saw the man with the scarf leaning over a low cot.

"Raven's Claw!" he yelled in a blinding rage. Grabbing the stranger's shoulder, Stephan whirled the man around and landed a solid blow to his jaw, sending him reeling back against the wall and crumpling to the floor with a moan.

"Stephan!"

He whirled around at the sound of Christiana's voice.

"Stephan! What on earth are you doing?" she gasped.

He immediately realized that the figure on the cot was not Christiana at all. She was standing behind him, staring at him in disbelief.

"Christiana?" Eric was at the door. "What's going on?"

Hurrying to the man's side she replied, "Mr. Richaux, are you alright?"

He moaned again as she helped him to his feet.

Stephan stood catching his breath, still poised for battle and trying to take in the scene before him.

"Eric, Stephan, this is Jean-Marc Richaux and this is his sister, Mariette. She's very ill," Christiana explained.

"You have a powerful fist, mon ami," Richaux managed with a pained smile.

"Stephan, why on earth did you hit him?" she asked again, still amazed by his actions.

Before he could answer, the young woman on the cot cried out again, "No! No! Please don't hurt them."

Christiana rushed to the woman's side and held her hand, speaking softly to quiet her.

"Well, what do you expect?" Eric finally broke the silence. "We find you've disappeared out the back door with a stranger, then hear cries coming from in here—"

Christiana realized her mistake. "I see what you mean. I'm sorry, but Mr. Richaux was so upset, and I didn't think you'd return so quickly. I'll explain it all later. Right now, we must get Mariette to the inn and send for the doctor."

Still slightly shaken, Stephan went to the cot and without a word, picked up the petite young woman to carry her back to the inn.

A short time later, Christiana sat at a table in the dining room with Richaux, Stephan, and Eric. Jean-Marc held a wet compress against his jaw. Stephan and Eric were watching Christiana so intensely she began to feel like the object of an inquisition.

"You see, Mr. Richaux and his sister were on their way back to Santo Domingo to their uncle's sugar plantation," she finally began.

"They had stopped in Boston, boarding another ship there. On their way from Boston they were attacked by a British sloop that chased them into Chesapeake Bay. The ship was just about to escape up the York River when they were overtaken. The crew and passengers were taken captive, but Mariette and Jean-Marc escaped, managing to make their way here."

"Why were you hiding?" Eric eyed Richaux suspiciously.

"Monsieur, it has been a most . . . uh . . . perplexing time for us. We have become very wary and distrusting, I fear. It is common knowledge that your country is divided in its sympathies, some for France, some for England. We were uncertain whom we could trust. Was it not you, monsieur, who was wanting to deny your French blood just a short while ago?"

Ignoring Richaux's reference to his own remark, Eric asked, "Why Christiana?"

"I heard the maid speak her name in the dining room. It would seem God led us to her. She is the second Macklin to come to our aid."

Christiana's blue eyes had brimmed with tears. She bit her lip and, blinking back the tears, swallowed hard. "You see, they were on the *Sea Sprite*—Alex's ship. My brother helped them escape just two days ago. He was wounded when the ship was captured, but he helped them over the side. They swam ashore. That's when Mariette caught a chill and became too ill to go on.

"When Mr. Richaux heard the news about Hampton and what the Frenchmen did there, he didn't know where to turn for help. I'm . . . I'm sorry I didn't stop to tell you, but he seemed so concerned for his sister."

Stephan had said nothing since bursting into the garden shed. Now he sat silently watching Christiana. He was thinking about her brother, a prisoner of the Royal Navy. The newspapers had carried horrendous stories about life aboard a British ship. The whole problem of impressment of American sailors had come about because life in the Royal Navy was such a hellish existence. Just when England needed to keep her naval power strong because of the war with France, British seamen were deserting to join the American merchant mariners whose lot was much better than those on a British ship of the line. Now, Alexander Macklin was their prisoner.

The Frenchman looked at Christiana. "Your brother is a fine man and we owe our lives to him," he said with his gentle French accent. "If I had not been responsible for my sister's safety, I would have helped him escape too. Even now, if I had a saber and pistol, I would board the *Sea Sprite* and fight to liberate him!"

Before anything more could be said, the doctor entered the dining room. "Mr. Richaux, your sister will be alright with some rest and good nourishment. Put two drops of this elixir in her tea morning and evening, and she should be feeling much better in two or three days."

He turned to Christiana to ask how she was feeling. When she replied that she was fine, he smiled. "I say, I haven't been this busy since Mrs. Kelley gave birth to triplets!"

"Doctor, how soon will Miss Richaux be able to travel?" Christiana asked.

"She should stay in bed a week, but if she's careful, she may be able to travel in four days."

"May I see her now?" Jean-Marc asked.

"Yes, she was asking for you, but see to it that she doesn't tax herself. I'll be back in the morning to check on her."

"Mademoiselle Macklin, please, I would like for Mariette to be able to thank you herself."

Christiana followed Jean-Marc up to the room. Christiana loaned Mariette a nightgown and promised to clean the young woman's grimy clothes. Then she joined the three young men waiting downstairs.

"Somehow we must get word to Gran to let her know that we're alright and only delayed a few days. When Mariette is able to travel, we'll take the two of you home to Dunston where she can recover completely."

"What'd we tell you, Richaux?" Eric grinned.

"What?" Christiana felt as if everyone knew something she didn't.

"Your friends apparently know you very well." Jean-Marc smiled. "They said you'd be very concerned about your grand-mère and that you'd insist on taking us home for Mariette to recuperate."

She smiled. "Well, if they thought of it too, it must be a good idea."

"Yes." Eric grimaced. "I seem to have drawn the short straw. I'll borrow a horse from Lemuel and leave for Dunston right away to tell Gran Barton you're okay, and about our expected guests."

"What about your arm? Will you be able to ride?"

He smiled smugly. "You've seen me ride, Christiana. I could ride with both arms broken, but I'm afraid I couldn't manage a team. Stephan will have to be the one to drive the carriage home."

# 9

The next morning, after taking Copper out for his early walk, Christiana went into the dining room to pick up Mariette's breakfast tray. She was on her way upstairs, when the innkeeper, Mr. Hatcher, handed her a note.

Upon receiving it, she returned to Mariette's room with Copper following close behind.

"I fear I am a dreadful bother." Mariette frowned when Christiana placed the tray on the bedside table and sat down in a chair nearby.

"Nonsense. It's nice to have a girl to talk to for a change. I grew up with four older brothers and not that many girls my age in our village. You must hurry and get well so we can really visit."

"A letter from your fiancé?" Mariette asked curiously, watching Christiana unfold the note.

Christiana laughed gently. "No, I have no fiancé. This seems to be from Stephan. How strange."

She read the short note silently while Mariette began to eat.

Miss Macklin, Richaux and I have gone on an errand which will take a couple of days. Stephan.

"An errand?" she thought to herself. "What sort of errand would take two days, I wonder? I must say, when it comes to writing, Stephan Page wastes even fewer words than when he's talking.

"Mariette, do you know anything about an errand?" Christiana asked aloud.

Mariette avoided Christiana's glance. "Mariette?"

"Oui, . . . uh, yes," came the reluctant answer.

"Do you know where they went?"

"To the *Sea Sprite*," Mariette whispered.

"The *Sea* . . . What?"

"Yes."

The young girl's dark eyes grew wide with apprehension. "Your Monsieur Page has gone to try to rescue your brother, and Jean-Marc has gone with him."

Christiana was too surprised to speak, and Mariette continued, "We must pray for their safe return. Monsieur Page and your brother must be very good friends for him to be willing to risk his life."

Christiana stared at Mariette in disbelief. "He hardly knows him. Alex has been living in Boston for nearly three years now. Are you certain about this?"

Mariette nodded. "Jean-Marc came in late last night and told me of their plans. He feels a great debt to your brother for saving us. When Monsieur Page began making plans for a rescue attempt, Jean-Marc of course insisted on going with him."

Christiana rose and walked over to the window. She stared out at the wide main street. Would Stephan Page ever cease to surprise her?

"If it is not for your brother's sake that he does this brave thing, then it must be for you," Mariette timidly suggested.

Glancing back, Christiana assured her, "You wouldn't say that if you knew how we get along." Still dumbfounded by the news, Christiana finally returned to the bedside table, poured a cup of tea and carefully stirred in two drops of medicine.

Mariette finished the broth and managed to drink the cup of tea spiked with the potent elixir prescribed by the doctor. Christiana placed the teacup back on the tray, then smoothed the covers over her patient as she settled back against the feather pillow.

"Jean-Marc was right." Mariette smiled. "It was God's hand that brought us first to your brother and then to you. You are so kind. I don't know how we . . ." Emotion choked off her words.

"Shhh now," Christiana soothed. "You just rest."

Mariette blinked back tears and nodded. Laying there quietly, she watched her new American friend walk over to the window to once again stare out at the street below. It was easy to see she was very distracted by the message in Stephan's note, for she had opened it again and studied it for some time. The effect of the elixir soon made Mariette drift off to sleep wondering why this young woman was so astonished that this man, Stephan, would try to rescue her brother. After all, hadn't he smashed down a door ready to fight whoever had taken her from the inn the day before? It ought to be obvious.

The only thing obvious to Christiana as she stood at the window staring down at Stephan's note was how the mystery surrounding him only became more complicated. He had confirmed her fears about her father's safety, but denied he was a spy and promised no harm would come to them by his hand, and yet she sensed he was hiding some dark, dangerous secret. Remembering the day before when he broke down the garden shed door and struck Jean-Marc, she could still see the fury blazing in his eyes. What name had he called? Raven's Claw? Who? Why? The questions whirled in her thoughts. Now this, an attempt to rescue her brother, Alex, from British hands.

Taken all together, none of it made any sense. Copper whined, breaking in on her mental turmoil. He was staring up at her as if to ask her what was troubling her. She stroked his head and glancing over at her sleeping patient, whispered, "I wish you could tell me why you like Stephan so much. I do hope he's worthy of your trust."

For the rest of that day and most of the next, Christiana and Mariette waited anxiously for Stephan and Jean-Marc's return. They passed the time chatting about their families and friends. Christiana found herself carrying on the major portion of the discussions since Mariette often became quite distressed when she would recall the happier days of her family life, now gone forever. The frail girl did tell Christiana that her family had left France during the Reign of Terror. They had taken refuge with her uncle on his sugar plantation in Santo Domingo. When their mother became ill, she begged her two children to take her back home. The voyage had been difficult but seeing their once beautiful estate in ruins had been more than their mother could bear. Already weak, she fainted in her son's arms and never awoke. After the funeral Mariette and Jean-Marc were returning to Santo Domingo when the *Sea Sprite* was captured and the Macklins suddenly entered their lives.

Each afternoon while her friend rested, Christiana strolled along Duke of Gloucester, the broad main street of Williamsburg, with Copper tramping proudly at her side. She loved animals so, especially dogs. They were wonderful creatures. No matter the circumstances, Copper only wanted to be near. A pat on the head, a kind word, and regular sustenance made his world perfect.

Although fiercely protective, Copper had a very gentle nature and somehow sensed that Christiana's new friend needed special attention. While the men were gone, he sat for long periods beside her bed, allowing her to stroke his silky coat, and listened to her speaking softly in French. As for Mariette, his presence helped calm her fretful spirit.

By the third day, Mariette was feeling stronger so Christiana helped her to the small flagstone terrace in the back garden for lunch. The Hatchers had taken the girls under their wing and were determined to hasten Mariette's recovery with the best menu the inn had to offer.

All morning, Christiana had noticed Copper's strange behavior. In the garden, he began pacing back and forth, then laid down for a few minutes only to stand and pace along the garden wall again.

"Copper, mon chiot, what is wrong?" Mariette called with a smile.

"Perhaps he's anxious to get home," Christiana commented a bit absently, for she too had felt apprehensive since awakening that morning.

Just then Mrs. Hatcher emerged with a tray. A huge smile beamed across her face.

"Here you are, young ladies. I hope you enjoy it. Oh, by the way, there's someone here to see you!"

Both girls turned. Instantly Christiana's heart leapt for joy as a tall young man with brown hair and eyes as dark as her father's stepped through the door.

"Alex!" Christiana jumped up and ran to her brother, throwing her arms about him and crying with relief, "Oh, Alex. Are you alright? They said you'd been wounded."

The young sailor was pale and thin, but he reassured her that the wound in his leg was not serious.

As Jean-Marc and Mariette greeted each other, Christiana looked around for Stephan.

Alex guessed what she was thinking. "He's okay, Chris. He's taking the horses to the livery. I was never so surprised or glad to see anyone in my life as I was when I saw those two fellows creeping into the cabin where I was being held prisoner.

"Hello, Copper boy!"

"I think he knew you were coming, Alex." Christiana laughed as the dog jumped up on her brother's chest enthusiastically. "He's been unsettled about something all morning." Again she glanced at the door.

Alex grinned. "Why don't you go on over to the livery and tell him to hurry up before his lunch gets cold?"

Christiana blushed. "I'm sure he'll be along in a minute."

"I'm not so sure. He said something about riding out to some farm to return the saddles or something. He may not be back for hours."

"Well, he should stop and eat before he does that!" Christiana said with determination. "Come on, Copper. Let's go find Stephan."

Stopping at the wide door of the livery stable, Christiana found the young man removing a saddle from one of the team horses. Copper didn't stop. Spotting Stephan, he ran full force, leaping up and nearly knocking the man down. Happily licking his friend's face, the animal finally settled down. Stephan ruffled the dog's thick fur.

Stepping into the shadowed building out of the bright sunshine, Christiana took a moment for her eyes to adjust to the dimness. The smell of dusty hay, old leather and wood, and the soft snuffling sound of horses nosing their oat bags created an atmosphere that was pleasant to her senses. It brought wonderful memories of times spent with her Grandfather McClaren and Uncle Robbie at Cherry Hills Farm.

The young lady walked forward slowly, clasping her hands nervously behind her back. Stephan's jacket lay across the carriage wheel. She noticed a large powder burn and hole through the loose fitting fabric of his home-spun shirt. It was just above the belt.

"He's not the only one glad to see you, Mr. Page," she said genuinely. "Were you hurt?"

The man shook his head no and grinned. "Just a close call; ventilated the shirt, not the skin."

"How can we ever thank you for saving Alex? I still can't believe you were able to rescue him, or that you decided to try," she continued.

Watching his strong profile, she wondered if he was remembering her accusations and was still angry with her. "How could I have ever misjudged someone so completely?" she thought.

"When Richaux suggested it," his voice broke through her thoughts, "I thought I'd go along and help."

"The way I understood it, the whole thing was your idea," she countered, now standing beside him.

"It doesn't matter whose idea it was as long as it was done. Your family has been very good to me, Chr—Miss Macklin. It seemed like a good way to repay your kindness."

She could detect no hint of resentment. On the contrary, the expression in the young man's blue eyes made her heart skip a beat.

"The Macklin family will be ever in your debt. Stephan, I'm very sorry."

"Sorry?"

"Yes," she replied softly. "Sorry that I've treated you so dreadfully ever since you came to our house. It was just that I thought . . . I felt . . ."

"You were the only one who was right in not trusting me," he said solemnly, still looking deeply into her eyes.

Her puzzled look did not stop him. He continued, "Perhaps I'll be able to tell you about it someday." Then almost adamantly, he added, "But be sure of this, I would not . . . I could not bring harm to your family."

"You have certainly proven that," she responded, unable to look away from his face.

Slanting in through the hayloft door, the afternoon sun's rays sent shafts of light in dazzling beams across the stable floor. A soft golden aura surrounded the two people for a moment. They seemed almost suspended in time.

Copper gently nuzzled Christiana's hand, reminding them of his presence and trying to get their attention. As Christiana looked down at him, a thought suddenly occurred to her, something she had been puzzling about the past three days.

"There's one thing I am a little curious about. When you broke into the gardener's shed the other day, you shouted something—a name maybe—Raven's Claw or something like that."

Before she could go any further, the man turned away. "It's not important."

Everything had been going so well. But just as the golden strands of light had shifted, so had the mood. Stephan's wall of reserve was suddenly present again. Christiana felt as if nothing had changed—except for one thing. At great personal risk, this apprentice had rescued her brother from the clutches of the British navy. This fact alone afforded him the benefit of doubt. Unless... Christiana's thoughts took a left turn. Unless, it wasn't a risk at all. If he were really a British spy, he might have arranged Alex's release...

She mentally readjusted her own protective shield. Rather brusquely she said, "You'd better come and have a bite to eat before you go riding off again."

Busying himself with the rigging on the saddle, he answered, "Thanks, but I'd better get these saddles back to Lemuel this afternoon so we can be ready to start home in the morning, if Miss Richaux is able to travel."

"Very well." She turned to go. Copper started after her then stopped, looking back at Stephan. Christiana could see the dog was waiting for the man to come along with them.

"Come on, Copper. Mr. Page won't be joining us right now."

Back in the Windham House garden, Christiana sat in the cool shade of a mulberry tree, listening to her brother and Jean-Marc relate the harrowing tale of the rescue.

"Your Monsieur Page is a very brave and cunning man." Jean-Marc addressed Christiana.

"He's not my Mr. Page," she interjected, "but do go on. I'm dying to know how all this came about."

"Not your Mr. Page? Hmmm . . . strange. Ah well.

"He spoke with me that first afternoon just after Monsieur Lowe left for your home. He asked many questions about the harbor where the ship was anchored and the number of guards we had seen and if any other ships were about. I told him as much as I could remember. I could begin to see what he had in mind and, though eager myself to liberate Alexander, I was most dubious about the success of such a venture.

"When it became apparent he was going to attempt it with or without my assistance, I could do nothing less than offer my own right arm.

"Page obtained saddles and bridles from young Lemuel and a few provisions from Monsieur Hatcher. We left shortly after you went up to your room for the night."

"Why didn't you tell me what you were doing?" she asked.

"Page thought it best not to get your hopes up in the unhappy event we should fail."

Hearing this, Christiana reasoned that if Stephan was working for the British, he would not have hesitated to tell her of his rescue plan. The fact that he wasn't sure they would succeed suggested that his motives were sincere. She listened eagerly as Jean-Marc continued.

"We rode most of the night and rested for a few hours before dawn. We followed the road to a few miles this side of Yorktown where we waited for the light of day. We skirted about the edge of town and found ourselves a short way from the place where the wharves first begin. You can only imagine my feelings when we first caught sight of the *Sea Sprite* still anchored in the middle of the York River. I had feared she had sailed away since our escape. The British admiral apparently had threatened to shell the waterfront if the people there didn't supply him with supplies and laborers to repair the ship.

"In the light of morning, it was easy to see that she wasn't seaworthy yet. She had lost her main mast and one more and had a large hole in the forward hull. But we could see that they were beginning the repairs. All morning long, we watched small boats ferry back and forth from one of the wharves carrying men and supplies."

Alex sat next to his little sister and shook his head. Sighing deeply he thought about his beautiful ship damaged and in British hands. His twin, James, would be upset. There had been long discussions about making this voyage. James had felt more uneasy than ever and had suggested waiting a few more days before trying to run the blockade. Alex had disagreed. Next time he'd pay closer attention to his twin's feelings.

Richaux continued his story.

"For hours your apprentice friend just sat there on the bank of the river, watching. I think it wasn't until we were actually there that he began making a plan. Toward the end of the day, we spotted two men rowing toward shore from the ship. Suddenly Page was up. It was time to move.

"It was nearly dusk as we made our way down to the wharf where the men tied their small boat. Page removed his jacket and rolled up his sleeves just like the workmen. After they'd gone, he told me to pick up some nearby planks and put them in the little boat. At last I could see what he had in mind. I removed my own jacket and rolled up my sleeves even though I wasn't certain we would succeed.

"As we rowed toward the ship, he finally explained his plan. I think we were both praying for divine help."

"Christiana and I prayed for you as well," Mariette added as she clutched her brother's hand. He patted her thin fingers, and she urged him to go on.

"All of a sudden a British officer hailed us from the deck. Calmly as can be, Page called up that we were bringing the last load of supplies so the workmen would be able to begin first thing in the morning without having to wait. The officer must have been on his way to his dinner because he merely waved and left. It was as simple as that.

"But that was the last simple task we faced. Once on board, we still had to find Alexander as well as some place to hide until dark.

"We carried the planks aboard with great effort, taking a great deal of time. It was mealtime, and the deck was clear except for two watchmen. Page warned me that one of the men was watching us very closely.

"Just as Page hoisted up the last board, the sailor came over to the side and looked over. I was nervous, but if Page was, he made a good show of hiding it. The sailor asked if we were from Yorktown. He told us his name was Twigs and was curious to know ours. Later, Page told me he instantly realized this was the friend of two deserters he had overheard at Shelton's Inn in Hanover! Before long, Page had promised Twigs sanctuary and a job on an American ship owned by Alexander if he would help us. The sailor was willing, even eager, but one thing stopped him—his fellow watchman. The sailor must have already distrusted his shipmate because he walked over deliberately to interrupt their conversation.

"Quick as a flash, Page hit him. Poof! The man was out, which was easy for me to understand." Jean-Marc smiled as he rubbed his own jaw.

Christiana returned his smile, but she was remembering Stephan's face contorted in rage as he struck Jean-Marc. He had told her that the name "Raven's Claw" was not important. However, to spark such fury, there must be something significant about it. She pushed these thoughts back as Jean-Marc was continuing his story. She didn't want to miss any of it.

"Twigs helped us tie the fellow up with some canvas strips. Then we carried him over to where the damaged sail lay in a pile and covered him with the canvas. It wasn't quite dark, but we couldn't wait. Twigs led us toward the stern to a hatch leading below.

"I must admit, my heart was pounding so hard I feared the whole ship would be alerted. Twice, we were nearly discovered, but Twigs was true to his word and led us to the cabin where Alexander was being held. He diverted the guard's attention and Page grabbed him from behind, dragging him into the cabin. We tied him up with Alexander's bonds.

"I was sure I was dreaming when they came through that door," Alex declared. He recalled the moment vividly. Still weak and in pain from his leg wound, he thought he was beginning to hallucinate. It had taken the two young rescuers a minute to convince him that they were real.

"Twigs led us out," Jean-Marc continued. "I helped Alexander, and Page guarded our rear. Miraculously we had reached the deck without a problem. Then, all of a sudden, the watchman we had tied up called out the alarm! Somehow, he had gotten loose and worked his way out from under the sail.

"Page grabbed Twigs. 'Make sure Alexander gets to shore!' he yelled, 'or there'll be no job!' Then he directed me to help while he kept the British busy. There was no arguing with him, so over we went.

"Jumping from a ship is not something I ever wish to do again, I might add. Just as I jumped, I spied Page struggling with a guard. While swimming, we heard two shots. I looked back to see our friend fall into the water. A host of sailors jammed the side and started shooting. Fortunately we were out of danger by then.

"Since Alexander and Twigs were alright, I circled back to see if I could help Page. Suddenly there he was swimming toward me! I was so happy I wanted to shout.

"So you have it. We spent the night in a grist mill along the shore because Alex was too weak to go any farther. Then yesterday morning, we found the doctor in Yorktown. He ministered to Alex's wound and recommended he rest there to regain some strength. Stephan was wary of everyone in the town. He had promised his help to Twigs, but worried some citizen sympathetic to the British might turn the young fellow back over to them."

"What happened to Twigs?" Christiana directed the question to Alexander, who sat comfortably beside her sipping a cup of tea.

"I gave a letter sealed with my signet ring," he grinned, "and directed him to a trustworthy friend in Yorktown who'll see to it he has a fresh start as an American seaman sailing from Baltimore."

"This morning Stephan persuaded Alex's friend to lend us a carriage to bring your brother back to Williamsburg today. He was most insistent that we needed to get back here as soon as possible," Jean-Marc concluded.

Christiana wondered if someone named Raven's Claw had anything to do with Stephan's sense of urgency.

The afternoon had slipped away, and Christiana realized that Mariette was very tired. She suggested that Mariette get some rest so they could get an early start home in the morning. No one felt the need of dinner, and everyone agreed that turning in early was wise. Jean-Marc escorted his sister up to her room.

For the first time in a long time, Christiana and Alexander had a chance to talk alone.

The twins, Alex and James, and Ram had all inherited their father's handsome dark hair and eyes, while Robert resembled their Grandfather McClaren's fair coloring. All four brothers had a keen sense of humor, although Ram and Robert were more serious-minded. The twins, however, had always been double trouble with teasing. Marriage and the responsibility of their own business had tempered this propensity so Christiana knew that Alex's first comment was sincere.

"Chris, you seem perplexed. Is something troubling you?"

"No. I was just so worried about you. A couple of years ago, the British could have had you and James both, with my blessing," she teased, "but now that you've grown into some rather nice fellows, it'd be a terrible waste of a perfectly good brother!"

"Well, thank you very much," he retorted with mock indignation.

"How is James?" she asked.

"Doing well. He's not going to be too happy with me losing the *Sea Sprite,* but then neither am I." He frowned. "For five months we've been running the blockade without a scratch. This is the second ship we've lost this month. Maybe James is right. Ever since we had that run-in with Rupert Harrod, the British have been especially alert to the movements of our vessels."

"I'm sure Stephan told you we were on our way back from delivering an order to the Caskells for Father. Mrs. Caskell mentioned her brother, Rupert, was still in sympathy with the British. Do you think he's the reason for your losses?" Christiana fed Copper a few bits of food scraps waiting for her brother's answer.

"We have no proof, of course. But he was very angry with us when his two most capable captains quit him to come work for us. They refused to carry any more cargo to Canada and England after Harrod lost a brigantine and her crew. They found out that he had accepted compensation from the British for his ship and cargo without demanding return of his crew as well. Seems as long as he makes a profit, his crews are expendable."

94

"It's a wonder that he keeps any employees at all," Christiana added.

"Apparently the attack on the brigantine was a mistake, and his fleet is generally left alone, so there's not usually as much risk for his crews."

"I wonder if the attack on Hampton was a mistake too?" she mused. "We heard yesterday that the Caskells' house was damaged by some of the sailors that got out of hand. Apparently Mrs. Caskell didn't have a chance to buy protection for their property before their place was besieged. She and Mr. Caskell weren't hurt because Colonel Beckwith stepped in just in time to save them but not the windows and some of the furniture on the ground floor."

"It will be interesting to see if they're reimbursed for their losses like her brother was. But enough of that," Alex declared. "Tell me now about everyone. How's Mother and Gran and the rest?"

Christiana was glad to speak of things other than the war, and quickly began to bring her brother up-to-date on the rest of the family.

"Gran is fine. She is remarkable. I don't know where she gets her energy. She'll probably outlive us all.

"Last week, Robert and Mother left for Mercy Ridge to be with Marianne when the baby is born. The last letter from Ram said that little Amy and Luke couldn't understand what was taking their new baby so long to arrive. Luke already has plans to take him fishing."

"He's sure it's going to be a little brother?" Alex grinned.

"Ram says he is. For only two years old, Luke already has very definite ideas. Amy is four now, you know, and says she wouldn't mind another little brother, but a sister would be nice.

"Uncle Robbie is quite well. He and Robert are excited about the new crop of foals at Cherry Hills Farms this year. Suzanne is fine, but still longs for a baby of their own. She feels she's letting Robert down by not giving him an heir."

"Heather would like to start a family right away too." Alex sighed. "But I think we should wait until this war is settled. James and Hannah have had the same disagreement, but James is even more adamant about it than I am." He gingerly touched his wounded leg and added, "If not for Stephan and Jean-Marc . . . ah well. It does certainly prove that we are right to only have one of us at sea at a time. After this, my dear wife will be more convinced than ever that I should leave the sailing to our crews from now on and stay on dry land."

"She has a point, at least, until our ships are safe from assault by the British," Christiana agreed.

They continued discussing the family and friends at Dunston until Mr. Hatcher came out to light the lamp standing at the corner of the garden. When he went back into the inn, Christiana could see that Alex was exhausted.

"You're looking a bit worse for wear, dear brother. Come on, you can lean on my shoulder and I'll help you up to your room."

"I am tired, but you still haven't told me what's troubling you. Since you've talked about everyone except Stephan, I have an idea it has something to do with him."

"What makes you say that?" she shot back, trying to avoid his questioning glance.

"Well, I know from your letters you were suspicious of him when he first came. What's the matter? Don't tell me you don't like to be proven wrong?"

"Don't be silly; I hope I have been wrong!" she said adamantly. "I mean—What do you think about him, Alex? Could he be a spy?"

"A spy?" Her brother laughed out loud. "Dear little sister, anyone these days could be a spy."

"I'm serious."

Immediately, Alex could see by the look in Christiana's eyes that she was very serious.

96

"I suppose he could be." He pronounced the words slowly, almost to tease. Then he added with a grin, "Of course, the lead that made the hole in his shirt was decidedly British, and Page certainly didn't make many friends aboard the ship!

"You know, Chris, there's something about the way he says your name though."

"What?"

"Oh nothing. You know I'm rather tired too. I think I'll turn in and try to get some rest. It'll be good to be home tomorrow."

"Alex! What did you mean by what you just said?" Christiana prodded him.

"Never mind. It's probably just my imagination. Good night, Chris. See you in the morning!"

Her brother winked at her with a smile as he limped to the back door of the inn, leaving her alone to contemplate what she had just heard.

# 10

The day following their return from Hampton, Andrew Macklin arrived home from Washington.

It had been an especially trying session with continued haggling over the necessity of establishing a standing army. While the Treasury could ill afford such an expense, many argued that if wisely spent, the money appropriated for the state militias would go far toward training and outfitting professional soldiers. Mac's appropriations committee had suggested that a smaller number of disciplined, well-trained men could accomplish more than a large force of militia comprised of farmers and tradesmen waiting out their six-month terms of service, especially when those terms often ended on the eve of an important confrontation with the enemy, depleting the ranks considerably. Much to Mac's chagrin, President Madison heeded Secretary of War John Armstrong's counsel in the matter of a standing army and chose not to accept the committee's recommendation. The first week of July 1813, thirty-seven years after the Declaration of Independence, Mac wearily wondered if the struggle might yet be lost.

Christiana was concerned about her father. He looked tired from the long ordeal. His handsome face was drawn in tight, haggard lines, and his broad shoulders seemed drooped with the weight of fatigue.

Expressing her concern to Alex, they agreed that a fishing trip would be just the right medicine. Alex's leg was much improved, and it had been a long time since father and son had been able to get away for a little fishing on the river between Dunston and Lynchburg. Mac agreed, and plans were made to leave early the next morning.

Late that evening Christiana had just finished packing a knapsack and was heading upstairs when she heard the door of her father's study open. Stephan emerged and closed the door quietly behind him. He stood at the door a moment, unaware he was being observed. With a slightly furrowed brow, he sighed and headed toward the stairs.

"You're up rather late this evening," he commented when he spotted Christiana on the stairs.

"So are you," she whispered so she wouldn't disturb anyone else. "Is anything wrong?"

He shook his head. "No. Your father and I were just discussing some things about the shop. I think it's a good idea he and Alex are going fishing. Your father could stand to get away for a while.

"Well, I've got some reading to do, and Eric grumbles if the lamp stays lit for too long. Good night."

Christiana watched him go down the hall to the room he shared with Eric. Curious, she turned and went back down the steps.

After tapping lightly at the study door, she opened it and peeked in. The study was a comfortably furnished room with a fireplace on one wall. French doors opened out into the backyard. A drawing table, smaller than the one in the shop, stood at one side of the doors with bookshelves lining the walls on the other side. A large desk and two wing back chairs stood in the middle of the room. Only the lamp on the desk was lit, leaving most of the room in soft shadow. A bouquet of fresh-cut flowers, gathered for her father's homecoming, sat on the corner of the desk. Their fragrance spiced the air pleasantly.

Christiana's father was leaning back in his chair behind the desk. In his hands he held a small silver figurine of two thoroughbred horses in full gallop with mane and tail flying. His brow furrowed in sober reflection, he didn't notice his daughter until she spoke.

"Father? Is something wrong?"

"Come in, Christa. You're up late."

"I was just packing a few things in the knapsack for you and Alex tomorrow.

"Uncle Rob was over yesterday when we got back. He said Princess of the Heather is ready to foal anytime now."

Mac fingered the figurine as he spoke. "Ahh yes, of course. Your mother will be anxious to see that new foal. Princess of the Heather was probably more like Lady than any of her offspring. But then, there's never been another pair like Lady and Sir Ettinsmoor. I don't think your mother has ever quite gotten over the day Lady went down." Mac sighed.

Christiana had heard the many stories of the two remarkable thoroughbred horses, Lady Heather Star and Sir Ettinsmoor, who had been instrumental in bringing her parents together. Her father had made the cast silver representation of the stunning pair and had given it to her mother on their first anniversary.

"You know, Christa," he said wistfully, "even when the house is full, it seems lonely when your mother is away."

"Mother says the same thing when you're not here," she replied lovingly.

A broad grin brightened his face as Mac forcibly shook himself free of his pensive mood. Standing, he walked over to the fireplace and carefully placed the figurine on the mantel.

"Well, as soon as your brother and I get back from our fishing trip, I'm heading for Mercy Ridge to fetch her back home," he declared with a twinkle in his dark eyes as he returned to his chair. "They'll just have to give her up a week early! It will also give me a chance to see Amy, Luke, and the newest Macklin. I'm glad it's not as far to Mercy Ridge as it was to Iron Mountain. These babies grow so quickly they'd be grown up without us ever seeing them. I still can't get over how much little Luke looks like Ram did when he was nearly two."

Christiana giggled, happy to see his spark of good humor again. She walked around the back of his chair.

"I saw Stephan just now. He's up rather late too. He said you were discussing some things about the shop. Anything I need to know?"

Mac grinned at his pretty daughter. What a delightful child she'd always been. Jessica had nearly died giving birth to the twins, so they had not planned to have more children. Christiana had come as a surprise, but such a precious surprise. From the moment her tiny fingers curved around her father's finger, she had been the apple of his eye. Telling her "no" had never been easy, but occasionally it was necessary. "Nope," he finally replied, and began to leaf through some papers on the desk.

Christiana's curiosity only intensified. However, she knew her father. If he wanted her to know something, he would tell her. If he didn't, there would be no chance of coaxing it out of him.

"How's Eric doing?" Mac asked, changing the subject.

"You know Eric. When he applies himself, he can do some very nice work. Of course, now that his arm must heal, he has the perfect excuse to stroll in the garden with Mariette."

"I thought he was paying close attention to Miss Richaux at dinner tonight. How do you feel about that?"

"Father, I suppose I did have a bit of a heart-flutter for him a while back," she admitted, "but to tell the truth, I'm a little relieved he's so interested in Mariette.

"By the way, has he mentioned the discussion he had with Mr. Caskell about his own shop in Roanoke when his apprenticeship is completed?"

"Yes, he did. I had thought that he could continue on here, but maybe that would be best for all."

"Well," she decided to take the step, "there's always Stephan. By the time Eric leaves, he should be as accomplished and a very able assistant." At the mention of Stephan's name again, Christiana saw a grave expression fill her father's eyes.

"If he's still here by then."

Mac's comment was more for his own benefit but it didn't go unnoticed. Before Christiana could pursue it though, he said, "I must say that's a very different attitude from the little spy-chaser I left here three weeks ago! A change of heart perhaps?"

"Well . . . ah . . ." she stammered, trying to find the right words. "After what he did for Alex, I suppose he does deserve a chance to prove himself, that is, unless you've learned something that might indicate I was right to begin with."

Mac stood up and put his arm around his daughter's shoulders. "That's my girl," he chuckled. "It never hurts to be cautious, but you can put your mind at ease. Stephan's no spy." Mac then kissed her on the forehead. "It's getting late. I think I'll turn in since Alex and I want to get away early in the morning."

With that he left her standing there, but she felt as much in the dark about Stephan as she had before. Mac had supported Stephan's claim that he wasn't a spy, yet there was something in her father's attitude indicating that his discussion with Stephan had left him disturbed about something.

Mysteries drove Christiana mad. She had always liked things well-ordered and predictable. It was bad enough to have the country in a turmoil of war, but to have a stranger enter their lives with some dark secret was unsettling to the point of distraction. To make matters worse, deep feelings she didn't understand were beginning to grow within her and she was having a harder and harder time denying their existence.

The next afternoon Christiana sat in the garden with Mariette and Jean-Marc. As they enjoyed cold lemonade and a cool breeze in the shade, Jean-Marc related his exploits on a sugar plantation in the steamy climate of Santo Domingo. Christiana realized that the nineteen-year-old Frenchman was about the same age as Stephan, and in fact only two years older than she! Now that they were safe and his sister had nearly recovered, Jean-Marc had been able to relax a bit, and the careworn expression that had made him appear much older when they first met had disappeared.

After a while Eric joined them, complaining slightly about being unable to work due to the pain in his arm. His plight was rewarded with the attention of a sympathetic Mariette, who gladly shared her garden bench with him.

The conversation then turned to the craft of silversmithing and to Christiana's artwork.

"I'd love to see your drawings, Christiana," Jean-Marc suggested.

Eric encouraged her to take Jean-Marc to the shop to see the illustrations she had just completed for her father. Christiana quickly took the hint and invited her French guest to follow her, leaving the young couple to themselves.

As she led her guest into the shop, Stephan stood at the far end near the crucible. He had just completed casting a pair of candlesticks. Not wishing to disturb him, they nodded a greeting, and Christiana led Jean-Marc to a large drawing table scattered with papers.

As he was admiring her detailed illustrations, Gran came to the door. Standing behind her was a tall slender young man in the smartly tailored, dark gray uniform of the Virginia state militia, a small group of full-time soldiers who commanded the various militia units around the state. He was a pleasant looking fellow with medium brown hair, a small mustache, and hazel eyes.

"Christiana, dear, this is Lieutenant Curtis Knox. He's come to see your father. When I told him that the congressman wasn't in, he insisted on speaking to you."

Gran then turned to the lieutenant. "May I get you a glass of fresh lemonade?" she asked.

The young man politely declined, entered the shop, and extended his hand toward Christiana.

"Miss Macklin," he said as he briskly shook her hand, "you probably don't remember me, but I escorted your family to the governor's reception three years ago."

"Yes, Lieutenant, I do remember. Please come in. May I introduce Jean-Marc Richaux and Stephan Page?"

The apprentice had already come forward and was standing behind Jean-Marc. After exchanging handshakes, Knox said soberly, "Miss Macklin, I have a bit of information I think your father should know." He glanced at Stephan and Jean-Marc. "If we could speak in private, please."

"Yes, of course. We'll go to Father's study. Excuse me, gentlemen," she nodded to Stephan and Jean-Marc, "I'll be right back."

In the study, Christiana offered the lieutenant a chair.

"I'm stationed in the quartermaster's office at Fort Stanford, near Fort Meigs," he began. "I recently learned about a strange case of a Natiri Indian by the name of Wolf Stalking. The story is rather absurd and is probably just a rumor, but I thought your father should hear about it anyway, especially after the attack on his party last winter."

"What is it?" she asked uneasily.

"I do wish your father was here so I wouldn't have to upset you with this," he said reluctantly.

"Please go on," she urged. "I'll be more upset if I have to sit here imagining what sort of rumor would have brought you out of your way like this!"

"Very well," he smiled. "Apparently this Wolf Stalking has sent his stepson on a mission to claim blood-vengeance against your father."

Unable to believe her ears, Christiana finally laughed and said, "You're not serious! Whatever for?"

"I wish I were not," he assured her grimly. "I learned of the story from an old trapper by the name of Chenault who interprets for the Shawnee and the militia from time to time. He was headed back to the northwest, but slipped on some ice and broke his leg and had to stay at Fort Stanford for a couple of months. He was there when your father was in February and said this Wolf Stalking and one of his stepsons were also there. Apparently there are two stepsons, both White, both taken captive as small children and raised as Indians.

"Nearly a month after the ambush of your father's party, the stepson who came to the fort with Wolf Stalking was bragging to Chenault that soon his father would be vindicated for a terrible wrong done many years ago by your father. He said then the old Indian could die in peace, sure of his place in their hereafter."

The story was so wildly unbelievable, Christiana half expected the lieutenant to laugh and confess it was all an extremely bad joke. However, the young man's serious demeanor quickly convinced her he wasn't joking.

"This is ridiculous!" Christiana declared, angrily coming to her feet. "My father could never have done anything so wrong as to warrant such a thing."

"Calm down, miss. I know that. But you know that sometimes these savages have some pretty strange customs. No telling what it could have been.

"Even though your father didn't actually kill anyone in Wolf Stalking's family or clan, the old Indian is claiming blood vengeance because he is considered dead to his people.

"The stepson sent to do this was educated at the Moravian Mission not far from the fort. He's about eighteen or nineteen now. Being White and able to speak English, he can travel anywhere without arousing suspicion.

"We are short of supplies and men there on the frontier; and I've been ordered back here to raise more funds for supplies and recruit more men and drill them to strengthen our defenses along Lake Erie. When Chenault heard I was returning to Virginia, he thought I could get a message to warn your father to be on alert for any strangers."

Her knees felt weak and she sat down slowly. "Do you know his name or what he looks like?" Christiana forced the words out of a tightened throat.

"He only knew his Natiri name, Yaro'ka-i, which supposedly means 'He Hunts with the Heart of the Eagle.' Have you seen any strangers or suspicious characters lurking about?"

She shook her head no.

The lieutenant stood to take his leave. "I grew up in this county and know how much the congressman has done for our district. I admire your father very much, Miss Macklin. If there's anything I can do, or if you hear of anyone suspicious coming to town, let me know. I felt I had to warn the congressman of the possible danger."

Trembling slightly, she stood up and extended her hand. "Thank you, Lieutenant. I appreciate your concern."

The man took her hand, holding it firmly a moment longer than necessary then added, "I'm truly sorry to have

106

distressed you. If your father had been here, it could have been avoided. Please don't worry, Miss Macklin. My unit will be camped outside of town for the next three weeks. We will be recruiting and training men for the northern campaign. If you need anything, please don't hesitate to call on me."

Bowing slightly, the lieutenant excused himself and left.

She sank weakly into the wing-backed chair again. Her head was swimming with questions. She hardly paid attention as Copper came ambling over to sit beside her chair. Why had she not told the lieutenant about Stephan? Then again, why should she? He couldn't possibly be this Yaro'ka-i. He'd been here for four months now. And, if he had come to harm her father, why hadn't he done so already? Despite this point in his favor, that engulfing tide of suspicion now resurfaced from the place Christiana had tried to bury it.

Just then, the sound of the study door roused her. She looked up to see Stephan standing there before her with the door closed behind him.

"What is it, Christiana?"

Stephan had called her by her first name only two other times: the night in the Caskells' garden and following the accident when he thought she was still unconscious. The sound of his voice saying it again pierced deep to the heart.

When she didn't reply, he walked over to where she was sitting. "Are you all right?"

"No," she finally managed, looking up at him. "Stephan, it's time to tell me what you're doing here. I have to know. I have to know now."

"What did the lieutenant have to say?" The young man's eyes narrowed as he studied her face, pale with distress, and her blue eyes dark with dread.

"He told me about a young man named Yaro'ka-i, and—" She swallowed hard to choke back the lump in her throat. She was determined not to dissolve into tears in front of him again. "And how this young man has pledged to destroy my father!"

Stephan closed his eyes for a long moment.

"Stephan. Tell me you're not this Yaro'ka-i." Her voice was barely above a whisper. She stood up and turned toward him.

"You've been suspicious of me for a long time," he replied defensively. "If you think I'm Yaro'ka-i, why didn't you turn me in to the lieutenant?"

Stephan faced her squarely.

Turning away from him, she walked over to the desk. "I'm not sure. I had to hear the truth from you first. After the past few days, after what you did for Alex, I had convinced myself that I'd been wrong about you."

Walking up behind her, Stephan placed his hands on her shoulders and turned her toward him. His grasp was firm but gentle.

"I told you I would never hurt you or your family. There are some things about me that I just can't tell you right now." Stephan kept his hands on her shoulders so she couldn't turn away. "In spite of what you've heard, I have to ask you to trust me a little longer. If you can't, well, you'll have to do what you think is best."

Stephan knew the depth of Christiana's devotion to her family, and he had no illusions that she would blithely accept some stranger's word simply because he asked her to. After discovering her suspicions about him, he was surprised that she hadn't at least mentioned them to Lieutenant Knox. He ignored the tiny glimmer of hope that there might be a soft spot in her heart willing to give him the benefit of the doubt.

Christiana sensed he was telling her the truth, and she discovered she wanted to believe him. Yet, could she risk her father's safety on some deep inexplicable feeling? He had not denied anything. And yet, had he not proven something by risking his life to save Alex?

As once before, time seemed suspended. The two people stood there intently searching each other's face for some sign of assurance. Yet a wide gulf of the unknown existed between them.

Just then a low, almost mournful, whine penetrated the curtain of tension. They looked down at Copper whose sad eyes signaled he was disturbed by what was happening.

Instinctively, they both reached out to reassure him and pat the animal on the head. Their hands touched.

Christiana stepped back. "Alright, Stephan, I'll wait until you can tell me. But I have to give Father the message that the lieutenant brought for him. Then, it will be up to him."

Stephan nodded. "Fair enough," he replied as they entered their uneasy truce.

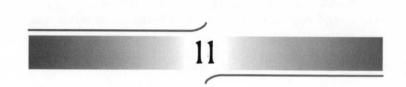

## 11

The summer night air was alive with the melodies of nature. The cricket and tree frog chorus was accompanied by an occasional owl a cappella. The fragrance of fresh dew mingled with clover and night blooming jasmine in the warm, still air.

The windows of the Macklin home were wide open, and strains of music as well as laughter drifted through the fragrant darkness. Friday, July 9, 1813, a welcome home party was being held to honor Christiana's mother and to celebrate Alexander's rescue from the British navy. Stephan and Jean-Marc were being honored as well for their heroic rescue.

As soon as Mac returned from the fishing trip with Alex, he had ridden to Mercy Ridge to retrieve his wife. As it happened, Marianne had delivered a new baby boy several days earlier and was already up and around, so Jessica could return home without worry.

Alex had developed an infection in his wound and remained in Dunston for an additional week to recuperate. As soon as Heather received word that her husband was recovering from a British-inflicted wound, she made plans to hurry to his side. James and Hannah accompanied her.

Friends and neighbors from all over the village and soldiers from the militia camp filled the house to overflowing. Robert, his wife Suzanne, and their Uncle Robbie had ridden over from Cherry Hills Farms. With the twins and their wives present, Ram was the only missing Macklin.

It had been nearly two weeks since the day Lieutenant Knox had delivered his upsetting message. Christiana had relayed it to her father as soon as he returned from fishing. He had made her promise not to mention anything to her mother, and he assured her that everything would be fine and not to worry about Stephan.

Because of this relaxed approach, Christiana tried to put the matter out of her mind. Having Jean-Marc, Mariette, and Alex around helped. Then the day after her father left for Mercy Ridge, Stephan had come into the study where she was working on the books and made a surprising statement.

"I've joined the militia," he had announced as calmly as if he'd informed her that he'd just finished polishing the candlesticks.

She'd been so surprised, her only reply was, "You did?"

"I'll just be drilling with them in the afternoons, so I'll take care of my duties here in the mornings. We're scheduled to head north on the fourteenth of July," he had explained.

"That's just two weeks away." The idea of him leaving had suddenly filled her with a strange jumble of emotions.

"It would be a good idea to be careful of strangers until you and your parents return to Washington on the fifteenth; but as far as worrying about your father . . . what you've been worrying about . . . you can rest easy. I'm sure that whole situation Knox told you about will be settled without any problem for the congressman."

"How can you be so sure of that?"

"Well, it's just that things have a way of working out and I'm sure this will too."

Without saying anything more, he had left the study. She had sat there a long time musing over the fact that conversations with Stephan Page always left her with as many or more questions than were ever answered.

The mystery surrounding Stephan still remained unsolved. However, Christiana had little time to consider it, for a few days later James, Hannah, and Heather arrived. Her parents returned two days after that. Now, the day after Mac and Jessica's return, this lively celebration was in full swing. With all the singing, dancing, and luscious food, Christiana was determined to put the puzzling situation out of her mind. She immersed herself in the energetic music of Elmer Tuttle's fiddle.

Even Stephan felt free enough to allow his good humor to escape a bit. He resisted the group's attempts to make a fuss over him because of the rescue and even pushed Jean-Marc forward to receive the plaudits. He laughed and sang a little, joining in the spirit of the party.

Christiana found herself oddly pleased to see him laughing. It was evident that Stephan was enjoying the evening.

The furniture had been moved out of the sitting room and the rugs rolled back for a dance floor. While many older folks sat in the dining room or on the wide front porch, a number of them gathered along the wall to watch the young people step lively to the music.

Christiana had just finished an energetic reel with Lieutenant Knox when the music started up again. Catching her breath, she asked if he would mind getting her some punch and taking a brief rest. Knox had been monopolizing her dances for most of the evening and, while he seemed nice, Christiana was glad for a moment to herself. Looking about, she spotted Stephan talking to Alex and Heather. She went over to join them.

"Stephan, I haven't seen you out on the dance floor yet," she commented.

Instantly she wished she hadn't called attention to this. Maybe he didn't know how to dance. Christiana had to admit to herself that she was a little disappointed Stephan hadn't tried to cut in while the lieutenant was so obviously trying to monopolize her attention.

The slight embarrassment on Stephan's face passed quickly. "You look as though you could use a breath of fresh air and a little rest," he replied. "Would you care to take a turn around the porch?"

The flash of his good-natured grin made her forget her comment and the lieutenant and the punch. She smiled with a slight curtsey. Stephan offered his arm and, begging the other couple's pardon, they left the noisy dance floor behind.

As they were walking down the hall toward the entryway, Stephan pointed to a large box sitting on the hall table.

"What do you suppose that could be?" he inquired innocently.

"I don't know," Christiana remarked, eyeing the large bow on the package.

Her escort picked up a small card tucked under the bow. "Miss Christiana Macklin."

"What in the world—?"

Before she could complete the sentence, Stephan interjected, "I suppose the only way you'll find out is if you open it!"

Christiana looked at him. A little gleam lit his eyes.

She quickly untied the ribbon. Lifting off the lid, she discovered a lovely bonnet of pale blue linen with tiny violet flowers clustered on one side of the brim and two lavender satin ribbons to tie under the chin. At a loss for words, she just stared at the gift for a moment.

"You don't like it," he said flatly. "Mariette said you would. But I should have asked her to go with me to pick it out. When I saw it in the mercantile window, it reminded me of the one that was ruined in the accident. I remembered how violet blue that one had made your eyes look."

She stopped him by putting her fingertips against his lips. "It's the most beautiful bonnet I've ever seen in my life," she declared softly.

The candles in the wall sconces cast a soft glow over the couple as he looked at her. A tear slipped down her cheek. He knew she was pleased.

Long ago, his father had told him how a woman can cry even when she's overwhelmed with joy. He had never seen it until now. Although this display of emotion was a bit unnerving, it was unmistakable evidence that he had chosen well and made her very happy.

Christiana carefully removed the bonnet from the hat box and put it on. Looking in the mirror over the hall table, she saw an attractive couple looking back at her. Stephan was nearly a head taller than she and stood behind her, looking handsome in his dark blue shirt. His light brown hair was neatly combed and in the soft light, his blue eyes looked almost black. Somehow the two of them looked natural together, and she felt the color rising in her cheeks as she noticed the look of admiration on his face.

"Christiana? What do we have here?" She turned at the sound of her mother's voice. Mac and Jessica were walking into the hall from the dining room.

"Isn't it lovely, Mother! Stephan bought it for me." She stopped a moment and looked at him. "It must have been terribly expensive. You really shouldn't have done it."

Uncertain whether the Macklins would approve, Stephan explained, "I promised her I'd replace the bonnet ruined in the accident."

Jessica smiled and patted his arm. "It's lovely, Stephan. That was very thoughtful of you."

Almost imperceptibly, both young people looked to Mac for a comment. All he said was "It's very nice."

The reservation in his voice signaled something amiss to his daughter. Christiana studied her father a moment and thought she caught a slight wrinkle in his brow. Could it be he was more concerned about Stephan and his situation than he wanted her to know?

"Wish Ram could have been here for the party last night," Alex said as he baited his fishhook.

"Yes, it's been a long time since you boys have all been home at the same time," Mac replied as he watched his fishing line suspended in the meandering current of the river.

Early morning sunrays were just beginning to tip over the treetops as Mac and the twins settled on the rocky bank of the river outside of Dunston.

"Mother said that little Luke was keeping Ram on his toes," James chuckled.

Mac grinned and nodded. "The little lad's more like his daddy every day, strong-willed, inquisitive. I'd say Ram and Marianne have their job cut out for them. Thank goodness Amy is so much like her mother. She'll be as pretty as Marianne and have that same calm strength. You can see it in her already."

"Hannah wants to start a family right away," James sighed. "But I think we should wait until this war is settled. Things are too uncertain."

"Well, James, if we answer Perry's plea for help, we'll not be running the blockade for a while," Alex said as he dropped his line in the water.

Mac glanced at James, the elder of the two young men by ten minutes. "Perry?"

"Uh-huh," James replied as he pulled in a pan-sized bass. "That's two you're behind, Alex." He removed the fish from the hook and dropped it in the wicker creel with one other.

"I'll catch up." Alex grinned, then nodded at his brother. "Go ahead and tell him; see what he thinks about it."

Before baiting another hook, James came to squat next to the rock where their father sat. The river slid silently by in a silvery ribbon catching the morning sunlight. It was a scene that often came to mind when far from home. As the four Macklin sons were growing up, this had been a favorite place to spend time together fishing and listening to stories of the Lenape people, as well as of the Scottish highlands and moors that had been passed down to their father from his father and grandfather. It was good being home again, but the troubles of the world intruded upon their conversation today.

"You remember we told you about our becoming acquainted with Oliver Perry last year when he was stationed at Newport in command of some of the gunboats there. Well, we got a letter from him just after Alex sailed on the *Sea Sprite*. You know he's supervising the construction of a fleet up on Lake Erie, and what a job he has trying to do the near impossible with few resources."

Mac nodded. He was well aware of the critical situation faced by the young O. H. Perry in a race to build a fleet strong enough to take command of Lake Erie. Control of the entire Northwest Territory would be determined by the nation in control of this lake poised between Canada and the U.S.

"He's in need of help training crews for the ships and overseeing the construction," James continued. "Alex and I've been talking it over since the girls and I got here. I think we've about decided to go. Hannah and Heather are all for it and are planning to set up house there in Erie. After Alex's close call, I think Heather is in favor of it most of all."

Mac studied both of his sons—tall, handsome young men of integrity, intelligent and courageous. He and Jessica had much to be thankful for with such fine sons. Aware of the danger they'd been courting with their blockade running, he was inclined to agree it would be much safer at Erie. But then he was also aware of the tragic comedy of errors being played out by the present incompetent military leaders along the Canadian border.

"And what about your company—Macklin, Macklin & Kendall, Limited?"

Alex pulled in a bass too small for the pan and released it back into the water as he began to answer his father's question.

"Losing two ships within a month has caused a serious cutback for a while. James says our fainthearted partner, Arthur Kendall, thinks it might be a good idea if the Macklin brothers are occupied elsewhere for the time being and maybe the British won't take such a singular obsession with our vessels."

"Well," Mac said. "It looks as though you boys have already made up your minds. Perry's task is a challenging one and may be more critical than anyone wants to admit. I know your help would be invaluable."

The twins nodded, the decision made.

# 12

On the fifteenth of July, two days before Richaux's and the Macklins' scheduled departure for Washington, a certain gloom had settled over the house. Eric and Mariette were obviously dreading the day they would be separated. Even Jean-Marc's usual jovial spirit was subdued. And Christiana had finally faced the fact of Stephan's departure with the militia the next morning. She didn't want him to go.

Early that afternoon, Christiana was sewing the finishing touches on a new dress for Mariette, whose baggage had been left on the *Sea Sprite* and who had been borrowing Christiana's clothes until she was able to make some of her own. Mariette and Eric had taken a walk into the village, and Christiana wanted to finish the dress before they returned.

As she was snipping the last thread, she heard the front door burst open. "Mr. Macklin! Mr. Macklin!" It was Eric's voice.

Christiana dropped her sewing on the settee in her room and dashed out. She reached the lower hall just as her father and mother rushed into the sitting room and Stephan and Jean-Marc burst in from the shop. Together they discovered Eric kneeling beside the chair with a distraught Mariette holding a shawl. Christiana recognized the delicate shawl of Spanish lace she had let Mariette borrow. James had brought it to her from a voyage to Barcelona, and it was Christiana's favorite.

On seeing Christiana, Mariette's pixie-like face clouded and she burst into tears. "I'm so sorry."

"Sorry?" Eric declared in exasperation. "Sorry about some bit of lace when you were nearly killed?"

"What happened, Eric?" Mac's tone was calm yet commanding.

"Some drunken drifter trying to show off, I guess. Threw this knife. It just missed her! See how close he came? It pinned part of this shawl to the post outside the mercantile."

"It made a dreadful hole," Mariette mourned.

Mac examined the knife and, with a sober expression, handed it to Stephan.

The moment the apprentice took the knife his heart sank a little. He could see the handle, which was made from the tine of a deer antler, had carvings etched into it and was blackened with charcoal. The one symbol that caught his eye was that of a sharp bird's talon. The other markings were unmistakably Shawnee.

"I tried to catch the blasted fool, but he got away," Eric lamented.

"Did you get a very good look at him?" Stephan asked.

"Not really," Eric replied. "I know he was a big man, probably a head taller than you. I think he wore buckskins."

"Did you notice anything else?" Mac asked.

Eric shook his head impatiently as he gently patted Mariette's hand trying to comfort her.

"Wait. I remember wondering why a White man would try so hard to look like an Indian."

"Are you alright, Mariette?" Jessica asked.

"Yes, thank you, just a bit shaken. I feel so very bad about the shawl."

"As long as you're alright," Christiana declared, "the shawl is of little consequence."

"Just rest there a minute, dearie; I'll bring you a nice cup of tea to settle your nerves." Gran hurried off to the kitchen.

Mac motioned to Stephan, and the two men left the room. Christiana and her mother exchanged glances filled with curiosity.

"Mariette, I'll be right back," Christiana said. "Eric, stay with her a moment, will you?"

Eric looked up at her as if she were crazy for thinking he would even consider leaving Mariette's side. Christiana grinned slightly, realizing the foolishness of her remark and followed her mother out of the room. Once in the hall, the two women went to the study to join Mac and Stephan.

"Mac, darling," Jessica said placing her hand on his arm. "Ever since I came home from Mercy Ridge, I've had the feeling you've been keeping something from me. This frightening incident has something to do with it, doesn't it?"

Mac looked at Stephan who nodded, then turned to look out the French doors into the garden.

"That's what happens when you've been married as long as we have." Mac grinned a bit ruefully as he affectionately touched Jessica's face. "You begin to know each other so well, it's nearly impossible to keep something hidden."

"Well?" Jessica pressed as she searched his dark eyes for a clue.

"Jess, remember when we first met—the journey from Charleston—when you received your Indian name Rea' na tani?"

"At the Natiri village," she recalled, baffled by the direction of his conversation.

"Do you remember the young brave I fought?"

"Yes, you spared his life, but what has that to do with anything?"

"Remember I told you I was afraid I wasn't doing him any favors by letting him live?" When she nodded, he continued. "Apparently I wasn't doing us any either, because he was banished and has been harboring a bitterness toward me all these years. That bitterness has led to this." Mac held up the knife.

Jessica slumped into a nearby chair. "You mean he's here, in Dunston?"

"Not him, his stepson, a fellow called Raven's Claw."

At the mention of the name, Christiana turned sharply toward Stephan. Their eye contact held their attention for so long they nearly missed the continuing conversation.

"Why didn't you tell me, Mac?" Jessica was asking.

"I didn't want to worry you unnecessarily. I don't think he was really trying to harm anyone, yet. I think it was just a warning."

Jessica glanced at Stephan. Now she became curious about his possible role, for he obviously knew all about this weapon and the man who had thrown it. She determined to ask Mac about it later when they were alone. "What are we to do about this fellow then?"

"Nothing for the moment," Mac replied. "Whatever he's up to, he'll have to come to Washington to do it because we can't delay our departure. I doubt he'll attempt to follow us. At any rate, I can't delay getting back to the capital."

Mac hesitated before continuing. He looked at his wife. "The news from Washington isn't good, Jess. I just received word that Armstrong has done it. I can't believe he can be so incredibly thickheaded! He is replacing General Dearborn with James Wilkinson immediately."

Later that evening, Christiana was in her room packing when Mariette came in and sat down on the bed. Christiana glanced up briefly and continued folding the last gown.

"This is the last, I think," she said. "Do you need help finishing with your bags?"

"No," came Mariette's reply.

"I'm not sure I'm prepared for this trip, Mariette, but there seems to be little choice."

"Christiana, I'm not going."

"I don't think there's a lovelier bonnet in all of Washington!" Christiana carefully placed her new bonnet in its box. "Can you imagine, he picked it out—What'd you say?"

"I said, I'm not going to Washington or Baltimore or Santo Domingo. I'm staying right here."

Christiana looked at her friend closely for the first time since she had entered the room and waited for her to explain further.

"Eric has asked me to stay here and marry him." Her face was shining. A radiance enveloped her.

"Mariette! He hasn't!"

"But he has," she insisted.

"I believe you. It's just I didn't realize Eric was quite that sensible."

"That frightening incident this morning—He said he suddenly realized what it would be like if something happened to me, or if I left and he never saw me again. I'm so happy I could cry!"

No sooner had she spoken the words than the tears spilled down her cheeks. Christiana's eyes filled with tears.

"We are to be married on the first of September. He's taking me to his family's home to stay while you're away. After what your papa told us, he says he wants me to be where his family can look after me."

"What does Jean-Marc think about all of this?"

"He has known for some time now that I love Eric very much. He's going to Washington with you, but I'll be very surprised if he makes arrangements to sail on to Santo Domingo. In the short time we've been here, he has become very fond of your America."

"Oh, Mariette, I couldn't be happier for you."

The two girls hugged each other gleefully.

Christiana then teased her friend gently, "You must love him very much to be willing to stay in the Lowe house for a month."

Mariette whirled around the room in a dance. "Oh, they're a wonderful family, so full of energy and fun. I feel as if God has given me a whole new life, a whole new family." She stopped a moment and looked at Christiana, her eyes shining. "Dear, dear Christiana, if it had not been for you and your brother, I never shall have found this new life. How can I ever say thank you?"

Christiana felt so happy. "Just promise that I can be your maid of honor in the wedding."

"But of course, there could be none other!" Mariette declared with glee.

The two women chattered for another hour until finally Christiana said, "You look exhausted, Mariette. We really ought to get to bed. I have a tiring trip ahead, and you'll be needing all of your energy to survive the next month with Eric's family."

"I'm so happy, I don't know if I will ever sleep again!" With that Mariette turned in a dizzying circle and flopped back on her bed.

"I'll go down and get us both some warm milk," Christiana offered. "I think we could both use it."

Having already donned her nightgown, the young woman tossed on her dressing gown and tiptoed down the stairs. Everyone had turned in early in preparation for the busy day to come, and the house was dark.

As she padded silently past her father's study, she thought she heard a noise. Remembering she hadn't seen Copper since just after dinner, she opened the door.

"Poor Copper, did you get shut in?"

Christiana stepped inside the room and called the dog's name.

Suddenly, she turned. Something had moved! A scream froze in her throat. At that instant a large form emerged from the deepest shadows. With the grip of a steel trap, a hand grabbed her by the shoulder and another clamped over her mouth.

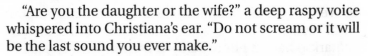

# 13

"Are you the daughter or the wife?" a deep raspy voice whispered into Christiana's ear. "Do not scream or it will be the last sound you ever make."

She nodded her intention to keep quiet, and the man asked his question again.

"Daughter," she gulped after he had moved his hand under her jaw. "And you no doubt are Raven's Claw." The man's grasp restricted her speech, and her voice was shaky.

"You know me then?" the shadow hissed. "That traitorous coyote Page has a loose tongue as well as a coward's heart."

"What have you to do with Page?" she stammered, still struggling for air.

"I have only come to complete the task he was sent for, the task he has lost heart to do himself—to humiliate and destroy Andrew Macklin."

"Yaro'ka-i?" Christiana could feel the pounding of her own heart. She swallowed hard.

"He doesn't deserve the name if he fails to honor the oath he sealed with his own blood. Old Father was deceived into thinking Page would kill the enemy and repay the old debt. He didn't see him as I did—strong, yes, and cunning, but a weak heart."

"Enemy?" she managed to ask as the Indian's grasp loosened slightly. "My father refused to kill Wolf Stalking in a fight. How could he possibly hate him so much for that?"

"Quiet!" he snarled, tightening his grip on her shoulder and jaw once again. "There are some things worse than the death of a brave warrior. Wolf Stalking was banished from the Natiri nation in disgrace. He wandered alone for a very long time, wanting to die yet fearing what awaited a coward in the afterworld. He swore he would once again face his enemy and bring shame and destruction on his head."

Christiana managed to speak despite the hold. "So this brave warrior sends a young man to do his killing for him?" She winced, expecting retaliation for her defiant remark. Surprisingly, the grip lessened.

"You speak boldly for one so close to death. Perhaps there is more to Page's change of heart than I thought."

Sensing that a show of fearlessness was the key to gaining time, Christiana rallied every ounce of courage she could muster. Fighting down the panic, she tried to keep the Indian talking.

"How can he send someone else to regain his pride?"

"You are an insolent female!" The brave almost spat his words. "Wolf Stalking has been wounded many times in battle and is unable to travel. It took him many years to find his enemy again. We went to the trading post where the spirits of his ancestors showed him his enemy. Macklin was there but did not recognize Wolf Stalking. The years have been hard and Old Father is now bent with age and bad health. Macklin still stands straight and looks much like he did when he was young. Old Father could never forget the face of the one who made him a wandering outcast. It was easy for Wolf Stalking to ask many questions and learn all about his old enemy.

"And now to steal into his dwelling and carry away his daughter will bring shame upon him. He will follow. Then he will die without honor."

Christiana struggled to maintain her composure, but with each passing moment it became more apparent that she could be carried off while everyone was asleep. Her only hope was that the man's iron-fisted grip would relax enough for her to escape. But that hope vanished when he abruptly picked her up and threw her over his shoulder. He obviously didn't care if she cried out. Indeed, it was what he expected.

Grabbing the edge of the door that was still ajar, she kicked wildly. Her efforts were laughably futile and, if she could have seen her captor's face, she would have seen a cruel, humorless smile.

Her fingertips slipped painfully from the door's edge as the man carried his bundle quickly toward the French doors opening onto the garden.

Suddenly she heard a low growl.

"Copper!" she screamed as loud as she could. "Help!"

The growl grew louder until it became a deep, fiercely savage snarling. Raven's Claw whirled at the sound. "Wolf!" he yelled in terror.

At that moment the big dog flew through the air and struck Raven's Claw with the full force of his ninety pounds. The power of the animal's lunge sent both captor and captive crashing to the floor. Christiana scrambled away from the furious struggle.

The sound of the man's cries and the savage snarling echoed throughout the house. Christiana could hardly believe the ferociousness of her beloved gentle pet.

"Copper, down! Down!" A light appeared at the door, and Stephan's loud voice punctuated the dog's snarls.

The animal finally obeyed and, scruff still raised like a great lion, stepped back. Low growls still sounded from deep within, but he backed up to where Christiana was crouching on the floor. When he had calmed down, she threw her arms around him, and his wide tongue happily licked her face.

Raven's Claw moaned. Stephan set the candle on Mac's desk and prepared to jerk the intruder to his feet. But, as he reached for him, a sudden flash of steel slashed through the air. Instinctively, Stephan drew back. Raven's Claw was on his feet like a rabid cat.

Copper tensed again, but Christiana clung to his neck. Stephan shouted, "No, Copper. Stay!"

Raven's Claw was poised with his back against the French doors. The flickering candlelight revealed a dreadful gash along the side of his face and blood trickling down his arm. Seemingly oblivious to his injuries, the Indian brandished his knife menacingly and, with a taunting grotesque grin, challenged Stephan to try to take it from him.

Suddenly yelling from the hallway and stairs signaled that the whole house had been alerted. Seeing the odds, Raven's Claw flung open the door at his back and disappeared into the night.

"It's not over," he cursed at Stephan from the darkness.

Christiana blinked as if she had just awakened from a nightmare. Realizing the danger had passed, she buried her face in Copper's ruff.

When Stephan rushed over to help her to her feet, she noticed the slash in his right sleeve and his arm. She winced. "Oh, Stephan! You're bleeding!"

"It's nothing. Are you hurt?" he said, pulling her up and closing his arms about her.

She clung to him tightly, trying to stop trembling and fighting back tears of relief. She shook her head. "No."

In no time, the room was filled with anxious people asking questions. Stephan stepped back to allow Jessica and Mac to hug their daughter. After everyone heard what had happened, Copper eagerly lapped up the lavish praise for his heroism.

After a long discussion and many questions, it was decided that the departure for Washington would continue as planned.

His wound bandaged, Stephan had assured them that pursuing Raven's Claw in the dark forest would be futile and dangerous. Further trouble from him tonight was unlikely, but the men would take turns keeping watch. The incident would be reported to Lieutenant Knox in the morning. As the new unit of militia was prepared to begin their march north then, it was likely some attempt to pick up Raven's Claw's trail would be made by a detachment of the new recruits.

Everyone except Stephan, Christiana, and her parents returned to their rooms. Stephan had volunteered for the first watch.

"Tell Eric to be sure and wake me at four o'clock," Mac reminded Stephan before he left. "And thanks again, lad."

Stephan took his extended hand in a firm handshake. "Copper is the one to thank."

"Accept our thanks anyway," Jessica added, "because if you hadn't decided it was a good idea for Copper to stay downstairs on guard tonight, he would have been left up in Christiana's room instead of with you in the shop. Christa, are you coming?"

"In a minute," she responded as she kissed her parents good night on their way out the door.

"Are you sure your arm will be alright?" she asked, turning toward Stephan.

He nodded. "It's really only a scratch."

Christiana walked over to the French doors and looked into the darkness. The soft glow of the candle on the desk was reflected in the glass panes of the doors and she could see Stephan's reflection.

"Yaro'ka-i. 'He Hunts with the Heart of the Eagle.' That's quite an impressive name to earn upon reaching manhood. My grandfather and his Cherokee blood-brother used to tell my father all about the eagle. They said he is wise enough to make the most of the abilities God has given him to fly the higher currents and take no more prey than needed; he's courageous enough to face the fiercest storms, and faithful to one mate for life. Many of the Indian nations revere the eagle more than any other creature. To earn such a name is about the highest honor you could win."

Stephan did not reply as he watched her standing there.

"Raven's Claw—" She shuddered with the vivid memory of his malevolent strength. "Raven's Claw said he had come to complete the task you'd been sent for. He said . . . he said you'd lost heart to . . . to kill his father's enemy."

"Christiana." Stephan stepped up behind her. His deep soft voice had a calming effect on her.

As she turned around, he closed his strong arms around her again in a comforting embrace. She welcomed their warmth and security.

"How long has Father known the truth about you?" she finally asked.

"I told him that night in the study, the day he returned from Washington," he answered, "but he knew already. When I first came, he had written to Brother Adams at the Moravian Mission near Fort Stanford. Brother Adams wrote back telling all about Wolf Stalking wanting me to avenge his honor so he would not be afraid to die being branded a coward. Brother Adams hoped your father could help me learn a trade to keep me away from Wolf Stalking's influences. Ironically, the good Brother had no idea your father was the very one Wolf Stalking hated so much. Of course, your father recognized that the facts of the story resembled your parents' experience too closely for coincidence."

"No wonder he wasn't surprised by the message from Lieutenant Knox!" Her head still rested against his chest. Finally looking up she asked, "Why wouldn't you tell me the truth that day Knox came?"

"I guess I didn't want to see that fear in your eyes again like the night in the Caskells' garden. I was getting used to your smile. I wasn't sure if you'd be able to believe I really wouldn't hurt your father."

"Can you tell me now what this is all about?" Exasperation edged her voice.

"It's a long story, and it's very late."

Christiana stepped back. The time had come for the whole truth and she must hear it. The stirrings deep in her heart could no longer be denied.

"Stephan—if that *is* your name—I think I shall scream if you don't tell me."

The apprentice turned and walked to the desk. Leaning back against the front, he folded his arms across his chest.

"I was born Stephan Page," he began. "Until I was seven years old, I lived with my parents on a small farm along the Kentucky frontier just as I told you.

"One day, I'd taken my father's lunch out to where he was plowing in the field when we were suddenly surrounded by Creek warriors." He took a deep breath. After thirteen years, he still found it difficult to talk about that dreadful day. "One of them was about to hit me with a club when my father struck him from behind. The Creek fell, dropping his club next to me. Instantly, two more Indians attacked him. Without thinking, I grabbed the club and began pounding at them. A third one then snatched me off my feet and carted me into the forest. I can still see my father laying there and our house in flames . . . my mother's body in the doorway," his voice trailed off.

Christiana sat down on a chair, her heart gripped deeply imagining such a traumatic experience for a child. "Oh, Stephan," she murmured softly.

"The brave carried me under his arm like a sack of flour. It seemed like hours until we reached their camp.

130

He threw me in a hut and tied me up. When the Creeks took me out the next morning, they tossed me back and forth between them in a little game of rough horseplay, a way of testing me I guess. I was probably still in shock because I wasn't afraid. I was just mad. In fact I was so angry, I was just waiting for a chance to get back at them. When one of the braves dropped me, I grabbed a broken limb and started flailing at him. He pulled his tomahawk and would have killed me then and there if Wolf Stalking hadn't stepped in.

"How did Wolf Stalking happen to be with the Creeks?" she asked.

"From what I've learned over the years, after he was banished from the Natiri village, he wandered alone for over two years. Just as a wolf survives best in a pack, Wolf Stalking hated living alone, not belonging with a group anymore. I think that part was almost harder to bear than the disgrace he suffered. He traveled farther west across Georgia and into what's now Mississippi Territory and settled with that band of Creeks. He lived with them for over ten years and had married a Creek woman named Blue Flower. After that long, he was still considered an outsider, by himself and the tribe. He still dressed with symbols of the animal totems the Natiri people feared and honored painted on his buckskin hunting shirt. Even a seven-year-old boy could see he was not one of them by the way he dressed and the way the front half of his head had been shaved with the remainder of hair pulled together in a hair lock at the back."

Christiana could imagine how frightened a child might be, but knew that Stephan must have shown extraordinary courage to have impressed the Natiri to challenge the Creek warrior on his behalf.

Stephan continued, "Anyway, he ended up fighting that Creek brave to see who would have the final say about me. Wolf Stalking won and announced that he would adopt me to help his grieving wife forget about their own young son who'd recently died."

"Wolf Stalking doesn't sound like a coward," Christiana interjected. "Why does he still consider himself one?"

"It's all in the point of view. As far as he's concerned, in a fight to the death—as he and your father fought—there's only a victorious warrior and a dead warrior. It's a very strict code of honor. Not being the victor, yet being alive, he stood in disgrace."

"Mother told me that she had been captured by the Natiri when they were on their way back from Charleston. Father overheard one of the Natiri warriors suggest that Mother might be a medicine woman because her horse killed two of their men. Father entered their camp, and playing on their superstitious nature, confirmed the warrior's idea. He warned them to let her go or a whole herd of wild horses would trample their village. They agreed that if he passed their test, their lives would be spared. During the test, Wolf Stalking's arrow drew blood giving Father the right to challenge him in a fight to the death. As you know, Father won the fight but refused to kill Wolf Stalking. It was a fair fight."

Stephan had to smile at the way her blue eyes flashed with pride in her father's victory. She took a deep breath, embarrassed at getting so carried away with her father's side of the story.

"Sorry. I just find Wolf Stalking's point of view completely unreasonable. Please go on. What happened after he won the fight with the Creek?"

"Come to find out, the Creek brave was Blue Flower's brother. Because he'd always been a troublemaker and because Blue Flower begged for her husband's life, her clan didn't claim blood vengeance, but they did say he was no longer welcome in their village. Blue Flower chose to go with him rather than stay with her people and once again he was an outcast. They took me with them and headed north. Blue Flower had a cousin living with a group of Shawnee along the Ohio River. Needless to say, I wasn't happy. I ran away several times, but each time Wolf Stalking found me and brought me back. I guess I finally decided I really had nothing to go back to. Blue Flower was kind, but very sad every time I ran away, so I finally stayed."

Stephan walked over to the glass-paned door and for a moment stood silently looking out into the night.

"There was another White boy with the Shawnee, but he'd been taken as a baby and was more Shawnee than White—if not by birth, certainly in spirit. His Shawnee parents had died shortly before we joined them. Blue Flower thought that having a brother might make me happier, so they adopted him as well.

"Raven's Claw?" Christiana asked, already knowing the answer.

He nodded without turning around. "We got along alright, but the older we grew, the more competitive we became. I suppose the breaking point was our manhood initiation.

"Being older by about a year, Raven's Claw went first. He spent three days alone in the forest without food or weapons and came back carrying the pelt of a large wolf that had been roaming the forest threatening anyone who strayed far from the village. He told us a giant raven had talked to him in a dream, telling him how to kill the wolf. There was a great celebration. He was given the name Raven's Claw and celebrated as a brave warrior who would have great strength to slay the people's enemies."

"What did Wolf Stalking think about that?" Christiana asked.

"Well, he wasn't very happy about it." Stephan turned to study her a moment. He still found it surprising that she was knowledgeable about Indian matters. "Do you know about animal totems?"

"Yes, I know that many of the Indian nations believe in having their real name decided by the shaman or medicine man or whoever they think has the gift for giving the right name," she nodded.

He walked to the fireplace and picked up the knife Macklin had placed there that afternoon. His arm was still stinging from the slight wound inflicted with a similar weapon brandished by Raven's Claw thirty minutes earlier in this very room. He'd seen this weapon with the blackened bird talon etched in its handle many times. He could almost hear the newly-named young Raven's Claw boasting to him as he waved this very knife handle in his face taunting, "Just because Old Father calls us brothers, doesn't make it so. I am the great Raven's Claw, bold and clever. What do you suppose you will be called?"

"It's a very solemn occasion," Christiana was saying.

"What?" he asked and turned his full attention to her.

"Names and animal totems. It takes a long time for the Name Giver to study on it, decide what the signs are according to the weather elements and any special appearance or any peculiar sighting of animal life when he's making the determination of the name. Then if you're given an animal's name, there's a special bond between you and that animal for the rest of your life."

"You're right," he finally agreed as he put the knife Raven's Claw had thrown at Mariette back on the mantle. "But with the Natiri, all of that has double importance. Apparently Wolf Stalking was born during a fierce winter storm with blowing ice and snow. Through the wind, his mother heard the howling of a wolf. Then when he grew older and was given his adult name, the Name Giver saw a lone wolf circle the camp as though stalking something hidden in one of the huts. When the Name Giver went to Wolf Stalking's hut and called him out, the wolf supposedly looked straight at the boy then disappeared into the forest. So, all his life, whenever he's seen wolf tracks or heard their howl, he's always felt he was being given some forewarning of some important event in his life."

"He must have been very upset with Raven's Claw, then," Christiana surmised.

"Yes, he thought it was a bad omen, especially for a son to have killed the totem of his father. Raven's Claw didn't agree and seemed satisfied that he had gained the highest praise. I'll never forget watching Raven's Claw receiving gifts from the tribal members on his big day. Old Wolf Stalking turned to me and said, 'It is a fitting name. His heart is as black as a raven's feather and he has always been a clever trickster just like Brother Raven is ... but he feeds on death.'"

Christiana shivered listening to Wolf Stalking's words being repeated. For although she knew ravens and crows eat carrion, she felt Wolf Stalking's reference to Raven's Claw had a much more sinister meaning, one which had become much clearer in the past hour. Pushing her terrifying encounter with the White Shawnee from her mind, she wanted to concentrate on Stephan's story now that she was finally able to hear it.

"Now, what about receiving your name?" she asked.

He walked back over to lean against the desk again and continued his story.

"When it came time for my initiation, the summer had been very dry and the crops meager. Because there was little food stored against the winter, when I returned after three days pulling a large buck on a travois, everyone was very happy. They asked about any dreams I had to indicate what my animal totem might be. I was ashamed and about to admit that I hadn't had such a dream when a large eagle I had spotted earlier that day began to circle over the camp. Each time it circled, its shadow passed directly over me. The whole thing caused quite a stir because you know how the eagle is greatly revered. That was when I was given the name Yaro'ka-i.

135

"Needless to say, I had nothing to do with the eagle, but it was a significant sign to everyone there, and Raven's Claw was angry for being outdone. That was the beginning of the bad feelings between us.

"During the celebration that followed, Wolf Stalking stood and proclaimed that he was proud of his son and heir, something he hadn't done for Raven's Claw. I was only thirteen and got so caught up in the excitement and pride of the whole episode I cut my right hand pledging with my blood to carry out whatever task he should name for me. I didn't realize what I was promising at the time." Stephan stopped for a moment and sighed.

"When I made the promise, Wolf Stalking didn't say anything, but the strangest look came into his eyes. I'll never forget it. It was the look of a man who has lived without hope for a long time and suddenly had a great prize within his reach.

"Not long after that, he took us upriver to the mission school near Fort Stanford. I couldn't understand why, but he said we had to learn to read and write and speak like the White people so that we could be interpreters for them if necessary. I stayed at the mission school for three years until I was sixteen. Raven's Claw stayed only a year.

"When Wolf Stalking learned that I'd become a Christian like my parents, he became angry and demanded I leave the school. He finally told me the real reason he had wanted me to relearn the White ways—"

At this point, Stephan stopped, reluctant to go on, but Christiana insisted he continue. "He wanted me to get close to your father and finally destroy him. I couldn't convince him that your father's death was not the way to heaven. He wouldn't listen. Since his health has been failing he's become even more obsessed with the idea that your father must die to dispel the curse of cowardice hanging over him. I'm his declared heir, so if your father dies by my hand, it's the same as by his.

136

"I went back to the mission one last time to talk to Brother Adams. He wanted me to remain there with his family, but I couldn't. Blue Flower wasn't well. I owed my life to Wolf Stalking, and I had made a blood oath to him. The only thing that kept Wolf Stalking from sending me out right away was the fact he had no idea where your father was.

"Then last February, of all things, your father showed up at Fort Stanford."

"Yes," Christiana nodded. "Being on the House Military Affairs Committee, it was their job to look into a possible case of misappropriating funds and supplies. Since mostly men with the Virginia militia were serving there, he was in charge of the investigation. Go on."

"Wolf Stalking declared that his ancestors had led him to the trading post at the fort so he could see his old enemy and learn what he needed to know. He saw your father talking to Brother Adams and later went to the mission where he asked all kinds of questions, and learned about the apprenticeship. Wolf Stalking told my old teacher that he was hoping I would be able to learn a trade to survive in the White world. Brother Adams was very glad to hear it and told Wolf Stalking that since your father was half-Lenape, he would be more inclined to help me than anyone else."

Stephan fell silent as he remembered watching the old Indian return from his visit to the mission. He'd never seen his adopted father, now frail and bent with arthritis, ever stride so purposefully through the village before. The young man had been cleaning his flintlock in preparation to leave with his good friend, Sings-the-Elk-Song, and the other Shawnee men to go north and join Tecumseh. He and his friend were discussing the success of their hunt earlier in the day as they worked on their weapons. Sings-the-Elk-Song spotted Wolf Stalking first and mentioned the old man's determined attitude.

"What has put new life in your step, Old Father?" Stephan had asked.

Wolf Stalking had studied him with a gleam in his eye and announced dramatically, "The time has come at last, my son. You will soon bring honor back to the name of Wolf Stalking. Then I will be able to go to my ancestors unafraid."

The old man explained his plan which meant Stephan would not be able to go with the others to join the great Shawnee leader, Tecumseh. Wolf Stalking seemed oblivious to anything except this opportunity for vengeance that he had feared would never come.

Raven's Claw, overhearing this plan, had looked at Stephan with a smug grin and said, "Don't worry, little brother, after tomorrow, you will be joining Tecumseh, and Old Father will have his revenge."

"Stephan?" Christiana's voice gently called him from the halls of his memory where Raven's Claw's voice still echoed.

"What?"

"You were mentioning Father's being at Fort Stanford?"

"Oh . . . uh . . . yes. After the attack on your father's party, Raven's Claw told me that he had been approached by someone from the fort asking him to kill your father. This was before Wolf Stalking ever found out about him. Raven's Claw thought it was a very funny twist and if someone hadn't warned the inspection party, he would have easily accomplished the task before I ever had the chance to even start out. He suspected an old trapper, Chenault, had warned them. Chenault has been a friend of the Shawnee for many years and used to visit the village we grew up in all the time. While he's not crazy about the Americans pushing west, if he got wind of an ambush, he's not someone to stand by and allow a massacre."

"Thank goodness," Christiana sighed, then suddenly remembered the incident at the garden shed. "That day in Williamsburg, you thought Raven's Claw was there, didn't you?"

He nodded.

"The look on your face when you broke into the gardener's shed really frightened me. You looked angry enough to kill someone!"

"If the situation had been what I feared, I might have," he replied honestly. "Raven's Claw followed me to Dunston. He confronted me one evening out by the spring house; wondered what was taking so long. I stalled him by telling him it was going to take time to find some way to humiliate your father. I was afraid Raven's Claw would take things into his own hands again."

Another piece of this mystery fell into place as she remembered Eric relating this very scene to her the evening before they left for Hampton.

"When did you decide that you wouldn't be able to harm my father?" she asked softly, closely watching the expression on his face.

Stuffing his hands in his pockets, Stephan moved back over to the French doors and looked out at the black sky filled with diamond-like stars. "I guess I decided the moment you opened the door that day I first arrived. Seeing you, I knew I could never go through with it. But I had to find out what kind of man your father was and somehow figure a way out. You know the rest."

Gradually, a wonderful warmth filled Christiana's heart. At last she understood.

The truth had proven he did deserve her trust. Her father had been right when he told her not to worry.

"From Brother Adams's letter, Father knew who you were and your real purpose for coming here. Yet he let you stay anyway, and he pretended my suspicions were wrong."

Stephan nodded as he continued to gaze outside. "He said it was better to have me close. He hoped the trouble could be resolved eventually. He's a remarkable man, Christiana."

"He and Copper are very good judges of character. What are you going to do now?"

"For the next six months, I'll be serving in the militia," he said purposefully trying to avoid the real reason for her question.

"That's not what I mean, and you know it. What are you going to do about Wolf Stalking?"

Stephan turned around to look at her. "I'll have to face him with my decision. While your father is in Washington, he'll be safe from Raven's Claw until I can settle the matter with Wolf Stalking."

He went on. "You mustn't say anything about this to your father though. He's talking about another trip to Fort Stanford next month and plans to face Wolf Stalking himself. I hope to have it all settled before then."

Christiana rose from the chair and walked over to stand facing him. With her hand on his arm, she looked up at him. "It won't be that simple. You forget, Stephan, I grew up spending a lot of time at Mercy Ridge. I learned about more customs than animal totems. The words 'blood vengeance' mean just that to the Indians. They demand blood, if not the initial victim then a substitute. You don't honestly expect me to believe you can talk it away with a man who's been obsessed by it his entire life! By refusing to honor it, you'll be forfeiting your own life."

Stephan covered her hand gently with his own and smiled at her, a look of pleasant surprise in his eyes.

"I should have told you the truth a long time ago."

She cocked her head in curiosity.

"Because," he grinned disarmingly, "it's much nicer having you on my side, being concerned about me, than ready to hang me as a spy."

Christiana grinned. "I'm afraid I was quite dreadful to you, but don't change the subject. You can't go back there. You simply can't!"

His smile was warm. "I can't do anything else; but knowing that it really matters to you makes it easier."

"Oh Stephan, for goodness sake. Please!" Christiana closed her eyes in exasperation and turned toward the doors, her voice barely audible. "If you go back there . . . I . . . I'm afraid I'll never see you again."

"You know, Christa," he finally said, "one of the first things I learned from Brother Adams was that if what you do is the Lord's will, he'll help you do it. I've got to set this straight with Wolf Stalking. Aside from diverting the danger from your father, perhaps there's more reason now than ever to want the past settled so I can think about the future."

Regardless of the cold fear that gripped her heart, she nodded slowly. "I'll be praying for your future, Stephan."

With that, Stephan touched her cheek. Placing his hand lightly under her chin, he turned her head and looked squarely in her eyes.

"I'll be leaving with Knox in the morning. If it's the Lord's will, I'll be back by February first of next year. Will I be welcome again in the Macklin home?"

"With open arms," she answered, a tear glistening on her dark lashes.

For the first time, their lips met in a long-awaited warm caress. It was a good-bye kiss with the promise of a new beginning when next they met.

# 14

Leaving Dunston, Stephan's militia company marched northwest, reaching Fort Stanford on July 28th. Two days later, the company was divided with half of the men staying at the fort and half ordered to march five miles to Webster's Cove along the shore of Lake Erie where they would board one of Commodore O. H. Perry's gunboats and sail to Presque Isle. Lieutenant Knox and twelve fellow Virginians, along with Stephan Page, were ordered to serve as marksmen on one of the vessels in Perry's fleet being built.

The day before they were to leave the fort for the cove, Stephan was approached by a familiar figure dressed in buckskins with an old felt hat topping a bushy mat of salt-and-pepper colored hair. The full-bush beard and mustache covered half the leathery, wrinkled face of the old trapper, Chenault.

A spark of recognition lit the hawk-like eyes.

"Yaro'ka-i, is that you?"

Stephan extended his hand. "Ho, Chenault. I thought you'd be headed to the north country by now."

"Best laid plans, m'boy," the old man growled as he shook the young soldier's hand in a steel-like grip. "I'm surprised to see ya here, and with the militia at that."

"I'm a little surprised myself," Stephan replied, his hand feeling as if it had been squeezed in a vise.

"I take it things didn't go exactly like ol' Wolf Stalking planned?" Chenault asked quietly as they walked away from the traffic of the crowded parade ground.

"Not exactly."

The old trapper spat, his hawk-like eyes scanning the bustling activity before them. Fort Stanford was a very busy place. They walked toward the gates, open to receive wagons and people coming and going to the trading post inside.

"Just came over from the Shawnee camp yesterday. Saw Blue Flower."

"How is she?" Stephan asked, thinking about the Indian woman who had been his adopted mother since he was seven years old. She had taken him into her heart as her own son, and had been bitterly unhappy when Wolf Stalking sent him off on the mission of vengeance. He was sorry that his duties would prevent him from going to the village to see her.

"She's well, but misses her sons," Chenault reported.

Stephan nodded sadly. "And Wolf Stalking?"

"The old fella has gone with Sings-the-Elk-Song and the rest to join Tecumseh. Don't know what he expects to do; he can hardly toddle along because of that rheumatiz'." The trapper scratched his beard. "Strange how things work out. Not too many moons ago, you were gettin' ready to go fight alongside Tecumseh yourself."

The irony of his situation had not escaped Stephan. He'd had a three-week march to consider the amazing turns his life had taken. If he hadn't gone to Dunston, Virginia, he would undoubtedly be in Tecumseh's camp preparing to fight the American military forces in which he now served.

"Somethin' mighty powerful musta happened to ya, boy. I know you wasn't too keen on carryin' out blood vengeance for Wolf Stalking, but . . ."

They'd reached the gates and walked out to stand on a small knoll overlooking the trail coming from the mission and Erie in the east and heading west toward the Sandusky River, then farther on to Fort Meigs. The mid-summer day was hot, but outside the fort they could feel the freshening breezes coming across from the lake.

Stephan couldn't explain everything that had happened since meeting the Macklins, so he only nodded, acknowledging the truth of Chenault's words.

"I'd be curious to see what happens if you should get Tecumseh or Wolf Stalking or Sings-the-Elk-Song in your sights across the battle line." Chenault pressed for an explanation, for he'd known Yaro'ka-i since about the time he'd earned his name. He didn't think the lad was one to switch loyalties easily.

"I pray that day doesn't come," the younger man sighed. Stephan had no qualms about going against the British, for he suspected their promises to the Indians would last no longer than the American promises of the past. And after studying the problems between England and America, he was more than willing to side with men like Andrew Macklin and his sons. But Wolf Stalking, his Shawnee friends, and Tecumseh were another matter altogether.

Tecumseh had made several visits to the village where Stephan grew up; each time the young Yaro'ka-i had been very impressed. He could still hear the compelling oratory of the hazel-eyed Shawnee chief as he addressed his people, laying before them his dream of a united Indian nation. With his charismatic personality and intelligence he had been able to rally the tribes of the Northwest Territory into an Indian confederacy. In addition to his leadership abilities, he was also a man of integrity and compassion. Although a fearless fighter and brilliant strategist, he hated senseless violence and torture. On at least one occasion he stopped his warriors from torturing their prisoners of war, calling his braves cowards for mistreating men unable to defend themselves.

The Shawnee war chief had believed British promises that any Indians fighting for the Crown would be able to keep their lands and any taken back from the Americans south of the Canadian border. Allying with the English was the best chance they had to stop the American advance into Indian territory. Stephan had witnessed the Indians' plight from their side. He had heard the wailing of sorrow from the burned-out villages of the Kickapoo, Miami, Ottawa, and Potawatomi, all members of the confederacy. He had been as angry as Tecumseh at General Harrison for his blatant disregard for Indian claims to their land. Now he was fighting under the same flag as Harrison and it troubled him.

Chenault could see it had taken something powerful indeed to prompt the young man, caught between two cultures, to make the choice he had. The old trapper was sure the decision had not been an easy one. Wasn't any business of his anyway, he told himself.

"Seen Raven's Claw lately?" he finally asked.

"Briefly," Stephan replied.

Chenault had been curious how things would end up between the two White boys raised by the Indians. The difference between the two boys had always been as big as the difference between their namesakes, the eagle and the raven.

"Still at odds, I reckon?"

Stephan nodded. "Things seem to have taken a turn for the worse."

He related the events in Dunston and his adopted brother's parting declaration that the conflict between them was not over. His story finished, he was curious to see the old man shaking his head.

"If this Macklin is the kind of man you seem to think, I'm glad someone warned him about that ambush. Looks like I'd better watch my back until I find out where your brother is, since he thinks it was me."

"You're probably right," Stephan agreed. He could tell by the twinkle in the man's eyes that Raven's Claw had been right in his suspicion that Chenault was the one who had warned the party. "I don't suppose you'd know who it was that hired Raven's Claw for that ambush, would you? I mean, you always keep your ears open, hear a lot."

Chenault removed his hat and beat it against his leg, releasing a small cloud of dust around him. Setting his gaze on the far horizon to the north, he said, "Seems I did hear somethin'. Mind you, that wouldn't be enough proof to do nothin' about the scoundrel; but could be I heard it was the quartermaster, Axel Harrod. Now, I'm headed to the far country and won't be able to repeat that for no one, but there it is."

"The name's familiar," Stephan mused. "He wouldn't be related to Rupert Harrod, would he?"

"I never been one to care about a man's family tree, so I couldn't say. I have heard that ships carryin' goods for the soldier boys here at the fort come in on a couple boats owned by some shipping company in Boston."

Stephan looked out toward the horizon and all the forest in between. A sudden longing for the freedom and simplicity of the life he had lived there with his adopted parents filled his heart.

"I thought I'd have a chance to go to the village and see Blue Flower and Wolf Stalking and get this thing about Andrew Macklin straightened out. I figured Raven's Claw would be there and that would be settled as well. But, there's no time. Was Raven's Claw at the village when you were there?"

Chenault shook his head. "Naw. Blue Flower said she hadn't heard from him since he left to follow you. She don't know where he is either."

"Will you be heading back that way?"

"Yup. Headed northwest at last. Came over here to pick up some supplies. Could stop back by there I reckon."

"Would you mind taking a note to Blue Flower for me?"

"I don't mind. After I leave the village, I'll be headin' on northwest and probably stop by Fort Meigs. If I hear any news of Raven's Claw, I'll send word to you."

Stephan nodded his thanks and took a deep breath. The warm breeze brought the faint fragrance of field mint to his nostrils. If he closed his eyes, he could almost imagine standing in the backyard of the Macklins' house and watching Christiana tend the garden. She had planted mint to ward off bugs that might spoil her flowers. Now that clean, sweet fragrance brought the memory of her, filling all of his senses, mind, and heart; and he knew he would never be able to return to the life he had known before. He would never be truly happy without her beside him.

# 15

Washington, D.C., in August of 1813 was a far cry from the capital city of the young United States that it was destined to become. The initial plan for broad avenues, marble monuments, and impressive buildings of stone to house the governmental offices drawn up by Major Pierre L'Enfant back in 1791, had been all but abandoned for the time being. Newspapers and officials complained that the new capital was too remote and inconvenient to the business centers of New York, Boston, and Philadelphia. Regardless of being disparagingly referred to as a "wilderness city" with its broad streets turning to a sea of mud during rainy periods, the city continued to expand until occupied by nearly twenty-five thousand people by 1813. This, of course, was when Congress was in session. During recess periods, a ghost-town atmosphere prevailed.

The housing situation in the city was bleak to say the least. While there were a few more houses to accommodate families than in the earlier years, they were still quite scarce. The construction workers working on the government buildings lived under difficult circumstances in a sprawling array of tents and lean-tos. The predominant sound heard throughout the city was that of hammers and saws as this army of carpenters and masons toiled. So far, only the Senate section of the Capitol Building had been completed, with the House section still under construction.

At the other end of Pennsylvania Avenue in the President's Palace, occasionally referred to as the "White House," President Madison and his wife, Dolly, were living in a few completed rooms. Many had yet to be finished. Abigail Adams, the First Lady preceding Mrs. Madison, had found it necessary to hang laundry in one of the incomplete rooms on the first floor. These inconveniences had not hindered the irrepressible Mrs. Madison, however, and she reigned capably as social head of the capital. Her grace and charm marked the many affairs of state, receptions, and weekly levees over which she presided. She had brought a vibrancy and lively air to the capital city and was a tremendous asset to her husband.

The Macklins had attended several of the Madisons' gala dinners. They were, in fact, to be included at such a dinner scheduled for the week following their arrival in the city. These were elegant affairs with new china and silver and servants stationed behind each guest's chair.

Four additional dinner invitations awaited attention upon their arrival Sunday afternoon at their Washington residence, a narrow frame house two stories tall but about half the width of their home in Dunston. Politely declining two other invitations for dinner that evening, they accepted the one from their long-time friends, the Nathaniel Burke family, and quickly settled in.

A fellow member of the House Military Affairs Committee, Nathaniel Burke had accompanied Mac on the inspection trip to Fort Stanford. A banker by trade, he had many eyes and ears throughout the capital city, Baltimore, and Philadelphia. If anyone could accurately fill Mac in on a current situation, Burke could. Mac was especially concerned about the appointment of Major General James Wilkinson to replace Dearborn. He wasn't upset that Dearborn was stepping down, for the old general was well past his abilities to handle such a position, but Mac felt that his replacement at this point in the young country's history was far from an improvement.

Winning independence in 1781 had only been the beginning of the struggle to develop the new government. Through all of the inner squabbling, frustrating economic difficulties, political intrigue, and personality conflicts, the tender government somehow managed to grow. While the majority of statesmen possessed a deep underlying sense of historic significance in reference to the decisions made during these developmental years, some used their influence for self-aggrandizement. One of these was James Wilkinson.

One reason Mac felt this way was Wilkinson's controversial history. Why a man with such a background was appointed to so vital a military position was baffling to Mac. Wilkinson's saintly appearance—white hair and soulful eyes—deceptively belied his total lack of principle. He had been involved in one plot after another, including one to replace George Washington in the "Conway Cabal" plot during the Revolutionary War. It was this treachery that had gained him Mac's enmity.

In 1804, another such incident occurred when Wilkinson turned States evidence to gain immunity for his part with Aaron Burr in a plot to cause the southwestern states to withdraw from the Union. It was rumored that he had even operated as a secret agent for the government of Spain. For Secretary of War Armstrong even to consider such a person for a leadership role left Mac shaking his head in disbelief.

Thinking about Wilkinson's dishonest dealings, Mac was reminded of the incident during the Revolutionary War when Wilkinson was Clothier General. An investigation into misappropriation of funds and supplies had revealed irregularities in Wilkinson's accounts. Although the slippery fellow managed to avoid charges being brought against him, he had been forced to resign. That incident brought Fort Stanford to mind. A letter received in Mac's office from a young officer at the fort cited suspicions that supplies meant for American soldiers were being diverted by someone at Fort Stanford to English-Canadian troops and their Indian allies.

Mac's February trip had failed to disclose proof of the young lieutenant's suspicions. However, after checking the young officer's background, he doubted that someone with such an exemplary service record and high recommendations would risk making false accusations. Further, the timing of the lieutenant's death, supposedly from pneumonia, just days before their inspection party arrived and the ambush of their party, left Mac convinced that there was something amiss at Fort Stanford. Therefore, he had continued to pursue the investigation against the advice of several members of his committee, having been warned that it would be unwise to antagonize the fort's quartermaster, Axel Harrod, because Harrod's father, Rupert Harrod, was a powerful shipping magnate in New England. The members felt like there was trouble enough with the New England States and no need to stir up any more over a few head of beef and some blankets sold on the sly to the Canadians. And it was true, the whole Northeastern section was on the brink of seceding from the Union.

No one had to tell him that Rupert Harrod could cause trouble. James and Alexander had found out firsthand, being competitors in the shipping business. Alex was convinced that Rupert had targeted the *Sea Sprite* for the British as a valuable cargo and strong crew in reprisal for hiring Rupert's two best captains when they quit working for him. About the only way to prove such a charge would be to have the testimony of someone from the British navy, a very unlikely event.

The situation at Fort Stanford, however, might be another matter. The type of operation in which Axel Harrod was suspected to be involved would require physical help to move the supplies being redirected to the British and their allied Indians. The more people involved, the more likely someone might let a bit of evidence slip. That's why Mac now had someone on the way to Fort Stanford who could inconspicuously watch Quartermaster Harrod and anyone with whom he dealt. Mac would be receiving monthly reports from this man on the inside until sufficient evidence was gathered to bring charges against the guilty parties.

That evening just before the Burke dinner, Mac was sitting at his desk reading over the latest report received from one of his colleagues concerning the situation at Fort Stanford when Jessica came in to remind him it was time to dress for the dinner. Still somewhat distracted by the report, Mac gazed out the window. Although the capital was a skeleton of a city, there was great promise here. He could feel it. The statesman hoped that the integrity of the country's leaders would rise above the greed and self-interest of a few power seekers.

Jessica watched her husband and along with her deep sense of pride came a nagging fear for his well-being. Her husband's dark hair was now generously streaked with gray and his strong, handsome face was furrowed with lines of care. For a moment, she reminisced about the few days they had spent at Mercy Ridge when he had come to take her home. He had seemed his old self, rested and relaxed, away for a brief time from the awful realities of the war. The lines of care had disappeared, and the sparkle of humor in his eyes had come out for the first time in a long time. It had been wonderful.

Now, he appeared as before. She couldn't help but think

of the November 1806 dinner party celebrating Mac's election to his first term in the House of Representatives and the words spoken by their friend, Harold Smythe, a district judge well acquainted with the many foibles of mankind: "It's a pitiful shame," he had said, "that our young men of principle are often sacrificed, worn to a ragged frazzle in their battle against the old (and not so old) greedy dragons intent upon devouring anyone or thing that stands in the way of their personal gain. I just thank God that on behalf of us village peasants, they don't shrink from the fight." Smythe's statement had been followed by a toast in Mac's honor. As glasses lifted, he continued, "To our young knights, may God grant them strength for the fray!"

Jessica also prayed for her husband's strength. She was looking forward to the end of this term of office when he would retire from the political scene. Many times she had wondered how much more serene their lives might have been without the tension and turmoil of service as a public representative.

Yet, through all this turmoil, there was the sense of accomplishment. With each new crisis, with each new step taken toward the successful implementation of the young Constitutional government, both she and Mac were aware that progress was being made.

"Mac, darling, Nathaniel will be pacing the floor waiting for us if we're much later."

He smiled and took her hand as they headed up to their room to change for the dinner.

Christiana was looking forward to their evening with the Burkes. She and their daughter, Rachel, had been close friends since their fathers had arrived in Washington to serve their first terms in Congress six years before. Rachel's hair was as fair as Christiana's was dark, and they had always attracted attention as being the "inseparable opposites." Tending to be a bit flamboyant, Rachel was outrageously witty and outspoken, able to make Christiana laugh no matter how melancholy her mood.

Rachel's work would be cut out for her this time as Christiana had not felt like even smiling since the morning Stephan had left with the militia. She could use a generous dose of Rachel's good humor.

As Christiana dressed, her mind wandered back to that dreadful morning with its monotonous drizzle and leaden gray skies. Finding it impossible to sleep after the night before, she was still awake when she heard Stephan close the door as he left the house just before dawn.

A short while later, she heard the sound of marching feet stomping along in the muddy lane in front of the Macklin house. She slipped out of bed to peek out her bedroom window. Although the morning light was still dim, she spotted one head toward the front of the column as it turned to look up through the drizzling rain toward her window. Her heart skipped a little beat. It was Stephan marching north with his unit. She thought she saw a slight smile as he touched the dripping brim of his battered felt hat. Raising her hand, she waved and watched the columns disappear into the dismal curtain of rain. From that moment on, Christiana's mood had seemed to match the weather that morning. Yes, her friend Rachel would have her work cut out for her this evening.

As the young lady descended the stairs, Jean-Marc stood at the hall mirror nervously straightening his cravat. When he saw Christiana, he smiled with obvious approval and offered his arm.

"You look lovely as usual, mademoiselle, perhaps even more so in that gown. That color matches the lavender blue of your eyes perfectly."

She smiled graciously. "Thank you, very kind sir."

"Having such a lovely young lady on my arm eases the apprehension I feel as I meet your friends tonight."

154

"There's absolutely nothing to be nervous about, Jean-Marc," she replied. "Knowing my friends—Rachel, especially—I have a feeling you'll be exceptionally well received."

After dinner that evening, Christiana and Jessica sat with Rachel and Carolina Burke on a small porch at the back of the Burke home. The August evening was stifling, without a breath of air, making the inside of the house extremely uncomfortable.

The Macklins had been happy to see their old friend Oliver Howe also present at the Burkes'. A senior member of the House from South Carolina, he had been very helpful during those first hectic months of Mac and Nathaniel's terms. A widower for many years, he often dined with friends and was a frequent guest at the Macklins' as well.

The gentlemen, Burke, Macklin, Howe, and Richaux, were talking at a rail fence that marked the boundary of the back garden a short distance away.

"Christiana," Rachel teasingly began, "how do you always manage to be in the company of the most attractive men? First your brothers, then Eric Lowe, and now this charming Mr. Richaux?"

Christiana laughed. "I had no choice about my brothers or Eric, Rachel, and as for Jean-Marc, well, like we told you at dinner, he and Mariette needed help."

"Perhaps, but nothing so romantic ever happens to me," she moaned. "He's so handsome. You'll be the envy of all the belles at the Madisons' dinner next week. Look, here he comes!" Rachel whispered behind her fan.

The French gentleman approached and bowed politely. "The congressmen are discussing some rather important matters. Would the mademoiselles care to join me for a stroll around the garden?"

Rachel almost jumped to her feet but smiled gracefully as she fluttered her fan coquettishly. "That'd be very nice,

Mr. Richaux. Christiana, you're not too tired from your journey from Dunston to join us, are you?"

Christiana had to hold back her smile. She knew Rachel wanted to walk with Jean-Marc alone. To Rachel's delight, she declined the invitation, claiming she was a bit weary from her trip.

As the three women watched the young couple stroll toward the garden, Carolina Burke directed their attention to her husband, Mr. Howe, and Mac who were still talking beside the fence.

"Nathaniel is so upset with this Wilkinson thing," she said. "Rumor has it that Armstrong plans to have Wilkinson and General Hampton lead a two-column attack against Montreal before winter."

The other two looked at her in disbelief.

Jessica asked, "General Wade Hampton? But everyone knows they can't stand each other! The last we heard, Wilkinson and Hampton weren't even on speaking terms. How are they going to cooperate in an attack?"

"Supposedly, all orders for Hampton from Wilkinson are to go through Armstrong."

"Surely not," Jessica said. "How will they ever manage that in mid-battle?"

While this surprising announcement sounded preposterous, Christiana and her mother knew that Carolina Burke was nearly as knowledgeable as her husband about such matters. Many of the Washington wives were every bit as concerned about governmental affairs. While some were not as careful about rumors and gossip as they should have been, Christiana and Jessica knew Carolina Burke was not simply passing on a bit of gossip. This was information she would not banter about lightly.

As her mother and Carolina continued discussing the situation, Christiana's mind was filled with thoughts of Stephan. The idea of him and his fellow militiamen being subject to the eccentric whims of such incompetent military leaders gripped her heart with cold dread.

"What about Brigadier General Jacob Brown?" Her mother's words reclaimed Christiana's full attention. "Mac has heard some very good things about him. And Dearborn's adjutant, Winfield Scott? Mac's convinced that although they're rather young, they'd be able to make good use of the small force we have."

Carolina nodded. "Nathaniel agrees. But how many times in the past, Jessica, have we seen good capable men passed over because of some pressure from who knows where!"

"Which reminds me. I didn't want to say anything at dinner when Christiana was telling us about her trip to Hampton. I know how Mac feels about Rupert Harrod, and didn't want to spoil his meal; but guess who is openly campaigning for appointment to replace William Pinkney as Attorney General?"

"I'm almost afraid to ask," Jessica replied.

"Chauncey Caskell, Esquire."

After the news about General Hampton and Wilkinson, little could surprise Jessica at the moment. "Well, when did this all start?"

Carolina swatted at a mosquito with her fan and answered, "Shortly after the attack on Hampton. They are staying with Clara's brother, Rupert, in Boston while repairs are being made to their house."

"I wonder if Mrs. Caskell is still so sympathetic to the British after what they did to her beautiful house," Christiana interjected.

"It took her some time to recover, apparently, but she now lays the blame entirely on the French sailors. Clara has never been one to be distracted by the facts—" Carolina stopped. "I'm sorry, that wasn't very kind. It's just that I've never seen anyone who could be so blind to so much as long as her social calendar was filled properly and tea was served on time."

Jessica and Christiana had to chuckle at Carolina's exasperation.

"As long as Chauncey Caskell has been the Burke family's attorney," she continued, "I have never known Clara Caskell to have an opinion of her own about anything that didn't have to do with the decor of their home or the status of their social standing. If she ever uttered a political opinion, you can be sure it's her brother, Rupert's. She seems to feel he is the expert rather than Chauncey."

Carolina stopped as she noticed the three congressmen moving slowly toward them, still intent on their discussion. As they approached, the ladies could hear the conversation.

"The attack is doomed before it even begins, Mac. It should be obvious to everyone by now that Canada will never be an easy conquest. Without competent officers, they'll never cut the supply line to Montreal. It's a waste of good men to try to do more than protect our border."

Mac agreed with Nathaniel. "It would appear that if we are to have any chance at all of gaining a decent position in the peace negotiations, the good Lord is going to have to shake up Armstrong enough that he'll finally appoint some competent leaders for our forces."

"That's a lot of shaking even for the good Lord, Mac." Howe's droll remark brought slight chuckles from the grim-faced men and helped to lighten the mood considerably.

August passed slowly as the dog days of late summer dragged by in a progression of hot, hazy days. The war news grew no more encouraging.

Christiana received three letters from Mariette about the wedding plans. Along with her mother and Jean-Marc, Christiana decided to return to Dunston three days before the special event. Since it would be impossible for Mac to get away, he was going to send along a bodyguard.

Jean-Marc's intentions following the wedding had changed dramatically. In a candid moment, he admitted to Christiana that he and his uncle had never really gotten along very well and the climate in Santo Domingo had never really been to his liking. "Although the United States is suffering serious difficulties in its war with England," he had told her, "I find an enthusiasm and optimism in the people here that is very appealing."

Having become acquainted with several people during their social events in Washington and impressing them with his gracious manner and quick wit, the Frenchman had made friends very quickly. Before long, he had been offered several jobs, including a position as a French teacher, manager of a furniture maker's shop in nearby Georgetown, as well as a French chef for a plantation in Georgia. He had declined these positions in favor of a post as a professor in French studies, history, and language at a small exclusive academy in Alexandria. He felt that this position comfortably preserved the dignity of his family name and offered him the chance to maintain a residence in Alexandria, not far from Washington but much more pleasant.

As Rachel had predicted, Christiana was the envy of the young ladies as Jean-Marc escorted her to the many functions. Since that morning she had watched Stephan march away, she had found him very good company. She knew she would miss him when he went to live in Alexandria after the wedding, but she realized it would not be the same feeling she experienced after Stephan left. Her loneliness for Stephan only seemed to grow.

In her ever forthright manner, Rachel had told her friend she was completely mad to be pining away for some strange young man off playing soldier while on the arm of the most fascinating young man in Washington. Rachel was one of those vivacious people who had a knack for saying the most outrageous things—for the most part true—without really offending. She freely admitted that at first she had sought Christiana's friendship because of her handsome twin brothers, James and Alex, who were then still a year away from leaving for Harvard. However, after the brothers left home for college and later married, the two girls had remained close friends. As flippant as Rachel might appear, there was never any doubt that she was Christiana's devotedly loyal friend.

Even with Jean-Marc's attention and their busy social schedule, Christiana's thoughts turned more and more to the young man who still remained a mystery. She still felt there was more to his story. She could not help wondering why. Regardless, she had to face the fact that she missed him more than she had ever thought possible.

Perhaps it had something to do with the plans for the wedding and Mariette's glowing letters of how happy she and Eric were. While Mariette was not as close a friend as Rachel, she had seen Christiana and Stephan together and had quickly recognized their feelings for each other. Her letters to Christiana always included some mention of her desire for Christiana and Stephan someday to enjoy the happiness she and Eric had found.

But this seemed to be an unlikely possibility. She had not received one word from him in nearly a month. While she didn't really expect any, somehow, whenever the post delivery was due, she couldn't help wondering if there might be some news of him.

At times she would wake at night from a dreadful nightmare, remembering vividly the overwhelming strength of Raven's Claw as he easily slung her over his shoulder like a sack of feathers. The memory of how powerless she had felt left her gasping for breath. Then she'd remember Stephan's gentle touch on her face and his comforting arms about her, the deep blue of his eyes and his warm smile in their mirrored reflection that night he had given her the new bonnet. A calmness would slowly encompass her and the terror of the nightmare would ebb away, replaced by the longing to see him again.

However, ever present with this pleasant recollection of his quiet, confident strength loomed her concern over whether he would be able to overcome the vindictive, cruel Raven's Claw when they met again. She knew that Raven's Claw would gladly accept the role of vindicator with Stephan offering himself as the substitute for her father. She also knew her father intended to settle the matter himself when he traveled to Fort Stanford in three weeks. Since hearing that Stephan's militia unit had been ordered to Erie, Pennsylvania, to reinforce the troops there, Mac was not expecting Stephan to be concerned any further with the matter of Wolf Stalking.

Christiana found it difficult not to discuss the situation with her mother, but she knew that if Jessica was aware of Stephan's intention, her father would somehow guess that something was afoot. It was impossible for her parents to hide things from each other after all these years. Not willing to betray her promise to Stephan, Christiana kept silent.

# 16

The journey back to Dunston for the wedding was pleasant. The weather had cooled with just the hint of an early fall spiking the breeze that whispered through drying grasses and leaves.

Due to a fall along the rutted lane in front of their Washington residence, Jessica had twisted her ankle and at the last minute was unable to go. Christiana suspected that her mother was deeply concerned about Mac and the injured ankle gave her an excellent excuse to remain with him. Rachel quickly offered herself as a traveling companion, and Christiana was delighted. Her witty bantering back and forth with Jean-Marc kept the mood light. It even brought an occasional smile to Wesley Coates, the grim bodyguard hired by Mac.

Jean-Marc enjoyed himself immensely in their company, finding both young ladies very attractive and most charming. He was much too gallant to express how dear Christiana had become to him, knowing her feelings for Page. "It'd be a loathsome thing to take advantage of the fellow's absence," he thought, "especially when he's away serving in the defense of his country. However, when he returns, ah, that might be another matter."

As customary in the nineteenth century, the wedding was held in the morning. Wednesday, September 1, had been chosen as the right day by Mariette following the rhyme:

Monday for wealth,
Tuesday for health,
Wednesday the best day of all;
Thursday for crosses,
Friday for losses,
Saturday no luck at all.

Only family and a few friends had been invited to the ceremony, which still meant a fair-sized crowd because of Eric's large family. However, nearly the whole village had been invited to the breakfast to follow. Eric's mother and two sisters, Gran, Christiana, and Rachel had been preparing food for the past three days for the post-wedding celebration.

As the ceremony began, Jean-Marc stood beside Eric at the altar of the old church, presenting his sister to her husband-to-be. Stepping back, he sighed contentedly as he watched the young couple exchange their vows. His sister would soon be very happily situated in her new home; he had a new, potentially challenging career and had made many wonderful new friends. Perhaps someday he would even have a wife and family of his own.

Christiana stood beside Mariette as maid of honor. Her heart brimmed with joy for the bride. Mariette looked like a petite porcelain doll dressed in a high-waisted gown of white satin. Her dark curls were crowned with a wreath of pink rosebuds and sprigs of baby's breath from the Macklins' garden. A long gossamer lace scarf, attached to this wreath at the mid-back of the bride's head, cascaded down her back. Turning to glance at Christiana, her dark eyes sparkled with intense joy. Christiana returned her jubilant smile and listened as the young couple exchanged their vows.

Eric looked more handsome than ever in his blue coat with silver buttons, white shirt with its high, starched collar, buff-colored waistcoat and trousers. The adoration in his eyes was unmistakable as he looked down at his tiny bride. The expression seemed to change his whole demeanor from the devil-may-care attitude to one more mature. It was obvious that the young man who had always been so interested in so many young ladies had irretrievably lost his heart to this pretty young French woman. For Mariette's sake, Christiana was very glad.

The vows completed, bride and groom kissed. Mariette turned to Christiana and hugged her tightly. "Someday it will be you and Stephan," she whispered.

Standing on the steps of the church after the ceremony, the bride tossed her bouquet directly to Christiana. The maid of honor caught it and placed the flowers to her nose to smell the sweet fragrance. Jean-Marc stood nearby and smiled, especially when he overheard several comments by onlookers wondering if the young Miss Macklin would be next to walk down the aisle with the bride's handsome brother. Something inside him told him, however, that Christiana wasn't thinking about him.

Jean-Marc was right. Her thoughts were miles away. Since coming home, she had become even more distracted.

At one point Rachel even scolded her for being so morose. "I don't know why I'm telling you to pay more attention to Jean-Marc," her friend finally declared. "I must be as mad as you. If you continue to be so distant, he'll surely tire of waiting for you to forget this mysterious Stephan. Then perhaps I shall have a chance to capture his heart!"

"Capture away, dear Rachel." Christiana smiled absentmindedly.

"Oh, Chris, for heaven's sake. Please cheer up," Rachel begged. "It wouldn't be any fun at all to capture Jean-Marc's heart if you don't even care."

Christiana was unable to resist her friend's teasing. "Well, I don't think you'll have to work very hard. He certainly seems to enjoy himself in your company."

"Do you think so?" Rachel asked hopefully. Then quickly assuming a more detached attitude, she added, "Of course, it is just one laugh after another."

"Never underestimate the power of a good sense of humor, Rachel. Mother always says that a healthy sense of humor can help any relationship. She's told me that more than once a silly spat has been kept from growing into something more serious between her and Father by laughter. It helped them see the foolishness of their disagreement."

The two girls were busily rearranging the room that had been Eric and Stephan's for the newlywed couple after their visit to Charlottesville to see Eric's grandfather who had been unable to make the trip for the wedding. Since Eric still needed to complete his apprenticeship, he and his new bride would soon take up residence at the Macklin house. Fortunately for the young couple, the rules that once strictly forbade marriage before completion of a silversmith's apprenticeship had become much more lenient. And, with the Macklins away in Washington much of the time, it would be a help to know Mariette was there keeping an eye on Gran Barton. When Mac retired from politics, the Macklins would be moving back to Dunston permanently and this would coincide with the time for the apprentice term to be over. It seemed a perfect plan.

With Jean-Marc and Wesley Coates's help, the girls had exchanged the twin beds in this room with the double bed in Christiana's room. They had just finished hanging the new curtains when Gran called up to them.

"Girls, as soon as you're finished, there's fresh apple cake and jasmine tea ready for you!"

"That sounds scrumptious," Rachel replied hungrily. "We'd better hurry down, if we want even a morsel. If Coates gets there first, we won't have a chance."

Christiana had to laugh. The bodyguard's appetite did match his massive size. Gran had been delighted to have someone in the house with such a robust appetite, who obviously enjoyed her cooking so much.

As they reached the lower hall, they heard a knock at the door. Jean-Marc was just on his way out for a daily afternoon stroll. He accepted an envelope from the messenger.

"It's for you, Christiana," he said, handing it to her.

Immediately, she recognized her mother's handwriting. Christiana opened it quickly to find a second envelope along with a note from her mother.

Dear Christa,

This letter arrived for you today. I thought you would want to see it as soon as possible. We miss you and are looking forward to your arrival next week. Give Gran a hug for us.

Lovingly, Mother

The handwriting looked vaguely familiar. Christiana turned it over and caught her breath. The word "Page" was written on the back.

"What is it, Chris?" Rachel asked.

"It's a letter from Stephan," came her answer as she studied the bold script.

"Well aren't you going to open it?" Rachel bubbled over.

"Yes. Yes, of course. Excuse me." The young woman walked with slow deliberate steps to her father's study and closed the door behind her.

Just then Gran came from the dining room. "Did I hear someone at the door?" she asked.

166

"It was a messenger with a letter for Chris," Rachel sighed.

Jean-Marc shrugged his shoulders, nodded politely, and excused himself for his walk. After he'd gone, Rachel turned to Gran.

"It's from that Page fellow. He must be extraordinary to have captivated her so."

"Yes," Gran smiled. "He is a very nice young man."

"Nice? Jean-Marc is nice, but she barely knows he's alive." Rachel almost whined.

"I think he's like another brother to her," Gran replied as they walked to the kitchen. "It's different with Stephan. You can see it in her eyes even when she's angry with him."

"I don't know why she refuses to just come right out and admit that she's madly in love with him!" Rachel declared.

Gran smiled knowingly. "You know Christiana. She's always been a cautious girl in many ways. She's never been one to make rash statements, especially about her own feelings."

In the meantime, Christiana walked over to her father's study desk and sat down. She still had not opened the letter. Finally, she carefully pried open the envelope.

The writing was bold. Before reading the words, she pensively moved her finger across the page, tracing the letters.

Dear Christiana,

We are at Erie and have joined up with a force of Kentucky riflemen. I was surprised to see Alex and James here. They've come to help Perry get the fleet ready to try to gain control of Lake Erie. They said to send their love and tell you that they miss you.

Sincerely, Stephan Page
P.S. So do I. Stephan

She clutched the letter to her. Jumping up, she twirled about the room. "He misses me!" she whispered with glee.

Just then, a knock sounded at the door, and Rachel poked her head in. "Is everything alright?" Seeing Christiana's face all aglow, she continued curiously. "My goodness. What did he say in that letter? Did he propose?"

"Propose?" Christiana laughed out loud. "Good gracious, no, of course not."

"Well, he must have said something wonderful to make your eyes shine like that. Let me see," Rachel challenged, extending her hand.

"He's just written to let me know that he's seen James and Alex." Christiana smiled, withholding the letter.

"Come on, Chris, let me see. Please? I'm dying of curiosity to see what magic words he's penned."

Rachel snatched the letter from Christiana's hand and quickly perused it. A bit disappointed, she declared, "He's not especially eloquent, is he."

"He misses me, Rachel." Christiana sighed dreamily.

"So do your brothers," her friend said flatly. "Obviously you're reading much more into these words than I can see. I can hardly wait to meet this fellow who can weave this powerful spell over you with so few, and such plain, words. I *am* going to get to meet him someday, aren't I?"

Rachel's question posed a sobering thought. Christiana's smile faded a bit as she replied, "Someday."

# 17

Three hundred miles from Dunston, Virginia, an American fleet of nine ships lay at anchor in Put-in-Bay in the Bass Islands along the southern part of Lake Erie. The moon shining brightly in the sky over the mammoth lake sent rays of light dancing across the dark waters.

In his cabin on his flagship, *Lawrence,* young Commodore Oliver Hazard Perry was writing letters. In anticipation of the battle with the British fleet anchored at Amherstburg, he was writing messages that perhaps would be his last. However, if in the will of the Almighty they were victorious, the letters happily would not be necessary.

While still suffering from the debilitating effects of the "lake fever" that had plagued him and many of his men, he had managed to build a fleet to challenge British control over Lake Erie. It had not been an easy task; however, they were as ready as they ever would be to meet their enemy. They had struggled short of men and supplies in a race of shipbuilding. His superior, Chauncey, headquartered on Lake Ontario, had all but ignored his repeated requests for able-bodied seamen. Chauncey had been reluctant to share his resources with the fleet at Lake

Erie, fearing he would need every man he had to defend against the British forces there.

Perry could not know that his British counterpart had been suffering the same inattention from his superior, Yeo, also on Lake Ontario. Barclay, the British commander at Amherstburg, was facing even worse supply problems than Perry.

In another example of the ironies of this war, Yeo and Chauncey, both having everything they needed, were sparring back and forth ineffectively, each fearing to fully commit himself to an all-out battle. Yeo was afraid that defeat would open Canada to American invasion, and Chauncey feared defeat and another humiliation for America. Neither was willing to take a chance on the capricious wind and weather, which play such an important part in a naval conflict between sailing ships.

Young Perry had no such fear. He had been champing at the bit to confront Barclay. During a meeting earlier in the evening, he had with near obsessive determination tried to impress his officers with the importance of maneuvering to fight in close. He was well aware that his ships had the advantage of firepower with their short carronades as long as they were within three hundred yards of the enemy. However, the British had the decided advantage with their long guns, effective at a distance of eight hundred yards.

Perry had efficiently used the material and men at his disposal in preparation for this battle, which involved not only a monumental effort of shipbuilding but also ingeniously floating the fleet over the protective sandbar at Presque Isle by using barge-like vessels called camels. Having done everything possible, they were ready.

The "weather gauge" would most certainly be a deciding factor, meaning they would also need the wind to be in their favor. Only God could help them there.

On this night of September 9, 1813, each man on board the nine ships of Perry's fleet considered what the next day would bring.

Aboard the American schooner *Tigress*, a young man in buckskins was leaning against the rail watching the moonlight dance across the dark ripples of the lake. Listening to the waves lapping gently against the hull and the crickets chirping along the shore, he was reminded of another moonlit night in a lush southern garden, an idyllic setting with a lovely young lady. Unfortunately the conversation had been less than idyllic and yet, it had been the beginning of breaking down the wall of suspicion and distrust. The fear and distrust in her eyes that night had been quite different from the look in her eyes the night that they stood in her father's study saying good-bye. Dare Stephan hope that look meant Christiana might feel about him as he had felt about her since the first moment he saw her?

Upon first arriving at Erie, Stephan and the Virginia militia had set up camp on the lakeshore near Presque Isle. They had practiced battle plans aboard the ships while construction was being completed. The militia would be supplying small arms fire as the ships closed in battle and, according to the way the tide of the conflict went, they were trained either to board another ship or to repel the advancing enemy from their own decks.

Coincidentally, Stephan had met James and Alex Macklin in Erie. They too had agreed to help Perry build his fleet and train the men to sail it. The brothers stood beside him now, both caught up in their own thoughts which, no doubt, included their wives, Hannah and Heather, waiting for them back in Erie. Both couples had been married less than a year, and the young wives had insisted upon accompanying their husbands to the small town of Erie while they helped in the construction of the fleet. Since moving to the Bass Islands down the shore of the lake, both Macklin brothers had been concerned about having to leave their wives so close to the battle area.

However, even more surprising than meeting the Macklin brothers, Stephan had discovered a long lost uncle and cousin among some Kentuckian riflemen sent by General Harrison to help man Commodore Perry's ships. Echoes of their meeting rang in his head now as he stood watching the campfires along the shores of Squaw Harbor.

The Virginia Company had only just arrived in Erie and set up camp next to the Kentucky Company. In the cool of the first evening, several men had gathered around a campfire between the two camps. It didn't take long to learn that the majority of them were militia from Kentucky. Oddly enough, the largest number of militia along the Canadian border between Erie and the Sandusky River to the southwest were from Henry Clay's home state. Following his stirring oratory, Clay's fellow Kentuckians saw this war with England as a "holy crusade" for freedom.

Perhaps because of some intangible tie to his distant childhood in Kentucky, Stephan had lingered by the fire, listening to the men's easygoing banter about hunting, fighting, and kinfolk.

While there, he had become aware of a particular figure across the fire who was watching him closely. A big man in homespun trousers and a buckskin hunting shirt was talking with a younger man yet seemed to be staring at Stephan. The older man and his younger companion finally stood and came around the fire beside him.

"Is there something I can do for you fellas?" Stephan had asked.

"If you ain't a Page from Kaintuck', I'll never see one agin," the older man said flatly.

The statement took Stephan by surprise. He slowly admitted that his name was indeed Page and he was originally from Kentucky.

"I told you, Cal. He's the spit'n image of Delaney Page. I could almost have believed he'd come back from the grave."

The two men studied Stephan, discussing him almost as if he were a statue unable to speak for himself.

"But Pa, Uncle Delaney's been dead near thirteen years since the massacre." The younger man spoke solemnly.

The second one squinted and then said, "But they never found the young'n, a boy of seven. Some figured he run off to the woods and got 'et by some critter. Sometimes though, if a child shows spunk, the Injuns take a young boy and raise 'em as their own or as a slave. I always figured that 'cause sister Alice's youngster was a spunky little fella for sure and certain."

Slowly a strange feeling grew in Stephan. Suddenly he realized that he knew this man. It had been years . . . no . . . a lifetime ago.

His mother's brother, Zephaniah Logan, had come to visit many times before that terrible day. And now, they were face-to-face again. The realization that he had been reunited with blood relatives after all these years was overwhelming. It was as if he had returned home from a foreign land to family members he had not seen for years.

With a slight catch in his voice, he asked cautiously, "Uncle Zephaniah?"

"Lord be praised!" the older man declared breathlessly, staggering back a step. In a moment, he recovered his composure, slapped his son on the back and smiled. "Shake hands with your cousin Stephan. Stephan, this here is your cousin Calhane."

The two young men clasped hands as Zephaniah hastily wiped away sudden tears.

The three men talked away the night, catching up on the lost years. After Stephan finished his story, they offered to come along with him to settle up the problem with Raven's Claw and Wolf Stalking. Then, when this little fracas with the British was over, Stephan could return to Kentucky with them.

Stephan declined their offer with thanks but told them it was something he'd have to attend to himself. His relatives understood, assuring him that the Logan farm was his home whenever he wanted to claim it.

Now, standing on the deck of the *Tigress,* Stephan thought about the overwhelming nostalgia he had felt as he listened to his uncle describe the farm Stephan had visited many times as a child. He could still see it in his mind's eye—its rolling fields surrounded on three sides by dense forests teeming with wild game and its sturdy barn with stalls enough for a milk cow and three horses that stood just off from the small but comfortable house. From the dim recesses of his memory, Stephan recalled climbing up to the sleeping loft with Calhane's older brother, Sam, when they had visited one Christmas, and listening to his parents and uncle and aunt whispering about the surprises the boys would find the next morning. Calhane had been just a baby at the time. His uncle told him that Aunt Sadie had passed away about ten years ago and Sam now had his own place with a wife and six children. Their farm was just across a small valley from Zephaniah's. Sam had already served a six-month tour with the militia. Now he was overseeing his father's farm while Zephaniah and Calhane were away, just as they had done for him while he was away. While he could not explain it, for the first time in thirteen years, Stephan had a strong sense of belonging and knowing where his future could lie.

A tap on his shoulder brought him back to the present. "Better get some rest, Page; tomorrow will be a very full day I think," Alex was saying.

"I'll be along in a minute," he answered.

As his two friends headed toward their bunks below, James clapped him on the shoulder and bade him good night.

Stephan stood for another moment, looking across the bay at the other ships at anchor. The Kentucky militiamen had been training for some time as marines in the unfamiliar realm of ships. As the Logans had proven expert marksmen, they had been chosen for the *Niagara* commanded by Jesse Elliott. Perry had been so glad for the reinforcement, he had offered Elliott his choice of crew and riflemen. There had been some talk about how discourteous Elliott had been in picking the very best of the lot for his command. Perry had let the issue slide, but Uncle Zephaniah had not been happy with their assignment. He told Stephan that he would much prefer serving under young Perry, who had already earned the respect of nearly every man at Presque Isle.

Looking up at the moon, Stephan wondered if Christiana ever saw this same moon and thought of him. He could not help but wonder what she would think of a small farm in Kentucky. A rare, wistful smile appeared as he imagined the two of them sitting on the front porch of the farmhouse watching a huge harvest moon climb high above them. It was a pleasant dream. "On the eve of battle, a fellow is allowed a dream or two," he thought.

Stephan held on to the dream for a while, reluctant to let it fade before the mountainous obstacles that may very well prevent any possibility of it ever coming true.

## 18

With the light of sunrise, the British sails were sighted and the signal to get underway was hoisted on the *Lawrence.* A dark blue flag with the white lettering, "Don't Give Up the Ship," was raised. Ladies from Erie had prepared the signal flag for Perry bearing the words he had chosen from the dying statement of James Lawrence, the naval hero lost in an earlier battle. A shout sounded throughout the American fleet.

As the American ships hauled anchor, the Americans were gravely aware that the wind was not yet blowing in their favor. Lieutenant Knox walked up and down the deck, giving last minute instructions and encouragement to the men in his unit.

Stephan stood next to James on the fo'c'sle; his grip on his musket tightened. Through narrowed eyes, he saw the two flagships draw closer. His mouth seemed dry as cotton.

Then a dark shadow briefly crossed the deck and drew his attention to the sky above them. There soaring in a wide graceful circle on powerful wings was a large eagle.

The sight stirred something deep within Stephan that caused his blood to race. He had always felt a special affinity with the regal denizen of the air, even before acquiring the name Yaro'ka-i. The sighting now gave him an inexplicable confidence in the outcome of the imminent clash.

The British were approaching in a tight line, no more than a hundred yards between each ship. The positions of the British were not exactly as anticipated so Perry made some last minute changes in the American formation. At Perry's signal, the *Lawrence* pulled ahead of the *Niagara* to encounter the British flagship *Detroit*. Elliott was in command of the *Niagara* with orders to engage the second largest British ship, the seventeen gun *Queen Charlotte*. He had fallen in behind the *Caledonia* which was assigned the task of the British brig, *Hunter*.

The two American gunboats, *Scorpion* and *Ariel*, were off the bow of the *Lawrence* to act as dispatch vessels. The other four small American vessels, *Somers, Porcupine, Tigress,* and *Tripp*, were to engage the British schooner, *Lady Prevost*, and the sloop, *Little Belt*.

At first the British long guns began to take their toll, smashing into the *Lawrence* still sailing against the wind. It was Barclay's plan to destroy the *Lawrence* first, then take each of the other ships one piece at a time. As cannonballs shattered through her hull and across her rigging, it appeared the plan was working.

Three hundred miles to the southeast, Christiana had returned to Washington and was about to sit down to lunch with her parents in their dining room just as the two forces were closing in on each other. As the schooner, *Lady Prevost,* came within range, Stephan raised his musket to begin firing with the other marines. Feeling a sudden chill, Christiana excused herself to take Copper out for a long walk. Oddly, she felt the need to be alone and say a special prayer for Stephan.

Back on Lake Erie, the *Lawrence* began pulling ahead of the slower gunboats. Then, without warning, the wind changed. The *Lawrence* closed in on the *Detroit*, well within carronade range. The exchange was brutal. Strangely, the *Niagara* held back behind the *Caledonia* while the *Lawrence* was nearly battered to splinters.

By 1:30 P.M. only fifty-four of the one hundred thirty-seven-member crew of the *Lawrence* were still alive. Miraculously, the well-known "Perry's Luck" was holding. As men were being killed and wounded all around him, Commodore Perry remained untouched.

The British command was not quite as fortunate in the fate of its leaders. Barclay, aboard the *Detroit*, was badly wounded, and the *Queen Charlotte* had lost its captain and first officer with the second officer wounded, leaving only an inexperienced lieutenant in command. The *Queen Charlotte*, Barclay's main support, was virtually useless.

From the unscathed decks of the *Niagara*, Zephaniah and Cal Logan watched as the sails of the *Lawrence* were reduced to shreds. It was irksome to be holding back when their support was so desperately needed. Grumbling through the ranks of marines and sailors on deck evidenced their chafing to get into the fray and come to the aid of their sister ship. When it finally appeared that Perry was dead, Elliott made his move to bring the *Niagara* up to save the day as Perry's blue and white flag was being lowered.

Ordering the *Caledonia* out of his way, Elliott prepared to join the battle. Much to his astonishment and the joy of the American sailors, they spotted a small boat suddenly emerge from the thick haze of the battle's smoke. Coming alongside, the young commodore climbed aboard carrying his blue and white flag. Eager hands hoisted it aloft as Perry assumed command of the *Niagara*. Elliott was immediately sent to call up the slower gunboats and take command of the smaller vessel, *Somers*.

As they watched Elliott rowing away through a heavy barrage of gunfire to relay Perry's orders to the gunboats to hurry forward, Zephaniah turned to Cal. "He's so bum-fuzzled and aggravated, any shells that hit him now would just bounce off!" Zephaniah commented with a wry smile. At that moment a volley of round shot exploded against the rail on the left side of Cal, peppering everyone within five feet with a spray of metal fragments and wooden splinters. To Cal's right, Zephaniah was knocked to the deck by the blast. Recovering his senses, the Kentuckian reached frantically for his son. Blood from a gash on his own forehead nearly blinded him, but he was gripped with horror as he was able to see Cal, lying a few feet away, mortally wounded. In his despair he hardly noticed the ugly wound in his own leg until he tried to rise. Unable to stand, he crawled to his son's side calling on God in his agony to take him too, for the pain in his heart was worse than any of the wounds in his flesh.

From the decks of the *Tigress*, Stephan and the twins could see the *Niagara* thrusting forward, intent on cutting through the British line. The sight of Perry's signal flag being raised had renewed spirits throughout the fleet.

Through the acrid smoke of burned sulphur and black powder, the crew of the *Tigress* exchanged fire with the British *Lady Prevost*. They were too busy with their own task to see that British commander Barclay's crew was trying to bring the *Detroit* around to train her undamaged gunside toward the *Niagara*, but the *Queen Charlotte*, in the hands of its inexperienced lieutenant, was following too closely astern and robbing what little wind they had from the *Detroit*'s sails. As the *Detroit* tried to come about, masts and bowsprits of the two British ships became entangled, leaving the *Queen Charlotte* unable to fire without hitting the *Detroit*.

The noise was deafening as cannons exploded and muskets barked incessantly. Through the din Stephan heard the whine of a musket ball whistling by his head. It caused him to dodge to the right just as another singed his left temple. The fiery sting brought the immediate realization of how closely he had just missed a rifle ball right between his eyes. Reloading, the militiaman resumed firing with a vengeance, more angry now than frightened.

Between the combined forces of the *Tripp, Porcupine, Tigress,* and *Somers,* the *Lady Prevost* and *Little Belt* soon capitulated. The *Niagara* pounded the British flagships, the *Detroit* and the *Queen Charlotte,* with shells landing on the *Hunter* and the *Chippewa* as well.

By three o'clock the white flag of surrender was finally hoisted on the *Detroit.* The battle was over and for the first time ever, an American fleet had captured an entire British fleet intact.

Perry quickly wrote a short note to General Harrison with the legendary words:

> We have met the enemy, and they are ours: two ships, two brigs, one schooner, and one sloop.
>
> Yours, with greatest respect and esteem,
>
> O. H. Perry

The situation aboard the *Lawrence* was a ghastly nightmare of shattered bodies. The price of the victory had been tragically high. However, Lake Erie was now under American control, and this would affect the coming battle between General Harrison and the alliance of Tecumseh and British General Proctor up along the Thames.

Stephan and the Macklin twins stood on the battle-scarred deck of the *Tigress* shaking hands in glad relief that the battle had ended leaving each of them in one piece. Gingerly Stephan touched the slightly bloody crease along the side of his head and grinned as his two companions noticed his close call. Surveying the carnage, their eyes stinging from the acrid smoke of gunpowder, they were each overcome by the inevitable question of why they had been spared when so many of their number had not. Their prayerful thanks for being alive came with sober remembrance of their fallen friends.

The next morning Stephan learned that his cousin, Calhane, was not so fortunate. He had been killed at Put-in-Bay in the last minutes of battle. Uncle Zephaniah had also been wounded but was expected to recover. Lieutenant Knox numbered among the wounded, having taken a musket ball in the shoulder. He would recover, but was to be taken back to Fort Stanford to do so.

Perry's orders to treat the British prisoners well was a pleasant surprise to the defeated sailors. An implacable foe in battle, Perry was charitable in victory. During his visit to the seriously wounded Barclay, he informed the British commander that he would request General Washington to parole Barclay unconditionally and allow him to return to his home in England.

As the Americans celebrated their victory, a message was delivered to Stephan. It was from his trapper friend. Chenault had gotten a soldier at Fort Meigs to write four words for him: Raven's Claw with Tecumseh. But Stephan had little time to consider the matter for within the week his unit was marching west to join Harrison's force to engage Tecumseh and General Proctor at Fort Maulden.

Stephan prayed he would not be in a position to be firing on the Indian allies of Proctor. He had trained and fought beside the other men in his unit and knew he could not let them down. He would have to fight and do his part, but he prayed no Shawnee would die by his hand.

As soon as the news about the defeat of Barclay's fleet reached Proctor at Fort Maulden, he immediately made plans to retreat farther north along the Thames. Tecumseh protested, wanting to stand and fight the intruding Americans. Tecumseh didn't respect Proctor like he had the late General Brock. When asked to stay behind to create a delaying action to protect the retreating forces, the Indian chief rebuked the British officer as weakhearted.

Brilliant reds and oranges of autumn emblazoned the forest as the American forces hurried north to catch up with Proctor. The heady taste of victory at Lake Erie spurred them on to yet another possible coup d'état in Canada.

Commodore Perry, desiring to join the battle against Proctor, had volunteered as General Harrison's aide. In pursuit of the British and Tecumseh, they found themselves the morning of October 3 at the mouth of the Thames River. As Perry stood beside General Harrison surveying the lay of the land before them, he noticed a large eagle soaring high above them. Drawing the general's attention to it, he was filled with a sudden excitement as he related sighting another such magnificent creature on the morning of their victorious lake battle.

Stephan saw the eagle too. He couldn't help but wonder whether Raven's Claw stood with the opposing forces and if today would be the day of their final, fatal meeting.

Two days later on October 5, Harrison's forces caught up with the British 41st Regiment as Proctor fled up the Thames River Road to Moraviantown. Marching in the second of three waves commanded directly by General Harrison, Stephan ended up on the side of the battle farthest away from the vast swamp where Tecumseh and the Indians that remained with him took their stand. The dreadful battle lasted a little less than an hour. Later Stephan heard some of the Kentuckians on the left arm of the attack in the swamp say that as long as the Indians heard Tecumseh's voice rallying his warriors, they battled fiercely. When their legendary leader's voice was suddenly stilled, the rest of the Indians slipped silently away through the swamp. By that time the British forces had been completely routed.

After the battle, in which Stephan had received a minor flesh wound in his side, he searched for the prisoners that had been taken captive. When he found them, one of their number was a friend from the same village where Stephan had lived. It was Sings-the-Elk-Song. When Stephan saw his buckskin shirt pierced by five or six rifle balls, it was tragically clear that the young warrior had seen his last hunt.

Gripping Stephan's wrist, Sings-the-Elk-Song greeted him with a wan smile. "Yaro'ka-i, the day has not gone well."

"No, my friend," Stephan winced as he raised the brave's head and held his canteen to the young man's parched lips.

Nodding his thanks, Sings-the-Elk-Song grimaced as he lay back. "I saw your spirit soaring above us and wished you were here to fight with us today."

Stephan choked back a lump in his throat and couldn't reply.

"Do not be sad, Yaro'ka-i. It was meant to be. Just as the eagle, your way was meant to be solitary. You were good Shawnee for a while, but it is not your way."

"Where are the rest?" Stephan asked. "You're the only one from our village I could see."

"Everyone from our village but Raven's Claw, Wolf Stalking, and I left two days ago when Walk-in-the-Water of the Wyandot took his people and the Miami. Proctor has betrayed us. He left us to protect his escape. Tecumseh never retreats; I fight with him and those who stayed."

"What about Wolf Stalking?"

"Your Old Father was too ill to leave with the others. He went to his ancestors last night."

"And Raven's Claw?"

"He fell just before Tecumseh's last war cry. Many times I wished you were here instead of him. He liked the death song too much."

"You should have gone back home too," Stephan sighed.

The young brave smiled. "No. It is better to die in the battle with Tecumseh. Someday, when you have sons, will you tell them how your friend Sings-the-Elk-Song fought beside the great Tecumseh?"

"Yes, I'll tell them about the Shawnee ways and about my friend who had courage to stand beside the great Tecumseh when others ran away."

The young brave smiled.

Stephan sat with him long after the Shawnee closed his eyes in death. Just before dusk, one of the Kentuckians who had been guarding the prisoners walked by and noticed the Indian was dead. He reached down and started to pick up the brave's feet to drag his body away to the mass grave that was being dug.

"Leave him be," Stephan growled as he saw several fresh scalps hanging from the soldier's belt.

"What the . . .?" the soldier exclaimed.

"I said, leave him be." Stephan stood and looked the Kentuckian in the eye. "I'll see to him."

The soldier studied Stephan a moment then said, "Ain't you Zeph Logan's kin?"

Stephan nodded.

"Well, then I reckon you can have this one." The soldier eyed him grimly and backed away.

Stephan then hefted his friend's body over his shoulder and disappeared into the forest. Sings-the-Elk-Song would have a proper Shawnee burial.

# 19

Mac's trip to Fort Stanford was postponed when he received a report regarding Axel Harrod from Colonel Sloane's clerk. Apparently, two days before Perry's victory, a small patrol from the fort out on an early morning fishing expedition at the lakeshore happened upon a curious scene. From a bluff overlooking the sheltered cove where they intended to fish, the militiamen saw a sloop anchored just off the beach. The crew was taking on board what appeared to be barrels of flour, bundles of blankets, and the kind of wooden boxes used for transporting bacon.

As they descended along the path leading down to the beach, the sergeant in charge of the patrol recognized Axel Harrod standing beside the half-empty wagon conversing with a man wearing the uniform of an officer in the British navy. It was obvious to all who witnessed the scene that the quartermaster of Fort Stanford was doing business with the enemy. The sergeant rushed his men forward in a hurried descent down the steep path to capture the renegade Harrod and the British sailors. Seeing his game was ended, Harrod hastily bargained with the captain of the sloop to take him aboard and by the time the militiamen reached the wagon, oarsmen had pulled the light ship nearly out of the cove and far enough for the wind to fill her sails. Muskets barked as the infuriated American soldiers cursed and aimed at the already unpopular Axel Harrod. The sloop was quickly out of their musket range, escaping with one small hole in the mainsail, and some splinters knocked loose from the aft rail.

Reading the report, Mac was disappointed the scoundrel Harrod had gotten away, but was glad his activities would at last be exposed and stopped.

Other pressing matters involving the war situation also delayed Mac from returning to Fort Stanford to settle the problem with the Natiri Indian, Wolf Stalking. Then a letter received from Stephan two weeks after the battle along the Thames River seemed to close that matter as well. Stephan informed him that during the difficult retreat north away from General Harrison's forces, Wolf Stalking's health had deteriorated dramatically and he had died. Mac remained in Washington.

The news of Perry's victory on Lake Erie was like a tonic to the disheartened Americans. The subsequent victory of General Harrison three weeks later along the Thames River when he defeated General Proctor and Tecumseh was even more encouraging. It had been an especially providential victory as the American forces had captured eight cannons and more than one million dollars worth of supplies from the British army retreating into Canada. For weeks Washington was abuzz with excitement and congratulations for one and all.

The celebrations were short-lived, however, for November and December brought dismal news. The border along lower Canada continued to blaze. While Harrison's victory at the Thames River virtually ended the Northwest campaign, from Sacketts Harbor on Lake Ontario along the St. Lawrence River to Cornwall and the Chateauguay River, the ill-fated Montreal campaign had met with disaster, just as Mac predicted. In mid-November Wilkinson temporarily retired, blaming General Hampton for the failure to capture Montreal and cut off supply lines to Kingston. The conditions along the border were frightful with as many American soldiers dying from illness due to rotten food and wretched sanitation as from the enemy's hand.

This phase of the war sunk to inexcusable acts against civilians as the Americans burned Newark and later York. The British retaliation would only just begin with the destruction of Buffalo and Black Rock. No one could know that the seeds of revenge planted during these ugly days would soon reach the very capital of the United States.

Christiana and Rachel had been back in Washington since the sixth of September when they went to help Jean-Marc find a small house in Alexandria. He had settled into his post as a professor of French studies.

Since returning, Christiana had noticed that her mother was indeed worried about her father. Christiana could see a marked intensity in his demeanor that left him quieter and more pensive than she had ever seen him.

The family returned home to Dunston for the Christmas holidays but were back in Washington on New Year's Day. News of the disaster with the Montreal campaign had not yet reached them.

One brisk morning two days after their return, Christiana was sitting at the secretary in the drawing room writing a thank-you note to Jean-Marc for a copy of a French edition of Moliere's *The Misanthrope,* given to her for Christmas. Glancing out the window overlooking the street, she saw her father riding toward the house, his jaw set firm. It was obvious he was very angry when he dismounted in front of the house instead of taking his horse around to the small stable at the back. She quickly signed the note she had just finished as the front door opened then slammed shut.

Jessica had seen Mac from the upstairs window and hurried down to see what the trouble could be. Her husband had infinite patience and it took a great deal to make him really angry, so she knew that something important must have happened.

Startled out of sound sleep by the slamming door, Copper jumped back beside the writing desk as Mac slammed his fist against the mantle.

"A stupid waste of good men, and for what?" the congressman declared angrily. "How could they rationally think they could take Montreal with poorly trained and equipped soldiers led by incompetents like Wilkinson! Neither side's stopping with soldiers now; even civilians aren't safe. Buffalo's been burned. The entire campaign's a disaster. The only good thing is that Wilkinson may retire, and now he's blaming it all on Hamp—"

Suddenly Mac's face turned ashen-gray, and he clutched his chest.

"Mac?" Jessica was alarmed by the strange look on her husband's face. "Mac, are you alright?"

"Jess!" he gasped.

"Chris!" Jessica cried. "Get the doctor. Run!"

Christiana hesitated a moment, frozen with fear, then quickly heeded her mother's frantic cry and raced from the room. Jessica helped her husband to the settee.

It seemed like an eternity as they waited. The doctor had been with Mac for nearly half an hour. Mother and daughter sat clasping each other's hands in prayerful silence. Carolina and Rachel Burke had come as soon as they had gotten word. Nathaniel Burke, along with their good friend from the Capitol, Oliver Howe, had just arrived when the doctor finally came down. The group stood to meet him.

"Jessica," he began with a sigh, "I've been trying to tell him and now it's happened. It's his heart, that old wound from the war. I think it weakened it, and now he's pushed it to the limit."

Jessica's knees went weak and she sat back down.

The doctor continued. "I'm not sure how he survived this one, but he won't be so fortunate next time. If he doesn't get away from this place—you can mark my words—there *will* be a next time.

"He's resting now. If he makes it through the night, he has a good chance of recovery. Jessica, he simply can't take the strain here any longer. You're going to have to convince him that it's time to let the younger pups do the scrapping."

The doctor patted Mrs. Macklin on the shoulder then turned to gather up his greatcoat. Shrugging, he grumbled, "I wish I hadn't promised to let him die rather than ever bleed him. It might help relieve the pressure. Even in his nearly unconscious state, he warned me to keep my promise or he'd scalp me. Stubborn man!

"Since I can't do anything more here and Mrs. Shaw is in labor, I'll be back in the morning to check on him unless you need me before. I'll probably be at the Shaws' place all afternoon."

After the doctor left, Jessica went to their room. She noticed that the doctor had drawn the drapes. Knowing how Mac always loved being able to look out and see the sky, she hurried over to open them wide again. Steeling herself, she turned and slowly walked to his bedside.

Mac lay very still, his face still that awful ashen-gray. It took every ounce of her self-control to fight back the cry of panic and denial welling inside. She felt as if her entire world was on the brink of destruction. It was hard to believe this was her Mac, always so strong, never seriously ill in the thirty-two years they had been married.

She had been the one who had been ill with the ague. She was the one who had nearly died in childbirth when the twins were born. Mac had always been there beside her bed, holding her hand, lending his great strength. Now, she could do no less for him. How dare she panic like this when he needed her beside him!

Pulling a chair next to the bed, she took his hand in hers and kissed it lightly. "I'm here, darling," she whispered. "Just as you've been here for me so many times. I wonder if you've ever truly known just how much I love you and need you."

For the rest of the afternoon she sat there watching him sleep, praying earnestly for his recovery.

Christiana brought her some tea and tried to convince her to rest. It was a futile request. Leaving the room, Christiana paused a moment, biting her lip and fighting back tears as she watched her mother holding her father's hand. There in the waning afternoon light, she could not—nor would she even try—to imagine her mother without her father. They were an inseparable pair, one incomplete without the other.

Quietly she left the room trying to swallow the lump in her throat and telling herself that it was up to her to see to everything while her mother cared for her father. She must remain strong for all of their sakes, even if she felt like hiding in her room crying until there were no more tears. But that would be senseless and selfish; there were too many things that must be done, like notifying her brothers.

Around three in the morning, Jessica awoke with a start. She had not intended to sleep, only to lay her head back and rest her eyes. Looking over at Mac, she discovered he was awake, watching her.

"Hello, Jess," he said softly.

Kneeling beside the bed, she kissed his hand, then softly stroked his face. "Hello, my darling," she whispered with a smile.

"I've been lying here watching you sleep. In this lamplight I was reminded of that first night beside the fire on our way to Charleston. . . . You're even prettier now than you were then . . . and I didn't think that was possible." His voice was low and very weak.

Jessica lightly touched a quieting fingertip to his lips. "You've always known just what to say to make my heart flutter, haven't you? Please, darling, rest now."

"We've had a great life, haven't we, Jess?"

"Yes, my darling, and we've still much left to do together."

"Have you ever been sorry, Jess? I know it hasn't always been easy."

Gently brushing his silver-streaked dark hair back from his forehead, she smiled wistfully. "I wouldn't trade a moment of our lives together for all the world. Even the most trying times have been bearable because you were beside me."

He smiled again and touched her cheek. "Jess," he said weakly. "I'm really tired." As he closed his eyes, his hand slipped slowly down to lay once more on the covers.

"Mac?" she breathed anxiously. "Andrew Macklin, don't you dare leave me," she declared in a desperate whisper, her throat constricted with fear.

Barely opening his eyes, he grinned. "I'm not going any-where, Jess, I promise. You just be sure and keep Doc away from me with those blasted leeches."

"I will, darling, don't worry."

With that, Mac closed his eyes and slept.

Jessica never moved from his side for more than a few minutes at a time during the next two days. The many prayers said for him by family and friends were answered as God permitted Mac to keep his promise to stay with Jessica. Slowly he began to regain his strength.

Two weeks after the frightening heart attack, Jessica was sitting next to his bed reading the letter Robert had written upon his return to Cherry Hills after visiting his parents. After she'd finished, Mac said thoughtfully, "Jess, would you be too disappointed if we went back home for good?"

She held her breath. Knowing how he never had liked the idea of quitting, she had avoided the subject of leaving Washington for fear of upsetting him. Now, looking into his dark brown eyes, she could see a light there that had been clouded by worry for a long time. Delighted, but curious about the change, she waited as he explained.

"You've put up with a lot these past few years, Jess. I've finally faced the fact that I've done all I can do here. I think the Lord's telling me it's time to take you back home and get on with our lives there. With the way things are going, he's the only one who can get this country through this trouble with England."

So it was. Mac was able to travel by the end of January and the Macklins left Washington, moving home to Dunston for good. The capital in 1814 would prove to be a very dangerous place even for those with healthy hearts.

# 20

Christiana remained in Washington for a week after her parents' departure. With the Burke family's help she completed the packing and arrangements for shipping the furniture and other belongings home. Since the Macklins didn't need any more furniture, they gave most of it to Eric and Mariette, who moved into a small house at the edge of town. Eric continued in the shop, planning to remain as long as Mac needed his help.

The month of February was ushered in by a bitterly icy wind and driving snow making venturing out nearly impossible. Although the weather was miserable outside, the Macklin home was warm and snug within as a constant fire burned cheerily on the hearth. Mac was improving daily, regaining his strength slowly but surely.

Jessica, Gran, and Christiana were busy making baby things because Alex and his wife, Heather, were expecting their first child in April, and Mariette had announced that she and Eric would be new parents in June.

Mac began drawing sketches for special baby spoons and cups and listened patiently to Eric's grand plans for his new heir, along with all the worries about every "what if" the young apprentice could think of. Mariette was serenely contented setting up their new home and preparing for their expected child. Other than Eric's frayed nerves, the only difficulty they seemed to be having was settling on a name for their bundle of joy. Just when everyone was sure it had been decided, someone would make the mistake of suggesting another possibility and the next few days would be spent discussing the merits and shortcomings of the new name. At last, they settled on Alexander Jean-Marc Lowe for a boy and Christiana Marie Lowe for a girl. It was finally agreed that the people responsible for bringing Mariette and Eric together in the first place ought to be so honored.

Christiana had received several short letters from Stephan since learning about Wolf Stalking's death. As February passed, she couldn't help but think about the night they had said good-bye. He had told her he would return to Dunston, if possible, when his enlistment with the militia was up. Since that time, however, a few things had changed.

His letters had explained about being reunited with his uncle and cousin, then losing Cal in battle. Now that his term had expired, he was going to take his uncle back to Kentucky and help Zephaniah with the farm while his uncle recovered from his wounds. Without his son, Zephaniah would also need help with the spring planting.

Stephan had also mentioned that during the Battle of the Thames he had heard that Raven's Claw had been killed. Although his company had been there, Stephan hadn't seen his adopted brother. Evidently, just as Tecumseh's body had not been found, Raven's Claw must also have been carried away by the Shawnee and buried in secret.

Christiana had reread the last lines of his last letter so many times she had nearly worn out the paper. In this one, Stephan had expressed his regret over her father's ill health and wished him a speedy recovery. He had also written:

It would appear that the past is settled even without the first confrontation. My only regret is that Wolf Stalking died feeling I had betrayed him. You must still pray for my future, for it seems much brighter now than before. I can even dare hope your words about me still being welcome in the Macklin household are still true. I think of you often.

She did feel the same, and she longed for the day when she would answer a knock at the door and find him standing there.

Stephan had promised to write again when he got his uncle situated. However, March and April came and went without another word.

For the country as a whole, April was a month of mixed blessings. The United States received the news that Napoleon had abdicated, ending the war between France and England. While some Americans cheered at this news, feeling it meant their war would also end soon, this wasn't especially encouraging news to those Americans who realized that Britain was now free to dispatch the Duke of Wellington's battle-hardened veterans to punish the impudent ex-colonists.

General Wilkinson had finally been replaced, much to Mac's delight. A fiasco at Lacolle Creek in March where Wilkinson had withdrawn his much superior numbered force from an attack on a fortress held by a relatively small number of British brought his demise. The announcement of the new leadership of the American regular army under Major General Jacob Brown and Brigadier General Winfield Scott had been very encouraging to Mac. Apparently Scott was working hard to create and train a disciplined force. By April it appeared that the regular troops of the army were showing real promise under young Scott's leadership and discipline.

Alex and Heather's baby was born the last week of April in Boston. They named their new daughter after the month that brought new life after a long cold winter. Alex wrote that he had forgotten when Christiana was a baby and he was amazed that such a tiny bundle could make so much noise, especially in the middle of the night. Aside from that, she was a wonderful gift from God.

Mariette was doing well. Eric was the one who worried, declaring that he wouldn't be happy until the whole thing was over and mother and baby were fine. Christiana could hardly believe what a difference the responsibility of a wife and expected family had made in Eric. He was almost like a different person now, although perhaps a bit too serious. Having been quite the ladies' man before, the apprentice was so completely devoted to his wife that his only fear was that some terrible trick of fate would take her from him.

With the fresh air and exercise, Mac continued to grow stronger daily. Jessica felt more content than she had been for quite a while. The sparkle of good humor and life had finally returned to her husband's eyes and she was happy. Every so often, he would become somewhat melancholy about the country's situation and the fact that Axel Harrod still roamed freely somewhere in Canada, but he realized that his friends in Washington were doing their best to resolve the problems. Mac had accepted the fact that his prayers for the country were his main contribution from now on.

June was ushered in with the exciting and safe birth of Mariette and Eric's son, Alexander Jean-Marc Lowe, who was born just before dawn on June second. Jessica and Eric's mother attended the birth in Eric and Mariette's small frame house on the edge of town. Mac and Eric's father kept the nervous father-to-be company during the long night. When the baby made his presence known with a healthy cry, Mac thought Eric was going to faint. He recovered quickly though and one would have thought Eric was the first father to have ever been so clever as to have a son. Christiana was especially happy for Mariette. She knew how important a family was to Eric's wife, and it was heartwarming to see her so happy after all of the tragedy she had experienced in her young life.

With the feared British veterans reported to be arriving in Canada, the war began to heat up again. The encouraging news of Winfield Scott's brigade winning victory at Chippewa on July 5 indicated that the training was beginning to pay off. The new Niagara campaign was attempting to cut British supply lines by invading Canada; however, the campaign ended in the defeat of Scott's troops at Lundy's Lane where they faced an overwhelming enemy force whose number had indeed been enlarged by the dreaded Wellington veterans.

While this campaign did not succeed, it was not the dismal failure of the previous campaigns. The U.S. Army had fought bravely and efficiently, exacting a high price from its enemy. Even in defeat, the men had gained a pride and spirit they had never possessed before.

Although the national scene was up in the air, everything was going very smoothly for the Macklin family. Christiana should have been quite content but with each passing day that she failed to hear from Stephan, she became a bit more unsettled.

The evening of July 13, the house was quiet. Everyone had gone to bed, but Christiana couldn't sleep. Finally, she came back down the stairs to get a book from the study, something to help her fall asleep. Scanning the books on the shelves, she realized she really wasn't in the mood to read. For a few moments she straightened a stack of sketches on the drawing table as Copper came ambling in and sat down beside her. He yawned and looked up at her as if wondering why they were up at this hour. She stroked his silky head and walked over to look out through the glass panes of the French doors. The night was clear with a half moon already casting a soft light over the garden.

Exactly one year ago this night she'd had one of the worst experiences and one of the most wonderful experiences of her life. On July 13, 1813, Copper had saved her from being kidnapped by Raven's Claw. Later that same night, Stephan had kissed her. He'd never been far from her thoughts since. Looking out into the deep slate gray sky, she wondered where he was and what he was doing, and most of all if she would ever see him again.

She knew he'd survived two momentous battles and had rediscovered his real family in his Uncle Zephaniah and his surviving cousin, Sam. Perhaps he'd met someone else in Kentucky. Perhaps Rachel had been right and she was foolish to allow her thoughts to dwell on him. The problem was, she had little control over trying to think of anything else.

In the meantime, Rachel apparently had taken her advice and captured Jean-Marc's heart. With each letter received from Rachel through spring and early summer, Jean-Marc's name was prominent on each page. The young Frenchman was doing well in his teaching position and visited Washington often. Rachel visited her cousin in Alexandria just as often and soon it was obvious that Christiana's two good friends were now a couple. While very happy for them, it only made it all the more difficult to cope with the emptiness caused by Stephan's absence.

On the first of August she was in the shop. Eric was working on a large salver for Judge Albee's wife. As Christiana showed her father the latest drawings she had completed, her mother appeared at the door with a familiar figure. It was Lieutenant Knox.

He smiled warmly. Christiana couldn't help but remember the last time he had come with a message. She only hoped this was strictly a courtesy call. Somehow, she knew it wasn't.

"Hello, Lieutenant, how are you?" Christiana asked.

"I'm doing well, thank you, since recovering from my wound received fighting with Commodore Perry on Lake Erie." He proudly patted the site of the wound on his shoulder.

"Yes, Stephan wrote saying you had been wounded," Christiana added.

"Did he?" He was pleased to find she already knew.

"Would you care to sit down, Lieutenant?" Jessica offered.

"Thank you, ma'am." After Jessica sat down, the officer took a seat on the settee, leaving a place for Christiana.

"Chris, perhaps the lieutenant would like some tea."

Christiana responded to her mother's suggestion and started for the kitchen to see about the refreshment. As she turned to leave the room, she noticed her father's slight scowl as he went to stand between his wife's chair and the fireplace rather than sit down.

When she returned, Christiana entered the room just in time to hear the lieutenant say, "I never would have suspected it of him. I really thought Page was alright. He fought hard, braver than most, through the battle on the lake. And although I was taken back to Fort Stanford to recuperate, the reports when they returned from the campaign along the Thames River were very favorable about him. He mustered out with a good record."

Christiana's heart began to pound as she set the tea service tray down. So distracted by the officer's words, she sat down without pouring tea for anyone.

Jessica, seeing the dread in her daughter's eyes, said nothing and handled the serving herself.

"When Page returned from the Thames," Knox continued, "he convinced that Indian woman who raised him to move over to the mission. Most of the people in her village had moved to the northwest right after word came that Tecumseh was dead; but she couldn't keep up since her health wasn't good. Then Page took his uncle to Kentucky and stayed there until last month. The Indian woman had Brother Adams send word to Page that she had only a little time left and wanted to see him once more before she died.

"Just before Page got there, the other one showed up. Everybody was surprised to see Raven's Claw again because word had come back from the Thames that he'd been killed with Tecumseh."

"We had heard the same from Stephan," Jessica responded, while Mac listened and watched the lieutenant in grim silence.

"Well, we surprised him too." Knox smiled triumphantly. "We caught him nappin' and had him all trussed up waiting for the hangman's rope when Page got the drop on the guard and cut that treacherous—" Catching himself before swearing, Knox apologized to Jessica and her daughter. "Sorry. Anyway, that was the last we saw of either of them."

"Have you come because you think there may be some danger from Raven's Claw again?" Jessica asked. She found herself a bit perturbed about this news for two reasons. It might distress her husband and Knox seemed to take particular delight in telling the tale.

"Yes, ma'am," the lieutenant replied with a crease in his brow. "I thought you ought to be alerted to the fact that he's on the loose."

"I doubt there's any danger, Lieutenant," Mac replied. He stepped closer to Jessica's chair and squeezed his wife's hand reassuringly, keenly aware of her concern for him. "Since the Indian's been alive when everyone thought otherwise, he's had plenty of time to come here if he intended to. Thank you for your concern."

After a cup of tea, Christiana ushered the lieutenant to the front door. He turned and smiled at her, asking if he might call on her. He was staying in Virginia for a while.

"I'm afraid I'll be leaving for Washington next week, Lieutenant Knox. You may remember my friends, Miss Burke and Mr. Richaux. They're having an engagement party on August twenty-sixth." Christiana abruptly changed the subject. "Do you really think Raven's Claw might come here after all this time, since Wolf Stalking is dead?"

He nodded solemnly. "But don't worry. I'll post guards. Your father won't even notice until the renegade is caught again. Will that help put your mind at ease?"

"Yes, thank you, Lieutenant. You're very kind."

"Another thing," he said as he turned to leave. "If Page should contact you, let me know. Be careful; he obviously can't be trusted anymore."

As she watched the young officer walk away from the house, the bright sunlit afternoon suddenly seemed to dim and a gray cloud like the one Stephan had disappeared into that last morning she had seen him settled around her heart.

The next week was busy with preparations for her trip to Washington. However, the old and familiar heaviness of heart she had experienced when suspecting Stephan of being a spy had returned.

Why in the world had she fallen in love with someone who seemed only to cause her distress? Love? Yes, she must admit it. She loved him desperately and facing it now only made her feel worse.

How could he have helped Raven's Claw escape knowing the danger not only to her father but to himself? As the months had passed since his last letter, she began to fear he might not return after all. He might have changed in all that time. Perhaps all of her suspicions about him had been closer to the truth than she wanted to believe. Perhaps she had been too quick to believe his story, to believe the look in his blue eyes. If he hadn't been sincere then she'd never be able to recognize sincerity in anyone, ever. However, facts were facts. And if he had jeopardized any of her family's lives by releasing Raven's Claw, she would never be able to forgive him.

"Christa?" Jessica repeated her daughter's name a third time before getting her attention.

"I'm sorry, Mother. What did you say?" Christiana turned away from her window where she had been staring down at the lane passing their house.

"I was just wondering if you needed any help packing. Eric will be by to take your things over to the stage office first thing in the morning," Jessica replied. She joined Christiana at the window and put her arm around her daughter's shoulders.

"Oh . . . I don't think so. We've been back and forth so many times, I could probably pack everything in my sleep now." She forced a smile and looked back out the window. After a long silence, she mused, "Why do you suppose I can still see his face so clearly after so long?"

Jessica had been aware of her daughter's heavy heart especially since Lieutenant Knox's visit earlier in the week, but Christiana had been reluctant to discuss it until now.

Responding to the question, Jessica sighed, "When you care for someone so much, time really has very little to do with it. During the Revolution I didn't hear from your father from the middle of July until New Year's Eve that year, yet not a day went by that I didn't close my eyes without being able to see his wonderful face."

"Yes, but you knew Father was doing something brave and honorable. There was no question about his motives or the goodness of his heart," Christiana lamented near tears.

"Do you really question the goodness of his heart, Christa?"

Christiana closed her eyes and tried to swallow the lump in her throat. "I've never felt this way about anyone. When I look in his eyes, deep down in my soul, I'm convinced his heart is sincere and good; and yet everything seems to be going just the opposite of the way I had dreamed it would turn out. The way things look now, we probably never will be together."

Jessica hugged her, sympathizing with her pain. "I know it's hard, dear. Perhaps there's some reasonable explanation for his actions. If it's the Lord's will that you be together, it will work out. If it isn't, then no matter how painful it might be now, there's a good reason and it'd be foolish to challenge God's wisdom."

Hadn't Stephan said something similar? At the present, it appeared that circumstances were working against them. Attempting to accept this, she tried concentrating on other things, but at unguarded moments she would find herself remembering his smile, his voice, and the touch of his hand on her face. And the ache in her heart would only intensify.

# 21

Christiana's mood remained dark as she traveled by stage to Washington. She had intended to leave Copper at home as a watchdog for her parents, but her father insisted that he go with her since she was traveling alone.

Nearing the capital for the first time since her father's heart attack, she thought of her dear friend, Rachel. She must be careful not to put a damper on this visit. Somehow, she had to push the entire subject of Stephan from her mind and lose herself in the joyful occasion she had come to celebrate.

The days with Rachel were like a whirlwind, and it was not difficult to put her own situation aside. However, in the quiet just before falling to sleep, she would find herself praying for Stephan and fighting back tears for the future they might have shared.

Thursday afternoon, the eleventh of August, found the girls across the Potomac in the home of Rachel's cousin in Alexandria, Virginia. Aside from the servants, the girls had the two-story brick house to themselves. Cousin and family were spending the scorching August days at their country home in the cooler climate of Smithtown on Long Island.

Jean-Marc came for a quiet supper that night and arranged to pick them up the next day for a picnic lunch, an afternoon of shopping, and then dinner at the home of the headmaster of his academy. It was a wonderful day, and the happy excitement of her two dear friends kept Christiana delightfully distracted from her melancholy thoughts of Stephan.

That evening after an elegant dinner with the academy's headmaster and his wife, Jean-Marc drove them home in the carriage placed at his disposal by the school. When they stopped in the circle drive of the two-story brick house, he assisted both young ladies down and walked them to the front door. He bowed deeply and kissed Christiana's hand as she thanked him for a lovely evening. He held the door open for her and as Rachel smiled coyly and started to follow Christiana inside, Jean-Marc caught her hand, gently pulling her back to his side. Christiana closed the door behind her to allow the young couple to have a moment to themselves. While very attentive to both young ladies during the day, his deep affection for Rachel was unmistakable. The sparkle in his eyes when he looked at her and the tenderness with which he touched her hand made it clear that his heart was in total captivity to the vivacious Miss Rachel Burke.

As the days passed, Christiana slowly became aware of a new degree of tension throughout the city. While Rachel seemed oblivious, Christiana frequently noticed a grim countenance on Mr. Burke's face. Coming down early for breakfast one morning, she found Mr. and Mrs. Burke sitting at the table.

"Excuse me, I didn't mean to intrude," she said, pausing at the doorway.

"Nonsense, come in, child," Nathaniel called.

Although he was a large burly man, the tough politician was amazingly tenderhearted when it came to his daughter and Christiana, who was nearly as dear to him as Rachel herself. It had been the Burkes who had helped her during those dreary days after her father's heart attack and later when she stayed behind to see to the packing of their belongings. The two families had been very close and their strength and support in that difficult time had been a blessing neither she nor her parents would ever forget.

As she sat down, Carolina rang for the cook to bring her some breakfast.

"I suppose you've heard all the rumors flying about the city," Nathaniel finally said.

"We haven't wanted to discuss such things in Rachel's presence," Carolina added sadly. "She's never been so happy, and we can't bring ourselves to dim her joy with bad news."

"I don't know if you have heard the rumor or not, Christa," Nathaniel began. "The British fleet under Vice Admiral Cochrane is headed this way. From what we hear, he has an especially low opinion of us Americans and plans to lay waste to the entire seaboard. Armstrong keeps insisting that Washington isn't in any danger of attack.

"Pray God, he's right, for we're practically defenseless here. Madison's appointed Joshua Barney to command what little naval force we have." He chuckled scornfully, "Naval force, hah! . . . Three gunboats, a few barges with cannons mounted on them, and five hundred sailors against the cream of the British navy and Wellington's troops."

Nathaniel wiped his mouth with a napkin as he spoke. "Do you remember Brigadier General Winder?"

Christiana smiled. "Yes. Remember how Rachel and I used to swoon over him at the dinner parties we attended? He always looked so handsome in his uniform."

"Good-looking fellow, maybe, but hardly the general I would have chosen to command the militia defending our capital. Of course, I'm not trying to please the governor of Maryland as Madison seems to be either."

"We probably should consider having the party at my cousin's home in Baltimore," Carolina commented thoughtfully.

"At least they're preparing their defenses!" Nathaniel's tone was irritated. "It would be the safer place, my dear," he added more softly.

"Cousin Eloise?" came a plaintive cry from the doorway. They turned to see Rachel entering. "Change the party to Cousin Eloise's house? Oh, Mother, not really!"

"Rachel, dear, it might be safer. We didn't want to worry you and spoil things, but this doesn't seem to be a good time to be planning it here."

"Oh, pooh. Those rumors about the British invading the capital have been flying about for the past year and a half. Secretary of War Armstrong insists we're safe, and he can't always be wrong. Besides, they wouldn't dare spoil this for me."

Rachel's remark was made in jest, yet Christiana knew how important this party was to her. She could almost imagine her friend standing on the shore shooing away the British navy with her parasol. Apparently she had not been as oblivious to the clouds of war closing in on the city as everyone had thought. She simply refused to believe anything could spoil this very special time for her.

A few days later on Saturday, August 20, as Christiana and Rachel were returning from delivering invitations, they heard a commotion on the street in front of the Capitol Building. A rider had just dismounted and was shouting excitedly to the people who had gathered around him.

"The entire British navy is sailing up the Patuxent River! They're not coming up the Potomac. We must evacuate the city!"

Fear spread through the quickly growing throng. Suddenly Rachel pushed through. "Stop that," she demanded angrily. "How do you know they're headed here? You'll start a panic if you don't curb your tongue."

Christiana grabbed her friend's arm and pulled her back through the crowd. "Rachel, we must wait for your father to tell us what's really happening," she admonished.

Later that evening Nathaniel returned home. The news was unsettling. Even though Armstrong continued to assure everyone that Washington was safe, the militia had been called up and General Winder was trying to form some sort of defense plan. Joshua Barney's flotilla had pulled back to the headwaters of the Patuxent so the British ships could not follow. Apparently, the enemy troops had disembarked at Benedict just forty miles from the capital without a single shot being fired to discourage their landing.

For the next two days, so many rumors circulated that it was hard to know what to believe. Through all the turmoil, Secretary of War Armstrong continued to declare that Baltimore was undoubtedly the target of this latest British raid. General Winder ran about exhausting himself trying desperately to muster enough militia to mount a decent defense of the capital. His repeated requests for help from Armstrong were ignored because he had not been the Secretary of War's choice to command the defense force.

The night of the twenty-third, the Burkes and Christiana listened to the rumble of wagons and carts as people began to evacuate the city.

"They don't know what a wonderful party they'll be missing," Rachel said as they lay in the dark listening.

"Rachel," Christiana said quietly as she fluffed the pillow on her part of the trundle bed. "I don't think I've ever seen you cling to an idea so tenaciously before. Would it really be so terrible to postpone the party for a while or even change it to another place?"

Rachel sighed. "You're right, Chris. I've been nearly obsessive about it, haven't I?" Then Rachel realized she had to admit her real fear. "I think I'm afraid that if we don't announce our engagement in front of all our friends, Jean-Marc may change his mind. He might find someone else or Stephan may not come back to you and Jean-Marc will want you instead—"

Suddenly, realizing what she had just said, she cried, "Oh Chris, I must be completely out of my mind. Listen to me . . . I'm sorry."

The comment about Stephan had pierced through Christiana like an arrow. Over the past several months she had come to believe it was true. Stephan was not going to return. Then, through her pain she heard Rachel's words.

"I'm sorry, Chris, please don't—" Before she knew what was happening Christiana found herself laughing.

"Chris! I can't believe you can laugh at a time like this."

"Rachel, after seeing you and Jean-Marc together in Alexandria last week, no one could ever imagine him changing his mind about you. He loves you more than you even realize."

"Oh, Chris, do you mean it? Do you really?"

"Yes, silly. Now go to sleep."

Rachel rushed over to Christiana's bed and threw her arms about her, hugging her tightly. "Oh, Chrissy. I love him so much I'd just die if . . . no, I won't even say it. Oh, thank you, Chris. I'm so glad you're here."

"I am too. Now we'd better get some sleep. You don't want any dark circles under your eyes when Jean-Marc arrives tomorrow night, do you?"

"You're right, you're right!" she replied, hurrying back to bed.

At breakfast the next morning Nathaniel handed his copy of the Wednesday, August 24, 1814, edition of the *National Intelligencer* to Christiana and shook his head with a grim sigh.

She read the lead sentence on the front page: "We feel assured that the number and bravery of our men will afford complete protection to the city."

After breakfast, they watched more wagons and carriages pass by laden with household articles and frightened people. Surprisingly, by afternoon the procession seemed to diminish. It appeared that the rest of Washington's population was waiting to see just what would happen next before dashing off in fright.

Later that day, Rachel and Christiana were helping the Burkes' cook prepare pastries. As they worked, the cook told the girls she had spoken with her sister who served on the domestic staff of the White House. It seemed that Mrs. Madison was calm as could be. While everyone else in the place was dashing about, she was calmly overseeing the packing of vital state documents, silver, and other valuables. Someone even said they overheard her call for a cannon to defend the White House. The President was at the moment out of the city with Armstrong and Monroe poised on the heights above Bladensburg reviewing the current situation. Mrs. Madison was determined to wait for his return before evacuating the city herself.

Rachel smiled triumphantly. "If she dares stay, can we run away like frightened children?"

"Never, mon cheri!"

"Jean-Marc!" Rachel gasped turning to see him entering the kitchen, instantly remembering she was covered with flour up to her elbows. She blushed vividly. "You've caught me at a terrible disadvantage! That's not fair you know. We weren't expecting you until tonight."

The young French professor came forward and placed a gentle kiss on her cheek. "You're lovely," he whispered, "even covered in flour. I could not wait until tonight."

Turning to see Christiana sitting at the table where she had been peeling apples, he smiled.

"Dear Christiana," he said in his soft French accent, "you'll never guess who I ran into yesterday."

Jean-Marc turned toward the door and with a sweep of

his hand drew her attention to a young man stepping into the doorway.

Her knife dropped on the table with a loud clatter. "Stephan!"

"Hello, Christa." His broad smile and the look in his eyes reflected an unmistakable delight.

Immediately her hand went to the white cap covering her hair and the apron covering her dress. Caught completely off guard, Christiana was speechless.

True to her character Rachel had quickly recovered. She turned to Jean-Marc and laughed. "Now that you've seen me like this, I suppose you'll want to call off the party."

"Hardly," he teased, picking up a tasty freshly-baked morsel. "We could never let such delicate pastry go to waste."

Rachel discreetly took Jean-Marc's arm and led him out of the kitchen. "Cook, perhaps you'd better set the table for dinner now," she directed over her shoulder as they left.

"Now, miss?" Cook asked. "Yes, of course, miss."

When they were alone, Stephan spoke first. "They make a fine couple."

Stephan looked different than he had that morning nearly a year ago. There was a maturity about him that comes to those who have survived the fiery baptism of battle. He obviously had not been eating as well as when he was partaking of Gran Barton's cooking, for his face seemed a bit thinner. Yet somehow the shoulders beneath his broadcloth jacket seemed broader than Christiana remembered. His face was tanned from hours of working in the fields and his bronze color caused the steel blue of his eyes to be even more striking. The look in those eyes had not changed nor had their effect on her.

Christiana's pulse was racing so fast she hardly heard him say, "I'm glad to hear your father is recovering. Jean-Marc said he had a very close call."

"Yes. He did." Forcing herself to look away, she added frostily, "From what I hear, you've had several yourself."

His initial enthusiasm at seeing her again was cut short. He had dared not think she would run to him with open arms, although for just a moment she appeared as if she might. On the other hand, after their letters and her attitude before he left, he had expected a bit warmer reception.

Uncertain of the meaning of this last comment, he said guardedly, "You're looking well." He wanted to say wonderful and take her in his arms, but she had picked up the knife again.

"You're looking fit yourself. Farming seems to suit you." Her attitude was as bristly as a porcupine.

"Is something wrong?" he asked warily.

"No. Of course not. Why?" She deliberately avoided his searching glance.

"Christiana, it's obvious you're upset for some reason."

"What makes you think I'm upset?"

Catching her hand, he cautiously removed the knife. "Because if you keep peeling away at those apples, there'll be nothing left but core."

She glanced down at the whittled remains of the apple in her hand and sighed irritably.

"I'm glad to see your arm is finally well," she said quickly, changing the subject.

"What?"

"Your arm, I was certain you must have broken it since the last time you wrote—let me see around the end of January, I believe."

"Letter writing doesn't come easy for everyone." The soldier smiled sheepishly.

"How difficult is it to write, 'I'm alive and well, hope you're the same'?" Giving him a withering glance, she took back the knife and began working again.

"Guess I didn't realize letters were so important to you," Stephan replied as he sat down on the edge of the table.

"Important? Not especially." Christiana picked up another apple and feigned nonchalance. "Just curious about how you were doing at farming with your uncle."

"Christiana, what is it? Are you angry because I went to Kentucky before coming back to Dunston?"

"Why should I care where you go?" Although she was trying to hold back her emotions, her words seemed louder. "I mean one would hardly expect you to pass up the opportunity to visit your uncle even though you were still under apprenticeship and Father was too ill to carry on the shop."

Instantly she regretted speaking so foolishly. In truth, she really wanted to confront him about Raven's Claw and learn what reasonable explanation he might have. But sparring about relatively insignificant matters would delay hearing something that might end forever the dream of them being together, a dream that she had stubbornly cherished.

She stood up to carry the peeled apples to the simmering pot hanging on the hook in the fireplace. As she passed him, Stephan reached out and caught her arm.

"Christiana, look at me." He tilted her chin up so she was facing him. "I knew Eric was able to handle the shop very well without my help, and I really didn't think you would begrudge me helping my uncle. There's something else. What is it?"

Just then, Rachel walked in. "Oh dear. Excuse me, Chris."

Startled by the sound of Rachel's voice at the doorway, Christiana quickly stepped back from Stephan.

"What is it, Rachel?" she asked, catching her breath.

Her friend smiled like a Cheshire cat. "You're a very popular young lady today. There's another handsome young soldier here to see you. It's Lieutenant Knox."

"What?" Quickly, she hurried to Rachel's side and pulled her into the kitchen.

"Did you say anything about Stephan being here?"

"No. Cook answered the door, and I overheard him ask for you. Why? What's wrong?"

"Nothing. Just don't say anything about Stephan being here and tell Jean-Marc not to mention it either."

Turning to Stephan she warned, "Stay here and don't make a sound."

Before anyone could say another word, Christiana was on her way to the parlor. She removed the cap from her head and patted her hair in place, then tossed her apron on a nearby chair. Stopping in front of the parlor door, she took a deep breath and entered. "Lieutenant Knox! What a surprise. What brings you to Washington?"

The officer stood, hat in hand, smiling broadly. "They called up my company, and we've just arrived to join General Winder in defense of the city. I managed a brief leave to come and escort you and your friends to safety."

"That's very thoughtful, Lieutenant. Is the danger really so certain?"

"I'm afraid so," he replied solemnly. "General Winder has formed a line of defense at Bladensburg, but it's doubtful we'll be able to hold against the invasion. There's rumors of spies in the city to clear the way to destroy it. You really must prepare to leave right away."

Rachel had followed Christiana into the parlor. "But Father hasn't returned from the Capitol yet," she protested. "We'll wait to see what he says. What about Mrs. Madison? Is she still in residence?"

"I'm not sure, Miss Burke. I've just ridden into town." Turning toward Christiana he said, "You really mustn't delay long. I'll go and try to find Congressman Burke. While I'm gone, please try to convince your friends to pack what they can and be ready to leave when I return."

After the lieutenant had taken his leave Jean-Marc sighed and took Rachel's hand. "Well, my dearest, it appears we must postpone our gala affair."

"I knew it," Rachel frowned. "It was the flour that ruined it all, wasn't it?"

Christiana watched Lieutenant Knox through the window as he made his way into the crowded street.

"What's wrong, Chris?" Rachel asked.

"I wonder about Lieutenant Knox—" she answered absently.

"What about him other than he seems quite smitten with you?" Rachel smiled broadly.

"I have the strangest feeling there's more to it than that," Christiana replied pensively.

"My, this is interesting: One beau in the kitchen and one in the parlor at the same time!" Rachel teased.

"Oh, Rachel, the British are on our doorstep and you're teasing about—" Then she remembered. Without finishing her sentence, she hurried back to the kitchen.

"Stephan?" she called quietly but the kitchen was empty. She returned to the parlor.

"Where is he?" Rachel asked.

"Gone."

"Gone?"

"As we all should be perhaps, mademoiselles. I fear that's rocket fire I hear in the distance." Jean-Marc remarked with concern.

Rachel refrained from her real thoughts about this Page character and said, "I'll go wake Mother from her nap. But we can't leave without Father."

No sooner had she left the room than Nathaniel Burke hurried in from the street. He quickly directed them to pack whatever essentials they could hand carry; then he hurried into his study to collect his important papers and valuables.

"Did Lieutenant Knox find you?" Jean-Marc asked following Nathaniel into the study.

"No, but it's a madhouse out there. The streets are so crowded we'd just be wasting time to try to get the carriage through." Nathaniel added, "Jean-Marc, if anything should happen to me, promise you'll take good care of Rachel and Carolina."

"Have no fear, sir. But nothing is going to happen to any of us."

"I tell you, Jean-Marc, if my family wasn't here to take away to safety, I'd stand and fight. You don't know the rage I'm feeling at the thought of those redcoats scarring one stone of this city."

"I understand, sir," Jean-Marc said solemnly. He held open the valise for Nathaniel to fill with portfolios of vital papers and correspondence. "Somehow I think even if the British burn the place to the ground, the undaunted spirit of your people—of this land—will only rebuild it even better than before."

Nathaniel clapped the young Frenchman on the shoulder. "I knew I was right in giving my consent to this marriage. Come now, we'd better get your bride-to-be to safety."

Within fifteen minutes, they had gathered some food and what few valuables they could carry and were ready to leave. The sound of musket fire echoed in the distance indicating there was no more time to waste.

"We can't wait for the lieutenant," Nathaniel directed when they finally gathered in the entry hall with their burdens.

As they hurried out into the street a cry sounded that sent chills to their bones. "The militia's in full retreat! Redcoats are entering the city!"

# 22

The scene before them was chaos. The street was clogged with heavily laden wagons that stirred up clouds of red dust choking the people on foot who were frantically carrying their backbreaking loads. The suffocating heat only intensified as panic drove the crowd to pandemonium.

Christiana searched the throng. Where could Stephan have disappeared to? Then, above the loud clamor and the dust, she thought she heard her name.

"Christiana, over here!"

Through the haze she spotted him! He was waving his hat from the corner of a nearby house on the other side of the street.

"Come this way!" Stephan shouted.

"Jean-Marc!" Christiana yelled as loud as she could. "It's Stephan!"

Within moments, the group joined the jostling stream of people and began to forge its way toward the narrow space on the opposite side. Christiana and Rachel linked arms to avoid being separated in the pressing throng. Suddenly, an earsplitting shellburst a block away caused the crowd to shriek. Instantly, the sea of people surged forward, and a young man carrying a wooden crate of squawking chickens plunged into the girls. When the sharp corner of the crate poked them at their linked arms, they lost their hold on each other and were forcibly separated.

Holding Rachel's other arm, Jean-Marc managed to pull her to the side of the seething river of frightened human beings. Escaping the crush the two finally reached the place where Stephan waited. The Burkes followed close behind.

However, Christiana was swept away like a leaf at the mercy of a river's current. Struggling to keep from stumbling, she was filled with the realization that she had no control. The crowd could carry her so far she'd never be able to find her friends again. Trying desperately to maneuver her way toward the other side, the young woman found herself wedged against a large hand-drawn cart piled high with household goods, its turning wheel moving slowly and groaning under its load.

Then she heard it. Her name! She looked up to spot Stephan with his hand outstretched working his way toward her. She reached back toward him. Their fingers almost touched when a sudden jerk pulled her to the side. The hem of her skirt had gotten caught in the wheel of the passing cart. Frantically, she pulled and tugged with all her might. The skirt didn't budge. Panic swept over her. She screamed, but she knew that even if the man pulling the cart could hear her, the momentum of the crowd was too great for him to stop. The fabric twisted and tugged, drawing her closer to certain death.

"Stephan!" she yelled as she struggled to tear herself free. "Stephan, help!"

Suddenly his arm was around her, holding her up. He pulled at the twisting fabric without success as the crowd pressed them forward.

"Stephan, look!" Christiana cried as she spotted an open box of utensils riding at the edge of the cart.

218

Quickly reaching into the box, he pulled out a large butcher knife and with a quick slash the tangled hem was separated from the rest of the skirt. Christiana was free.

Gasping with relief, she clutched the lapel of his jacket as he protected her from the crowd and they pushed their way toward the edge of the street.

"Are you alright?" he asked when they reached the side.

She nodded, still unable to speak.

"Come on. We've got a farmer's cart I borrowed. I've hitched the two horses Jean-Marc and I rode from Alexandria to it. The others are doubling back behind the houses. We'll cut across the back fields to the road along the river."

Wasting no time, he snatched her hand, and the two of them dashed back between the houses to the lane that ran behind the rear gardens. At that moment, the horse-drawn cart galloped toward them. But the happy reunion among the friends was cut short by another shellburst. Quickly they clambered into the wagon.

The bone-jarring effect of the cart's bouncing across the uneven ground was hardly noticed in their dash away from the repeated volleys of cannon fire raking the city. When they finally reached the river road, they heard shouting. Billowing gray smoke rose into the sky at the far end of the bridge over the Potomac.

"They're burning the other end of the bridge to keep the redcoats from crossing into Virginia!" Nathaniel exclaimed.

"We'll have to take cover in the woods," Stephan directed.

Immediately, Jean-Marc reined the horses from the river road. He stopped at a small clearing of gray-barked beech trees on the side of a gentle knoll. Through the trees the group had a clear field of vision across to the city and could detect any advancing troops in time to retreat farther into the forest.

Alighting from the wagon, they had just caught their breath when they heard a tremendous series of explosions.

Almost instinctively Christiana grabbed Stephan's arm. He pulled her close in a protective embrace. For a long moment they held each other tightly, watching the columns of smoke rise ominously from the city.

"The Navy yard," Nathaniel explained aloud.

Christiana buried her face against Stephan's shoulder, thankful that her parents were not here to see this terrible destruction.

Nathaniel expressed everyone's thoughts. "This must be the darkest hour of our country's history. Will we ever recover from this humiliation?"

Turning toward Stephan he added, "Our thanks to you, young man. Without your help, we'd still be plodding along the road. I take it you're Christa's friend?"

Keeping one arm wrapped around her, Stephan shook Nathaniel's hand.

"Yes, thank you, Stephan." Rachel stepped next to them, clinging to Jean-Marc's arm. "I really must apologize. I'm afraid I misjudged you. I thought you'd abandoned Chris. Please forgive me."

"Forgiven." Stephan smiled slightly. Then, clasping Christiana's elbow he said, "Excuse us, Rachel, we have something we need to talk about."

Stephan quickly ushered Christiana a short distance away.

"Did you think I'd run out on you too?" he asked bluntly.

She looked at him trying to appear stern. "I didn't know what to think, except that you were running from Lieutenant Knox."

"You have such a low opinion of me that you think I would leave you in danger just to save my own hide?" A deeply disturbed frown furrowed his brow.

"I . . ." she began.

"You obviously still suspect me of some dark deed," he interrupted, "yet you tried to shield me from Knox. I don't understand you at all! I thought we had resolved all of that past history. I thought you realized I care for you. How could you possibly think I'd just run off?" With that, he turned around and headed back toward the horses.

"Stephan—" She trailed after him.

Watching silently as he removed the harness from one of the horses, she realized he was preparing to leave. She stepped forward. "Where are you going?"

He didn't look at her. "Back to the city," he stated flatly.

"What?" she gasped. "Why?"

He swung up on the horse's bare back. "We have no arms to defend ourselves. I have a pistol and rifle with my luggage back at the boardinghouse. There wasn't time to go back for them before, but we may need them and any others I might find along the way."

Without further explanation, Stephan wheeled his mount and rode off across the fields toward the besieged capital.

"Where in the world is he going?" Rachel said when she spotted him leaving.

Christiana explained. Nathaniel nodded his approval while Jean-Marc exclaimed, "That Page is either the most foolhardy fellow I've ever known, or the most brave."

Stephan would have denied either claim as he guided his horse across the wide fields. He had always thought of himself as being fairly levelheaded and possessing no more courage than any other, but their situation was desperate and he knew they needed some way to defend themselves if the British pursued them. He chose to ignore the fact he was so agitated with Christiana he had ridden off without giving much clear thought to how he would retrieve his weapons or to the possibility of encountering Lieutenant Knox before he was prepared.

Christiana watched him disappear in the distance. Absently she reached down to stroke Copper's head. Suddenly she realized she had not seen him since . . . since . . . she tried to remember just when she had seen him last! In all the excitement, she had forgotten all about Copper.

"Rachel!" she cried. "When did you see Copper last?"

"Copper? Oh dear, let me see. I think I saw him just before you went down to the cellar for the apples."

With a sinking feeling in her stomach, Christiana suddenly had a good idea of what happened.

"Of course," she moaned. "He must have followed me down there. You know how he loves to lay on that cool stone floor when it's as hot as it is today. He must not have come up before someone closed the door on him."

"Oh, Chris, I'm sorry." Rachel placed her arm around her friend's shoulders.

Nathaniel and Carolina Burke both expressed their sympathy. Carolina tried to cheer her. "He'll probably be just fine. No doubt he's asleep and won't even know about all the commotion."

With a forced smile she tried to agree, but as she turned to look at the smoke rising above the city, all she could imagine was the Burkes' house in flames and the ceiling and the floors crashing down.

As Jean-Marc joined them after removing the harness from the other horse to allow it to graze, Rachel quietly explained what had happened. All of a sudden, the couple heard her father shout, "Christiana!"

Rachel looked up. To her disbelief, Christiana was galloping away toward the city with her skirts flowing in the breeze.

"Chris!"

"What on earth?" Jean-Marc exclaimed. "She'd rush into jeopardy for the sake of a dog?"

"Copper isn't an ordinary dog to her," Rachel replied. "He's a dear friend. She'd never abandon him nor ask anyone else to risk going after him."

With the wind whipping at her dark hair, Christiana was so intent on reaching the Burkes' house before it was put to the torch, she didn't even notice the darkening sky and the black storm clouds gathering in the distance.

# 23

Drawing closer to the outskirts of the city, Christiana was surprised to hear very little musket fire—only triumphant shouts and breaking glass. A pall of smoke drifted across the rooftops and the acrid smell of burning sulphur from the explosions at the naval yard stung her eyes and throat.

Slowing her horse to a walk, she planned to ride quietly up to the back of the house, hide her mount in the stable, and then quickly duck in through the back door to the cellar. She felt relieved when she realized that most of the smoke appeared to be coming from the main government buildings rather than the residential area.

It only took a minute to tie the horse in the stable and hurry toward the back steps. Christiana quickly let herself in and, with pounding heart she ran to the door leading down to the cellar. Immediately Copper came bounding out, greeting her with frantic enthusiasm and nearly knocking her down. Hugging his furry neck, she tried to calm him.

Heading toward the back door, a rumble of thunder sounded outside and Copper stopped in his tracks. He hated thunder. She patted his head to reassure him that he was alright. He danced nervously a moment then pressed against her leg looking up at her anxiously. Stroking his head, she urged him to follow and stepped toward the door just as a loud shriek and blast of a Congreve rocket sounded nearby. Running into the dining room to look outside toward the street, Christiana could see flames begin to billow up from the roof of the Bordens' house across the street and two doors down.

Filled with terror, Christiana grabbed for Copper, but he had whipped around and she saw him tearing up the back stairs. She knew he was headed for his safe haven under her bed in Rachel's room. Looking about frantically, she would need some kind of leash to keep her precious pet from bolting away once they got outside. Rushing into the parlor, she grabbed one of the long drapery cords holding back the drapes. Cautiously peeking out the window, she could see the street was clear in front. Farther down the street she could see redcoats talking to one hapless citizen who had chosen to stay in his house rather than run.

Hurrying by the window, she dashed up the front stairs to Rachel's bedroom. More thunder rumbled across the sky overhead. Rain was beginning to patter against the bedroom window and the sky grew darker. Getting down on her hands and knees, she looked under the trundle bed to see Copper cowering there in the corner. When he saw her his tail flapped up and down, but he didn't move.

"Come on, Copper, we have to go, boy," she called to him softly.

He crawled a few inches toward her, his tail still flapping the floor nervously. She crawled in under the bed herself to reach him and cooing to him softly, she managed to tie the drapery cord around his neck. She was backing out from under the bed and coaxing him to follow when a lightning bolt struck so close the window panes rattled; with a whine Copper scooted back into the corner as far as he could go.

"Oh, Copper. Come on, please," she begged going back in after him. This time it took her longer to convince him to inch his way out with her because the thunder was rumbling almost without a pause between lightning bolts.

She was finally out from under the bed herself but still on her knees and he was following her when she heard loud voices and stamping feet downstairs in the entry hall. Her pulse nearly stopped and she put her hand on Copper's head to stop him where he was. She could hear at least four different men's voices, all speaking with British accents. At first she couldn't hear what they were saying until a deep voice came from the staircase saying, "The way things is scattered about, looks like they've skittered away, sir."

Another voice from the entry hall replied, "Well, search it anyway, and be quick about it."

Christiana quickly pushed Copper back under the bed and crawled in after him, pulling the coverlet back down over the space. Copper started to growl deep in his throat and she put her hand on his muzzle and whispered, "Quiet."

"Be quick about it," she heard the redcoat soldier grumble as his heavy boots clomped along the hallway outside Rachel's room. "I've spent the last five days marching forty miles through wretched heat, nearly had my ear torn off by a rifle ball, and now come close to bein' struck by lightning; and he says 'be quick about it.' There's no one here. Ahh, doesn't that bed look soft. If only . . . Heh?" he called back to the voice downstairs. "Yes, sir."

She could see the toe of his boot under the edge of the coverlet and held her breath, praying Copper wouldn't decide to lunge at it.

The soldier patted the mattress wishing he could just lay down and sleep for a day or two. But no, duty called.

Looking out the window as he turned and left the room, he saw the rain coming down harder now. He'd never seen such a storm where he came from and it made him edgy.

The voice called up the stairs again saying, "There's some fancy tea cakes down here, soon's you're through up there. Corporal says we'll wait the storm out here, prob'ly spend the night."

"Well, what d'ya know," the soldier sighed. It's about time."

Christiana was afraid to move as she listened to the heavy boots moving down the hall. Then as they clomped heavily back down the stairs, she allowed herself to take a deep breath. Releasing Copper's muzzle, he panted and licked her hand. She pressed her face in his fur and told him what a good dog he was. The house still held the heat from the August day, since they had closed the windows as they prepared to leave earlier. Therefore, the bedroom was stifling. It was even hotter under the trundle bed, but she dared not move from her hiding place. All she could think of was the terrible stories they'd heard after the attack on Hampton. Being careful not to make a sound, she laid there under the bed wondering about her friends the Burkes and Jean-Marc out in this terrible storm. She remembered a farmhouse not far from the clearing and hoped they had been able to make their way to it. But what about Stephan? Where was he?

The combination of the heat, the lack of sleep the night before, the terrifying exodus from the city, then the race back for Copper finally took its toll and Christiana fell asleep listening to the rain falling heavily upon the roof.

"She did what?" Stephan exclaimed as he hopped off his horse landing next to Jean-Marc. The rain had nearly stopped, but it was now dark. He had been unable to get into the McKeowin's Hotel to get his guns because it was filled with British taking shelter from the storm and set-

226

tling in for the night. Narrowly escaping capture, he had returned to the clearing with one old flintlock he'd found along the road where someone had dropped it in the panic leaving town. Jean-Marc was at the clearing alone, waiting for Christiana and Stephan's return so he could take them to the farmhouse where the others were taking shelter for the night.

Stephan's heart sank when Jean-Marc told him about Christiana.

"She was away before we could stop her. I would have followed, but without a horse, it seemed impossible to catch her. Nathaniel begged me to stay and help him get Rachel, Mrs. Burke, and their cook to some shelter because we could see the storm coming. I have been standing here waiting and hating myself for not at least trying to catch and stop her."

Stephan shook his head. "Even if you'd had a horse, I doubt you'd have caught her or persuaded her to come back. Her father says she's inherited her mother's determination. I think she's just plain stubborn," he declared.

"You are going back to find her?" Jean-Marc asked as he watched Stephan swing up on the horse's back again.

"Yes, and if I miss her and she comes back here, tie her up if you have to, but don't let her leave again."

Jean-Marc agreed and watched Stephan disappear into the darkness. The rain had doused most of the flames that had raged earlier, but here and there a glow of light from something still blazing or rekindled marked the shadowy outline of the city in the distance. The young Frenchman was as deeply affected by the sight as the others, for he admired these unique people. So provincial in many ways, there was an astounding brilliance in their concepts of freedom from tyranny for the common man as well as nearly limitless opportunities for those willing to make the effort. Somehow they must recover from this humiliation and fight back to avoid returning to British colonial status again.

Christiana felt like she was suffocating. She awoke to find herself still in the restricted space under the trundle bed, with Copper still beside her. She wondered what time it was. Laying there listening, she could hear noises in the street and see a line of soft light showing beneath the edge of the coverlet.

She couldn't believe that she had slept through the night, but with her limbs so cramped that she could hardly move, she knew it was true. Her left leg and right hand were numb. Copper whined and licked her face. He wanted out from under there now as much as she did. She waited a minute or two more while the feeling returned to her leg and hand. Still no sound from within the house. Carefully she raised the hem of the coverlet to look out at the room. No one there. Slipping out from under the bed, she tiptoed to the window and peeked out to see the sky was clear with a pale blush along the eastern horizon. Smoke still rose from the direction of the President's mansion and Capitol Square. In the street below, she could see four soldiers leaving the house and joining three others coming from another house. They exchanged a few words then moved off toward the center of town.

Christiana took a deep breath and prayed that all of the soldiers had left the house. Turning to go to the door she noticed the other trundle bed with its covers all mussed; with a cold shiver she realized one of the soldiers had slept there sometime during the night. Trying not to think about the close call, she made her way to the door with barely a sound, Copper at her side on his drapery cord leash. At the top of the stairs as she was just about to step down from the top step, Copper began a throaty growl. At that moment she heard voices from the kitchen, then suddenly the intruders were in the hall below. Holding her breath she quickly stepped back and pulled Copper with her.

"Hurry up, Kinney, the corporal doesn't want to miss out on the smashin' and burnin'."

Peeking around the stairwell corner, Christiana saw a young soldier pull on his red tunic and sling his musket strap over his shoulder as he walked briskly toward the front door.

The soldier trailing behind complained, "What's the rush? The city's ours. What about breakfast?"

In a moment they were out the front door, not bothering to close it behind them. Christiana waited a few more breathless minutes, listening to the voices out in the street. Copper whined.

Hurrying to the back stairs and down to the kitchen she was relieved to find that the house was empty. The kitchen was a mess. Every morsel of pastry was gone and the simmering pot of applesauce left to cool on the work table had been scraped clean. The faint aroma of cinnamon, apples, and baked pastry still lingering in the air made her realize she hadn't eaten a bite since lunch the day before.

Copper sniffed at the floor, lapping up crumbs under the table. She checked the pantry to find it ransacked. Copper found several crackers scattered on the pantry floor and quickly devoured them. The noises in the street kept her on edge fearing some of the soldiers might return. They'd have to eat later, she decided, and headed for the back door. Through the window she could see the back garden was clear. So was the lane beside it where the stable stood. The sun was up now. It was going to be another sweltering day.

Leading Copper on his leash, Christiana quickly slipped out the door, hurried across to the stable and inside. It took a moment for her eyes to adjust from the bright morning sunlight to the dimness of the stable. When she could see, she was suddenly dismayed to discover the building was empty. The soldiers had apparently found her horse and taken it along with them. The distance she'd covered the day before in a fifteen-minute gallop had suddenly stretched into a very long walk through rolling wooded hills and open meadows. She sat down on an old trunk to think a moment of what to do next.

Stephan shifted, trying to find a more comfortable position than the one he'd been scrunched in for the past two hours. The small cupola in the second-story attic of the house directly across the street from the Burkes' was cramped, hot, and dusty, but he was able to see an unobstructed view of the front of the house where he was sure Christiana had to be hiding.

Daylight was finally creeping over the city as he saw the front door of the Burkes' house open and two redcoats step out into the street. They were soon joined by two more from the house and three from down the block. His heart was pounding faster. He knew there were two more soldiers in the house and had a strong feeling that Christiana Macklin was there as well.

After talking with Jean-Marc, he had raced back to the city. Finding the Burkes' stable, he discovered Christiana's horse still there, but no sign of her or Copper. He could see the house was occupied by soldiers. His ability to move silently, learned from his Indian tutors, now allowed him to circle the house looking through the windows to see who was where downstairs. He had to wait until the lantern lights were turned down before he boldly slipped inside to search for Christa. One soldier dozed at the kitchen table, and Stephan moved like a silent shadow to the back stairs leading to the second floor. He knew that another soldier was stretched out on the settee in the parlor while a third sat by the front door nodding off.

Upstairs, he crept into each bedroom and found one soldier asleep on one part of a trundle bed, took a quick look in the wardrobe, then back out in the hall. Moving to the other bedroom, he found two soldiers snoring on the one wide bed, and again no one hiding in the wardrobe. He found the narrow stair leading to the attic and a quick search left him scratching his head. He'd had such a strong feeling that she was hiding somewhere in the house.

At least he was consoled by the fact that she was not a captive of the soldiers, not here anyway. Rather than go back down through the house, he climbed out the shuttered cupola at the back of the attic and along the edge of the roof, then lowered himself down to the back porch roof. From there he lightly dropped to the ground. For the next four hours, he dodged from shadow to shadow searching for the most stubborn, most foolhardy, most wonderful young woman he had known or ever would know.

Stephan's long, exhausting, and futile search had brought him back here to this attic. He had discovered there were still a few civilians who had not evacuated and were being allowed to stay in their houses. He prayed Christiana had found shelter with some friends, but had to be certain she wasn't still hidden somewhere in the Burkes' house.

He was relieved to see the sixth soldier ambling out of the house stuffing a piece of bread in his mouth. Still no sign of Christiana. Unless other soldiers had entered the house after his search, it should be empty. Waiting until the redcoats cleared on down the street, he then hurried down through the empty house he'd been hiding in and dashed across to the Burkes' place. Unbeknownst to him, as he was entering the front door, Christiana and Copper were slipping out the back, heading toward the stable. A quick, fruitless search of every nook and cranny left him perplexed. The only answer could be she'd found shelter with other friends in the city or she had slipped away while he was searching for her elsewhere. He decided it was time

231

to return to the Burkes and Jean-Marc. She was probably already there herself. The decision made he peeked out through the side window of the entry hall to see if the street was clear to cross over to where he'd left his horse the night before. The sight before him quickly changed his plans for there riding by, apparently unconcerned about being taken captive, was Lieutenant Knox.

# 24

"When I heard the rockets had fallen on Fourth Street, I feared the worst." Oliver Howe sighed with relief as he watched Christiana eat a generous portion of ham and eggs just prepared by his cook. Copper lay on the wide porch just outside the kitchen door happily gnawing on a soup bone. "That's why I sent my steward over there this morning to check on the Burkes and you."

"The Bordens' house was hit last night just before the rain started," Christiana explained as she finished the last delicious morsel on her plate. "I was certainly glad to see your steward this morning. I'd just discovered my horse gone and wasn't quite sure what to do.

"You said there were still quite a few people left in the city?"

The frail little man who had been such a good friend to her father and Nathaniel Burke was slight in stature but his spirit was as bold as brass, and he was most disgusted with the entire situation surrounding the invasion.

"Yes, not everyone could get out once the rush started, and then when Major-General Ross and that dadburn Cochrane were in the street, it was too late. I have to admit Ross is a gentleman and apparently has no intention of hurting civilians. I can't be so sure about the admiral. I sure wouldn't turn my back on him.

"You look a bit frazzled, my dear. Would you like to go up to the guest room and rest? If Ross is true to his word, this house is safe."

She looked down at her yellow linen dress, part of its skirt slashed when Stephan freed her from the cart wheel. The dress and petticoats showing beneath were grimy and beyond repair.

"A bit frazzled, indeed, Mr. Howe. You're much too kind. I look a mess. Since it appears the British intend only to destroy the heart of the city . . ." her voice broke slightly; the truth of what was happening still incomprehensible, ". . . and spare the civilians, I suppose I'd be safe enough to go back to the Burkes' and change my clothes."

The old gentleman rubbed his chin. "Well, I don't know that we can depend on that, my dear. It's those blasted Congreve rockets, too, you know. They make the darn'dest racket and there's no controlling where they go. I think it's best you stay here. Besides, though Ross is a gentleman, no tellin' what some of his men are capable of."

As if to punctuate his point, a shrill shriek sounded just a block or so away, ending in an explosion. No others followed immediately and Mr. Howe said, "See what I mean? You'd best stay here. I couldn't face your dear parents if I allowed you to leave and you were injured in any way."

Bowing to his wishes for her to stay, Christiana decided at least to go up to the guest room to sponge off some of the grime from yesterday's ordeal.

Throughout the morning and early afternoon, they continued to see new fires kindled around Capitol Square and even into the residential areas. Christiana could only pray that Stephan had found his guns and returned to the Burkes and Jean-Marc. About two o'clock that afternoon, Mr. Howe had retired for a nap and Christiana was looking through the window at the dismal scene outside when a tremendous explosion rattled the windows and knocked over delicate porcelain figurines on shelves. Mr. Howe's steward came rushing out of the kitchen and joined her at the window.

"Now what?" the man declared.

"I'm not sure. Look! It seems to be over by Greenleaf Point. They must be destroying the fort there," she replied.

"I'd heard our militia did that. But don't s'pose they did a very good job, what with the hurry they was in to get outta town."

Christiana could only watch in further disbelief as another huge cloud of black smoke billowed into the sky.

"Miss Macklin! Miss Macklin! Your doggy's run off!"

Christiana whirled around to see one of the maids wringing her hands excitedly. "He wanted outside and I opened the door. Then there was that awful noise and he lit out fastern' anythin' I ever did see."

"Oh dear!" she exclaimed. "He's probably gone back to the Burkes'. He's terrified of loud noises. I'd better get him."

"No, Miss. Mr. Howe wanted me to be sure you stay right here," the steward declared. "Too dangerous out there on the streets now."

"But, I really must go after him. As frightened as he is, he probably thinks I'll be there at that house like he's used to. I know exactly where he's gone to hide if he can get in the house. The front door was standing slightly ajar when I went out the back this morning and you found me."

Her explanation had little effect. The gentleman in charge of Mr. Howe's staff was not about to let her leave after being told she was to stay.

About that time, the old congressman came hurrying down the stairs, grumbling and shaking his head.

"Now what in tarnation was that?" he demanded.

"We think it was over at the fort at Greenleaf Point, sir," his steward replied.

"Mr. Howe, I'm afraid I must leave for a little while," Christiana began. "Copper seems to have run away frightened by that dreadful noise. I'm sure he's gone back to the

Burkes' and it will just take me a few minutes to go over there and bring him back," she explained as she edged her way toward the entry hall.

"Now, just hold on there, child. Until we know what this newest catastrophe is, I don't care if the President's cat has run off, you will stay put. Why I'd never be able to look your father in the eye again if anything happened to his little girl while she was in my care. No. You just set yourself down, and we'll wait for the news. It spreads quick enough with these things."

Christiana could see the steward was relieved it was not going to be his task to go out and find out what was happening now. She could have chewed nails having to sit in that room waiting to be allowed to go after Copper. Apparently, to Mr. Howe she would always be a little girl. Out of respect for him and her parents' good name, she gritted her teeth and sat waiting for the news. Outside, she could see storm clouds beginning to gather again this afternoon.

Nearly an hour passed before the message came for Mr. Howe telling them that when the fort at Greenleaf Point was destroyed by the retreating American militia, the powder magazine had not been touched. Without the means to transport it, the redcoats decided to destroy the 150 barrels of black powder by throwing them down a deep well so the Americans couldn't use them either. Somehow, it ignited causing the tremendous explosion that killed from twelve to thirty men and injured at least 44 seriously, all British soldiers. Major-General Ross had ordered the injured to be carried to the empty hotel on Carroll Row for a temporary hospital. The message completed, Christiana was on her feet.

"You see, Mr. Howe, it was their own accident. It's not some new assault. Won't you please let me go after Copper?"

"Well, all right," the old gentleman agreed, then started to add, "but wait until . . ."

Christiana didn't hear his last few words; she had rushed from the room the moment he said "all right."

Halfway down the front walk of the large house, she remembered she had removed the drapery cord from Copper's neck and left it in Mr. Howe's parlor. She dared not go back and decided she could always use the other one that still held back the drapes in the Burkes' parlor.

As she dashed down two blocks and turned down Fourth Street where the Burkes lived, she was brought up short by the sight of four British soldiers walking down the street with their muskets poised as if looking for someone. She quickly decided it might be safer to go down the lane at the back of the houses and ducked in between the first two houses to take the back way.

Opening the back door carefully, she slipped inside the kitchen and with heart pounding and out of breath she quickly went into the parlor and retrieved the other drapery cord for Copper's leash. Within another two minutes she had hurried up the back stairs and into Rachel's room.

"Copper boy, come here," she called softly and kneeled down to look under the bed. There he was. This time he was so happy to see her, he crawled to her wagging his tail vigorously.

"What am I to do with you," she scolded gently as she tied the new leash in place. Going over to the window, she peeked out and could see the four soldiers had moved on down the street. Still she decided it would be safer to go down the back stairs again. Leaving the bedroom, Copper trotted beside her as they passed the stairs going down to the entry hall. A sudden crash sounded that made her stop in her tracks. Someone was in the house again. Just as she had earlier, she listened at the stairwell trying to determine who and where the intruders were this time.

She could hear a scuffling noise in the study and then an angry voice.

"Who else, Knox?"

It was Stephan!

She and Copper hurried down the stairs and into the study. There she saw Lieutenant Knox sprawled on the floor with Stephan holding a pistol against his chest.

"Christiana! What the devil are you doing here?" Stephan was stunned.

By this time Christiana was kneeling on the other side of Knox looking at his torn jacket and blackened bloody shirt. His face was bruised and bleeding.

Christiana looked at Stephan in disbelief. "What have you done?" she demanded.

"I didn't do this," he shot back angrily. "He did it to himself. Tell her, Knox," Stephan said through clinched teeth. "Tell her you nearly blew yourself up setting fire to the powder store."

"What?" Christiana was now bewildered.

"It exploded quicker than we expected," Knox groaned.

"Well at least the British won't get their hands on our arms," she replied more sympathetically.

"Tell her, Knox. Tell her you're *with* them. Tell her you did it for the redcoats."

"Stephan," she reprimanded him sharply. "How can you say such a thing?"

The air in the study was deathly still, hanging like a heavy blanket all about them. Just then Knox's battered body shuddered with a coughing spasm. Christiana started to ask how badly he was injured when a rush of wind slammed against the open study door banging it back against the wall so hard the glass shattered.

Looking out through the windows, Stephan saw debris flying through the air. The sky had grown so dark it looked like late evening. He turned back to Christiana.

"I think we'd better get to some shelter—"

No sooner had he pronounced the word than a board smashed through the window striking Stephan across the back of the head. Fragments of glass peppered the room. Taking advantage of the painful diversion, Knox thrust a sharp uppercut at Stephan's chin, cutting into it with the ring on his hand. The lieutenant then grabbed the pistol.

Knox had appeared to be too badly injured to have the strength to stand, let alone attack Stephan, but not any longer. He pulled himself to his feet and grinned.

Stephan was still kneeling, dazed and holding his head. The crashing window had frightened Copper, who had jumped behind Christiana. The dog stepped over to Stephan to lick his face. Stephan patted him as the animal sat down close by, growling at Knox.

"Miss Macklin, get your dog and hold him away," Knox abruptly ordered. "Then go get the other cord like that one you're using for a leash and help me bind his hands."

Christiana eyed both the lieutenant and Stephan.

"Hurry, Miss Macklin," the lieutenant continued. "He's a dangerous man."

Stephan remained silent. A bright red streak ran down his chin from Knox's ring. Suddenly Christiana remembered Stephan's furious attack on Jean-Marc. She knew he could be dangerous but it wasn't the kind of dangerous the lieutenant was implying. Stephan was threatening when he needed to defend something he held dear. Christiana knew what she had to do.

"I can't help you, Lieutenant," she answered sternly as she walked to Stephan's side and knelt down to check his head wound.

The lieutenant waved the pistol angrily. "Do as I say!" he shouted.

Just then an unearthly roaring noise that grew increasingly louder punctuated his command.

"Cyclone!" Stephan yelled as he struggled to his feet. "The cellar!"

Christiana recognized the terrifying sound.

"Page!" Knox warned, aiming the pistol at him.

"If we stay here, we'll all be blown away!" Stephan shouted.

It didn't take long for the ferocious noise to convince the lieutenant he'd better go too. He scurried after them with Copper following behind. Another loud crash sent the dog running down the stone steps past the three of them.

Reaching the bottom step they could hear deafening crashing noises above them. Then all of a sudden, a rush of air and light poured in. In the same instant, the cellar door and part of the floor peeled away. Stephan pushed Christiana against the wall and wedged her tight to shield her from the falling debris. Copper hid himself behind Christiana's skirts next to the wall.

The cacophony seemed to last much longer than the few minutes it actually took for the funnel cloud to pass by. Above them a swirling maelstrom of dust and the fragments of shattered houses swept by in a wild flurry created by the tremendous vacuum of the black snaking funnel. Then the sounds and roar moved away.

"It's over now," Stephan said as Christiana still clutched his arm. "Are you alright?"

She nodded, and they both looked over at Knox who sat huddled against the wall on the floor across from them.

"Don't try anything, Page," he said waving the loaded pistol. "I have nothing to gain by letting you live. On the contrary, if not for Miss Macklin, I would have already finished the job, but I'm not uncivilized. With the British in control of the city, I can stay with them when they move on to take Baltimore. It appears my usefulness to them on this side has come to an end, and I'll have to join them outright. I don't relish a hanging rope, which I'm sure Miss Macklin's father will demand when she tells him about this."

The lieutenant stood up. "Don't worry, I may be a traitor, but I'd hardly stoop to killing a woman. That is, unless you try something stupid, Page. Then who knows where a stray shot might go. Come on, let's go introduce you to your new masters."

Before they reached the steps, a downpour of huge raindrops suddenly dropped out of the sky. Within an instant, a torrent from a cloudburst following the tornado was pounding down on them.

Stephan shouted, "This place'll be full of water in a few minutes. We've got to get out of here!"

Before he'd finished the sentence, the water was already ankle deep. A waterfall cascaded down the steps and over the opened sides at the top.

"Alright," Knox agreed. "But you go first and remember— I'm ready for any false moves."

Reaching the top of the stairs, they realized that half of the house, including the study where they'd been just minutes earlier, had been ripped away as if some giant hand had torn it in two and removed one side. The other half was practically untouched by the wind. But now the driving rain was flooding everything.

Through the dense wet veil, they could see the stable still standing.

Knox followed the couple as they climbed around and over the debris outside the house. The battering rain on the stable roof was deafening, but at least it was dry and warm inside. It was an immense relief to be out of the hammering deluge. Copper whined, and Christiana stroked his head. Stephan led her over to an empty stall where the two of them sat down on a stack of feed bags. Knox settled on a small pile of hay just a few feet away.

Copper curled up at their feet soaking wet and shivering. Christiana was shivering too, as much from shock as from being drenched. Stephan wrapped his arm around her shoulders, and she leaned against him wearily. In her exhaustion, his nearness provided welcomed and comforting strength. For the moment, as she closed her eyes, there were no British soldiers, no Raven's Claw, not even a Lieutenant Knox, only Stephan with his sheltering arm around her.

# 25

The sound of coughing brought Christiana back to reality. It was Knox. He looked terrible. "You're badly hurt, Lieutenant," she said. "Let me see about your wounds."

He shook his head. "No. Thank you for your concern, but we're going to wait right here for the soldiers. Don't worry, Miss Macklin, they won't detain you long.

"Now Page there . . . They're going to hang onto him for a very long time." The lieutenant focused on Stephan. "I remember you saying on Lake Erie, Page, that the life of a sailor would never suit you. Well, you'd better get used to it. Prisoners of war serve very long terms aboard British ships. Americans have an especially trying time, I hear."

"Why are you doing this?" Christiana couldn't help asking. "How can you betray your own country this way?"

"Actually it wasn't all that difficult, Miss Macklin. I joined the militia to get away from home. Not a fancy home like yours, a drafty shack on the backside of a tobacco plantation. It didn't take long to gain my rank since I was willing to stay on past my enlistment time over and over again.

"I was transferred to Fort Stanford the end of March, just after your father's party was ambushed up there. I was assigned to take the place of the quartermaster's assistant who had died rather suddenly. It wasn't long before I discovered Quartermaster Harrod's second set of records that showed the profits he and his father, Rupert, were making selling army supplies to the Shawnee and the Canadians. I was careful when I confronted him about it, not wanting to die suddenly like his last assistant. He made a very persuasive argument against my turning him in. He paid very well for my silence—" A spell of hard coughing interrupted the lieutenant again. He raised the pistol warning them not to move.

"How did you go from simple bribery to helping destroy your country's capital?" Christiana asked almost bitterly.

"I fear I'm cursed with more ambition than fancy background. It didn't take long to get acquainted with some of Harrod's British and Canadian friends. I proved to have some valuable information for them from time to time, and they paid well.

"In fact, I've been promised a pension and even a medal when this is over. I plan to move to England and marry a young lady of fine breeding and perhaps even a title. Over there the young ladies like you pay attention to men with medals and pensions. They won't ignore me, like you have, because I'm a mere plantation laborer's son."

"I had no idea what your background was," Christiana declared with disgust. "Even if I had, it would have made no difference in my opinion of you. I'm sorry if you felt I was ignoring you, but my heart already belonged to . . . I mean, I—" She quickly stole a side glance at Stephan. She saw him cock his head slightly as a quizzical expression appeared on his face.

Knox's hacking cough filled the silence in the stable again. Christiana softened the tone of her voice. "Lieutenant Knox—Curtis—please let Stephan go, and I'll help you get to someone who can tend your wounds. You need help."

Stephan started to object, but she ignored him and repeated her request.

Knox grinned. "No . . . he's been chasing me too long now. I want him out of the way for good."

"Chasing *you?*" Christiana's eyes opened wide with surprise.

Knox shifted uncomfortably. "That's why I had to turn the tables on him with the Raven's Claw story."

"I don't understand." She really felt confused now.

"You can tell her, Page. I'm going to rest. But I'm not going to sleep, so no false moves!"

Christiana looked at Stephan.

"Your father kept a close watch on the personnel lists at Fort Stanford and paid particular attention to Harrod's unit. Knox sent supply reports in to your father's committee without ever mentioning any shortages that other officers complained about.

"After I told your father the truth, Knox arrived with the warning about me. Since he had arrived at Fort Stanford after Wolf Stalking sent me to Dunston, he didn't recognize me."

"But if he was working for Axel Harrod, why would he bother to warn Father about you, especially if he was behind the ambush as Father suspected?"

"Don't you see," Knox broke in impatiently. "Harrod was furious when your father refused to give up the investigation. When he heard about the blood vengeance against your father, he thought everything would be taken care of."

"How did he know about the blood vengeance?" Christiana interrupted curiously.

Knox shifted to a more comfortable position. "Not long after I started working with Harrod, I went to Chenault to have him do some interpreting for me with one of the Shawnee about some supplies they wanted. He was there recovering from his broken leg, but he refused to help me, saying he wouldn't do any more work for Harrod and the

244

Shawnee, especially Raven's Claw, because of this thing with Wolf Stalking and Yaro'ka-i." The lieutenant smirked at Stephan. "When I told Harrod, he was so happy about it, he didn't care about losing Chenault as an interpreter. The only trouble was, Yaro'ka-i didn't carry through and your father was still alive. So, to divert attention away from us, Harrod sent me to warn your father, thus removing suspicion from us; and at the same time sent Raven's Claw to finish the job himself." Knox leaned his head back against the stall wall and grimaced in pain. "Go ahead, Page, finish your story."

Stephen continued the explanation with, "Your father was still suspicious about Knox because of all the circumstantial evidence against him and Harrod. We didn't know about Raven's Claw being sent by Harrod at the time, and he asked me to join the militia to keep an eye on Knox and see if I could come up with any solid evidence."

This fact surprised her as much as the rest of the story, and made her wonder why she hadn't been told about it.

Guessing what she was thinking, he explained. "Mr. Macklin thought it'd be best if no one else knew about it. But then Knox and I were unexpectedly ordered to Lake Erie and he was wounded. Just before the battle, Harrod was caught delivering a wagonload of supplies to a British ship on the lake and he escaped with them. Knox was sent back to Fort Stanford to recuperate and I was sent on to fight with General Harrison at the Thames. With Harrod gone and Knox wounded, a new quartermaster took over. Since Harrod got away and Chenault had gone off on one of his hunting journeys, there wasn't any solid evidence against what Knox had done. Without Harrod, he wouldn't be able to continue, so my job seemed finished for the time being. My enlistment was up and as you know, I took my uncle home to Kentucky."

Christiana only had half of the story. She still wanted to know about the latest incident with Raven's Claw.

"When Brother Adams sent for me because Blue Flower was ill and wanted to see me again before she died, I went back to the mission," Stephan began. "She told me that Raven's Claw had come to see her. He had only been wounded at the Thames, and was determined to avenge Wolf Stalking against Mr. Macklin. He was also going to come after me because Old Father had died without me keeping my promise to him." Stephan sighed, remembering his last meeting with his adopted mother.

Christiana laid her hand on Stephan's. He looked at her, and was touched by the understanding he could see there in those beautiful blue eyes. She was soaking wet, her dark hair hanging loose. There was a smudge of dirt on her cheek and he was reminded of the day she'd fallen in Copper's bath, the day he first dared to touch her lovely face.

"Do go on, it's just now getting interesting," Knox grumbled sarcastically as he watched this exchange of tender glances.

Christiana nodded for she too wanted to hear the rest.

"While I was talking to Blue Flower, Brother Adams came in and said Raven's Claw had been captured by the soldiers and they were going to hang him after a short trial.

"Blue Flower asked me to go over to the fort to see him and try to make peace between us. She had always been disappointed that we didn't get along better. I went to the fort and ran into Old Chenault. He had just returned from the north country with furs to trade. Knox happened to see us talking and was afraid Chenault had told me about his connection with Harrod. He knew Chenault would never go to the American authorities—he's a lone wolf more sympathetic to the Indians than to the Americans pushing west.

"But Knox knew I'd tell your father about him and was afraid it would be enough evidence for his committee. So he came up with the idea of letting Raven's Claw escape and blaming it on me. He figured if Raven's Claw didn't get me, the militia would. Knox went to the captain with

246

the report then asked for a transfer to Falls Church with the 10th Virginia militia.

"The captain believed his story—" Stephan stopped abruptly, a sudden revelation having occurred to him. "And you did too, didn't you?" he looked at her. "Somehow you heard the lie that I helped Raven's Claw escape! I guess that explains a lot." He understood now what had been troubling her since his return.

Christiana could feel her heart beating. "When he placed guards at the house to protect Father from Raven's Claw, they were really waiting there to catch you, if you came."

"Probably." Stephan nodded. "Chenault found out where Knox was headed and told me. I was avoiding your place just in case Raven's Claw did follow me. I didn't want anyone at Dunston to get caught in the crossfire like last time. I still have an occasional bad dream about that night."

"I do too," she mused softly.

He hoped her dream was not as disturbing as was his. It was the same each time. The heart-stopping vision of a cruelly grinning Raven's Claw walking quickly away with Christiana tucked under his arm like a sack of flour, just as a small boy was once carried off by Creek Indians. And just as in the scene of his distant past, the Indian was walking away from the body of a man laying on the ground. The difference between his dream and the reality of his abduction by the Creeks, was that in his dream, the man laying on the ground was himself. A knife with a Shawnee-carved antler handle was buried deep in his heart. Unable to move to save the girl, he would wake up gasping for breath with Christiana's voice screaming his name still ringing in his ears.

He closed his hand tightly around hers and took a deep breath to help dispel the overwhelming anxiety the dream always instilled. Sitting there beside her, holding her soft warm hand, helped him push aside the memory of his nightmare, and he picked up his story once again.

"Anyway, I got to Falls Church just after the 10th Virginia had been ordered to Washington. After your letters telling me Jean-Marc had settled in Alexandria, I decided to look him up and see if anyone over there had any better idea of what was going on than I'd heard so far. When he told me you were here, I couldn't resist the temptation to come see you. It looked like Knox was occupied for awhile anyway.

"Last night when I got back to the clearing, Jean-Marc told me you'd come after Copper." He shook his head in exasperation. "So I came back looking for you. Searched everywhere for you, including in here, then thought you had either slipped back out of the city or had found some friends to stay with. I was just getting ready to head back myself when I spotted Knox riding as proud as you please down the street. I followed him and saw him stop and visit with several of the redcoats and even an officer or two. It was pretty clear they already knew him."

"How?" she asked still unable to believe the man's treachery.

Knox smiled smugly. "As soon as I left your place two weeks ago, instead of reporting to Falls Church, I went on to the bay coast and made connections with Admiral Cochrane at Yorktown. Sailed with them up the Patuxent to Benedict. I was sent ahead to see what kind of defenses were being set up in the city. I don't think Ross believed me when I told them that they could waltz into the city without a problem."

Stephan took up his story again. "The longer I followed him, the madder I got and decided to catch him alone if I could and bring him back to the militia authorities. I lost track of him for a little while, then happened to see them bringing the injured away from the explosion site. I could see he was hurt, but he was walking on his own. I couldn't get him away from them, so I let him see me.

"He and two other soldiers came after me. I lost the other two and ducked back here figuring he'd guess where

I'd go. When he came in, he swung at me, but he was in pretty bad shape and fell down. I didn't even hit him."

Christiana's eyes lit up and her mouth curved into a soft smile. "I believe you," she said. "Do you forgive me for misjudging you again?"

He didn't respond immediately. Finally, with a gleam of pleasure in his eyes he replied, "What's really curious is that three times now when you thought I might be guilty of something, you didn't turn me over to Knox. That's encouraging because it must mean that even though you've had your doubts about me, when it comes right down to it, you're ready to at least hear my side."

"It means more than that, Stephan," she spoke softly now, looking down at her hands in her lap and even blushing a bit. "I've cared deeply for you for a long time. I couldn't bear to see you taken away without hearing your side first. From the beginning, I've hoped my doubts were wrong. I guess by being unpleasant, I was really trying to protect my own heart from being hurt if my suspicions were true."

Stephan gently cradled her right hand in his and lightly kissed her palm. Then he closed her slender fingers over the kiss. "Hold on to that," he whispered.

"Isn't that touching," Knox grumbled, watching through narrowed eyes. "You'll have to consider that a good-bye kiss as soon as the soldiers come this way."

"They're taking their time, aren't they?" Stephan chided. "Perhaps they're eating dinner. It stopped raining some time ago."

"They'll be along," Knox declared rather nervously. "Just settle back there and wait."

"It'll be dark soon, Knox," Stephan stated.

"I've been thinking about that." He looked at Christiana. "Miss Macklin, go over and get that lantern and bring it over here and light it. I may be hurt but not that bad. I'm a light sleeper, so if either of you make a move, I'll know it.

"The redcoats have probably made camp for the night and will finish searching the city in the morning." Leaning his head back wearily, the lieutenant closed his eyes for a moment. Then he roused himself and glared at Stephan. "Just to make sure you don't try anything, Page. Miss Macklin, get that rope from the wall over there and bring it here."

When she hesitated, Knox grinned humorlessly and raised the pistol toward Stephan. His hand seemed quite steady. "If you don't do as I say," he warned, "I'll just have to go ahead and shoot him now to make sure he doesn't give me any trouble tonight."

She reluctantly retrieved the rope from a peg on the stable wall and, following Knox's instructions, made a slip-knot. After placing the loop around Stephan's right wrist, she handed the other end to the gun-wielding soldier.

Pointing the pistol at her, Knox then ordered Stephan to move to the front of the stall where a tether ring was attached to the wall. Next he grabbed Christiana's arm and pulled himself up. Keeping the girl between them with the pistol pointed at her, he directed Stephan to pass the rope through the tether ring and sit down. Knox then ordered Christiana to tie Stephan's wrists together securely, warning her to be sure the knot was tight.

After doing this, Christiana plopped down on the hay next to Stephan. Knox smiled with satisfaction. Stephan couldn't catch him off guard now.

All the while, Stephan was watching the lieutenant's every move. He was getting weaker, and Stephan felt it was only a matter of time before he collapsed. He decided to relax and wait. He certainly did not intend to be turned over to the British, and it looked like he didn't have to worry about that until morning. Considering Knox's appearance, he probably wouldn't have to worry about it at all. But whatever happened, he had Christiana to think about now.

The shadows within the stable deepened as night crept silently over the ravaged city. The night was long and unpleasant, but at last the shadows receded with the silent intrusion of a gray morning mist.

Stephan stirred. His head still throbbed from the blow he'd received from the flying board. His arms ached numbly from being tied. Glancing down, he saw Christiana still sleeping on her thick bed of hay with Copper curled up next to her.

Knox was leaning back against the stall. He seemed to be asleep. For a moment Stephan thought the young officer might be dead, but the moment he moved, Knox opened his eyes and raised the ever-present pistol.

"Well, Knox, I almost thought you'd left us during the night," Stephan commented quietly.

"I told you I wasn't hurt that bad. Now wake Miss Macklin and we'll go introduce you to the admiral."

The man's voice sounded weak but was edged with a dangerous resolve. Stephan knew he was in a deadly frame of mind. He had little to lose by killing Page and only a twisted sense of satisfaction to gain by turning him over to the British. Stephan could see that with Knox feeling as badly as he did, at this point it didn't really matter to the traitor which way it went.

At this point, Christiana awakened. She frowned with dismay when she saw Stephan still tied to the tether ring. When she started to reach for him, Stephan tilted his head slightly toward Knox to remind her of their predicament.

"Good morning, Miss Macklin. You slept well, I hope." The lieutenant's voice sounded cold. She detected the deadly no-nonsense mood of their captor too.

Knox pulled himself up to a wobbly position and directed Christiana to untie the rope from Stephan's wrists. "Lead the way!" he ordered. "Enjoy your walk, Page. It'll be your last one on land for a very long time."

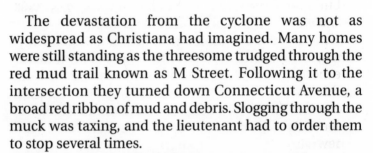

# 26

The devastation from the cyclone was not as widespread as Christiana had imagined. Many homes were still standing as the threesome trudged through the red mud trail known as M Street. Following it to the intersection they turned down Connecticut Avenue, a broad red ribbon of mud and debris. Slogging through the muck was taxing, and the lieutenant had to order them to stop several times.

After they had walked about ten minutes without seeing the first bold red uniform, Stephan finally asked, "Where are all of your redcoat friends, Knox?"

It was easy to see young Knox had been wondering the same thing. Except for the storm's garbage strewn along the streets, the city seemed deserted. It was an eerie sight.

"Stephan, look!" Christiana gasped.

The words caught in her throat as she pointed toward the end of the avenue. There in the bright morning light was a heart-wrenching sight—the blackened shell that had once housed the President of the United States. Tears blurred Christiana's vision as she spotted several government buildings in charred ruins. The sight before them was infuriating.

Christiana turned on Knox with a searing look in her eyes. He stepped back. With some difficulty she controlled her rage.

"I hope you're proud of yourself and your redcoat friends. Well, you haven't won yet. We'll build it again. We will! Better than ever."

Knox smiled weakly, his attitude somewhat less than contrite. "If you do, it'll be with English pounds. Right now General Prevost stands with more than ten thousand British troops at Plattsburg ready to march on New York State."

The lieutenant reclaimed his boldness. "This attack and the one planned for Baltimore were mere diversions and retribution for burning Port Dover last year. Do you expect me to believe that the cowards who wouldn't even stand to defend their own capital will have strength enough— let alone backbone enough—to turn back the British tide?"

He motioned for them to move on. Christiana stuck out her chin and stiffened her back. With her hand tucked in the crook of Stephan's arm, she clutched desperately at his sleeve. Inside she was devastated by the overwhelming news.

Stephan squeezed her hand and whispered quietly, "Remember your father said the redcoats were cocksure of their strength in '76 too."

She smiled gratefully through the tears welling up in her eyes. Although his face was drawn in tight lines, Stephan managed an encouraging grin. And somehow, inexplicably somehow, she knew he was right. No matter how bleak things appeared now, the United States would remain the United States, never again a colony of England.

As the group approached the gutted White House, a voice hailed them from the porch of a nearby house.

"Hello there!"

They turned to see an elderly little man scurrying down the front steps toward them. Through her tears, Christiana realized it was Mr. Howe. She was relieved to see his home had not been damaged by the storm.

"Mr. Howe," she exclaimed with relief. "Where are the soldiers?"

"Christiana, child, are you alright? The Burkes are worried sick. They were just by here looking for you."

"Oh dear. Yes. Yes, I'm fine. Are they alright? Where did they go? And where are the British?"

He chuckled, his eyes dancing with merriment. "Well, my dear, they appear to have tucked their redcoat tails and run. It looks like the good Lord took his hand in this one. He must have figured that if our militia couldn't stand to protect the city, he would have to. So he sent his mighty wind to stop their fun.

"The redcoats took off so fast they left their wounded behind! In fact, what with the storm and the explosion they set off, there were more British soldiers hurt than anybody else. The wounded have been rounded up over by the Patent Office. That's where the Burkes went looking for you.

"Your friend can put his pistol away. There's no one to shoot now." He directed a stern face at the lieutenant. Then he added, "He doesn't look well. Better get him over to the doctor. I heard that Doc Beanes was arrested and taken along with the redcoats, but Dr. Thornton is still here. In fact, he's the one who talked the British into sparing the Patent Office."

The lieutenant's pistol-holding arm had dropped to his side. Stephan thought the young man was going to collapse, but he only stood there with a far-off look in his face, gazing toward the horizon where the people who had promised him a medal had sailed away.

General Ross and Admiral Cochrane had delivered a humiliating blow to Washington, D.C., and were satisfied to march on toward Alexandria. Then Baltimore would feel the blast of their cannons. A freakish wind and rain storm, while it had temporarily unnerved their forces, wasn't going to be taken by them as a serious indication they could not attain their goal of punishing these upstart colonists and regaining a good bit of territory in the process.

The British sailed away from Alexandria after being bribed with goods such as tobacco, cotton, and flour to leave it untouched. They were in high spirits. There was apparently little substance to these so-called independent Americans.

Admiral Cochrane stood on the deck of his flagship bound for the port city of Baltimore. He had been especially eager to wreak havoc on this nest of pirates, the home port of the majority of the privateers who still plagued the Royal Navy and caused embarrassment to the pride of England. He eyed the distant silhouette of the star-shaped fortress at Fort McHenry with a sarcastic smile wondering if it too had been abandoned as Fort Washington had a few days earlier. In his contempt for these ruffian Americans, the admiral found it difficult to understand why it had taken so long to subdue them.

This haughtiness was short-lived. Within the week, Ross was shot and killed by two daring boys of the American militia as he led his troops toward Baltimore. Although the two boys paid with their own lives, their sacrifice helped save the city and deprive the British of a valuable leader. Ross was an especially popular and forceful commander, and his death seemed to take the heart and direction out of the invading land forces. They approached the defenses surrounding the city but lacked the drive to press forward. They finally withdrew.

Admiral Cochrane discovered that not all American officers were as inept as Winder and Wilkinson. Major General Sam Smith, a sixty-two-year-old veteran of the Revolutionary War had been preparing for the attack. His five thousand militiamen were more determined than those who had been caught flatfooted in Washington. In addition to the determined Smith, Fort McHenry had not been abandoned. Under the strong capable leadership of Colonel George Armistead, the thousand soldiers within the fort had supreme confidence. The siege of Baltimore soon gave Cochrane a new outlook on this strange American breed.

Two days later, on September 13, Francis Scott Key awakened to find the American flag still waving above Fort McHenry after a long night of bombardment. The Americans had repelled Cochrane's strongest attack. The thrilling sight inspired Key to write a stirring poem that would soon give the nation a national anthem and a renewed sense of pride.

Yes, things were beginning to look up.

# 27

Further disappointment awaited the British when General Prevost had to retreat without attacking New York. The young American Lieutenant Tom Macdonough soundly defeated the British fleet on Lake Champlain cutting the supply line for Prevost's large invading force. Macdonough's ingenious battle tactics once more proved the excellence of the American navy. By turning Prevost back, Macdonough had broken the impetus of England's invasion attempt through Canada.

On December 24, 1814, peace negotiations were signed in Ghent, Belgium. Most of the hostile activity had ceased. Although it would take three weeks for the news to reach the U.S., the war was over at last.

After the attack on the capital, there was some discussion about changing the seat of government to another city. However, it was not seriously considered. There now seemed to be a strong feeling against giving up the site.

When Mac learned of the decision to rebuild the capital without changing its location, he replied, "As disheartening as it was at the time, perhaps this is what it took to bring a sense of unity to our country. Along with the shame that we allowed it to happen, our people can take pride in the fact we didn't give up there. God still has his hand on this land. Thanks to him, there's finally a stronger sense of nationhood . . . of being Americans."

The holidays promised to be a joyful time and preparations at the Macklin household had been going on in earnest since the first of December.

Christiana looked out through the French doors in the study. Threatening clouds hung low above the bare trees in their back garden. She prayed that the threat of snow would hold off just a few days longer.

The young woman couldn't remember a year when so many people were traveling for the holidays. Travel under perfect weather conditions was not always easy, and wintertime could prove to be especially trying in the lower elevations when roads could change from rough frozen ruts to a shifting sea of mud during unseasonable thaws. As long as travelers were not caught in blizzard conditions or an early thaw, winter travel was not too uncommon, however. Many settlers moving into the frontier west of the Appalachians began their journey before the frozen ground had a chance to thaw, transporting their possessions on sleds across the snow and ice.

So far this winter had been fairly mild. The ground was still frozen with a few patches of snow left behind from the last storm. If it snowed now Christiana knew it still could cause traveling difficulty for everyone converging on the Macklin home.

For the first time in eight years, the whole family was gathering together for the holidays. Ram and Marianne had already arrived with Luke, Amy, and the new baby, making the long trip from Mercy Ridge early enough to allow for weather delays. The twins, their wives, and baby April had just arrived, having sailed from Boston to Yorktown and then overland by stage. Robert, Suzanne, and

Uncle Robbie were driving over from Cherry Hills Farms and scheduled to arrive later today, Christmas Eve.

Eric's family, the Lowes, had gone to Charlottesville to visit his grandfather and had graciously offered their home for overflow sleeping accommodations. They knew the Macklin house would be bursting at the seams. Eric and Mariette had taken their new son to Washington to spend the holidays with Jean-Marc and the Burke family. Plans for Rachel's spring wedding to Mariette's brother were going to be a major subject for discussion during the visit. The engagement party had finally taken place in October and, as Rachel had desired, in Washington.

Christiana had not seen Stephan since the first of September when he had escorted her back to Dunston. His mission for her father concerning Lieutenant Knox had been completed with the arrest of the young traitor. They had later learned that he had escaped the hangman's rope by a few days when he succumbed to lingering complications caused by his injuries from the explosion in Washington. However, his testimony had implicated Rupert and Axel Harrod and several of their employees involved in the treachery of aiding the enemy while making personal profits.

Knox had explained in detail how Rupert had imported many of the supplies from British suppliers, sold them to the U.S. Army and state militias, then siphoned them off gradually, and ultimately sold them to the British Canadians and their Indian allies for inflated prices. His son, Axel, was his main contact for both sides along the Canadian border. Although Axel had escaped to Canada, the publicity about the Harrods alerted the Canadian government to the double dealing; and Axel was arrested by the Canadians and sentenced to live in a bleak little village on an island off the coast of Nova Scotia. Rupert never actually came to trial. Before the case was placed on the court docket, the flagship of his fleet went down in heavy seas off Newfoundland carrying him with it.

Jessica and Christiana couldn't help but feel a little sorry for Clara Caskell. She couldn't quite grasp why there'd been such a furor over her brother and nephew doing business with the Canadians; after all, their money was as good as the next person's, she reasoned. She was sure that someone was badly mistaken that they had any dealings with the Indians at all. Her brother was quite above that sort of thing, she knew for certain. Mr. Caskell while having nothing to do with his brother-in-law's affairs found that the scandal played havoc with his law firm's business. They had gone into seclusion at their Roanoke home to wait out the storm of scandal touching Mrs. Caskell's family. Needless to say, their offer to Eric had long been forgotten; but Mac's apprentice was very happy right where he was now.

Stephan had returned to his Uncle Zephaniah's farm in time to help with the harvest, promising to try to write at least once in a while to let her know he was still among the living. The last note Christiana had received indicated that he planned to be in Dunston by the twenty-third and was bringing his uncle. Stephan's cousin, Sam, had volunteered to send one of his farmhands over to his father's place to oversee the care of the livestock for the holidays. Zephaniah's older son felt it would be good for his father to be away from the farm this Christmas since this was the first Christmas back home without Calhane. Stephan's uncle was finding it difficult to adjust.

Christiana was having a hard time concentrating on anything as the day drew to a close. The excitement of seeing the twins and the newest Macklin child had helped. The house was bursting with life with the addition of two babies, two small children, four young couples, and Uncle Robbie all trying to catch up on each other's lives. In the few spare minutes when Christiana was unoccupied, she caught herself peeking out the windows for some sign of two approaching travelers.

Today, those low-hanging clouds held a snowy burden. She knew it was only a matter of time. Threatening snow in Dunston meant the mountains were already under a thick blanket. She hated to think about Stephan trekking through the gap just west of Roanoke near Big Stone Mountain along the old Kanawha Trail and fighting a snow storm.

After a warm supper of a hearty vegetable soup, everyone gathered in the drawing room to sing carols and sip eggnog. A roaring fire blazed on the hearth. The air was fragrant with the fresh pine boughs of the gaily decorated tree and the many spices mingling with the savory aromas from the kitchen.

As they sang, Christiana looked around the room at the smiling faces touched with the warm glow from the fire. Gran and Jessica each held one of the grandchildren and were obviously delighted to be surrounded with the whole family.

Everyone was especially thankful Mac was with them after his heart attack. These were the dearest people in all the world to her. Her heart was filled with a wonderful joy and yet, it wasn't quite complete. Something—someone—was still missing.

The evening wore on and the candles burned low. One last chorus of "Angels Trumpeting," an old Scottish Christmas chorus, echoed through the house with the Macklin men's deep rich voices blending pleasantly with the dulcet notes of the women. Copper dozed contentedly on the floor beside Christiana.

At the end of the first verse, the dog suddenly raised his head and pricked up his ears. Christiana noticed him leave the room. Thinking he wanted to go outside, she too slipped out of the drawing room.

In the hallway, the big dog stood at the door wagging

his tail excitedly. Her heartbeat quickened as she heard a knock. Holding her breath, she ordered Copper to stay and reached for the doorknob.

The soft glow of the hall candles washed over two men, hats in hand, standing on the threshold. Her heart leapt for joy. She smiled and tried to speak but could only whisper breathlessly, "Stephan."

"Christiana," he returned. The sparkle in his eyes and his smile reflected a delight equal to hers.

Time stood still as the couple drank in the delicious sight of each other. Finally Copper whined and Uncle Zephaniah cleared his throat.

"Oh, my goodness. Forgive me," she blushed, stepping aside to let them enter the warm house. "Please come in."

Copper danced around the two men barking excitedly, at last dissolving into a jubilant bay almost like he was singing. Ruffling the dog's fur, Stephan introduced his uncle.

"I'm so glad you could come, Mr. Logan," Christiana smiled, taking his hand. "I've heard so much about you."

"Thanks for the invite, but just call me Uncle Zeph. Well, son, she's ever' bit as purty as you said. You'd better grab her and give her a hug a'fore I do."

Before Stephan could take her in his arms, the hall filled with people streaming out of the drawing room. In a moment, family members were happily greeting Stephan and meeting Zephaniah, everyone talking at once. After some warm soup, the two weary travelers accompanied Robert, Suzanne, and Uncle Robbie to the Lowes' house.

Christmas day dawned gray and cold with low hanging clouds still threatening snow. Inside the Macklin home, however, the fire burned cheerily in the large kitchen fireplace as a few of the early risers sat around the table drinking coffee and visiting. One by one the others drifted downstairs.

The day sped by quickly with presents and a game of darts and a lot of laughter. After their huge Christmas dinner, Christiana was carrying away the last bit of silverware just as Uncle Zeph walked through the dining room. "That was a fine meal, Christiana. I haven't had the likes since my missus passed to glory."

"I'm glad you enjoyed it, Uncle Zeph. Is there something else I can get for you?"

"Oh, no, no. I'm stuffed to the gills," he declared, patting his sides.

It was then that she noticed Uncle Zeph seemed to want to say something else.

"Is something wrong?" she asked.

Tugging at his ear nervously, he finally decided to come straight to the point. "I wanted to talk with you a minute, alone. That's not easy around here." He grinned affably.

She had to smile.

"It's about Stephan," he added haltingly.

"Yes?"

"He's a fine young man. A girl couldn't do no better. Now, I know he inherited his mother's Irish temper and his father's Scot stubbornness, but he's got a good heart. Even all those years with the Injuns couldn't change that . . . not that I've got anythin' agin' the Injuns. It's just some are a bit more likeable than others."

"I know." She was touched by his attempt to be careful of her feelings since she was part Indian herself.

"He's a hard worker, and you'd never go hungry."

"Uncle Zeph . . ."

He stopped a minute. "You're quite the matchmaker aren't you," she said. "This almost sounds like a proposal."

"In a way it is," he admitted. "He's been pinin' away fer you ever since he come back. Now, I know if you won't come with us to Kaintuck, he'll come back with me alright because he knows I still can't handle the farm by myself, but he won't be fit to live with."

"But Uncle Zeph, he hasn't even asked me to come!" she declared.

The man snorted with an exasperated grin. "He does appear a might slow 'bout speakin' his mind, but then he hasn't had much of a chance that I can see."

Just then, Amy and Luke ran in and dragged Christiana away to the drawing room to read them a new book of children's verses. This went on for nearly a half hour when finally Marianne took Ram aside. Ram smiled as his young wife went to Christiana's rescue. "Come on, children," she said. "Your Aunt Chris has some other things to do now."

Ram returned to his dart game with Stephan but deliberately stopped him in the middle of his turn. He took the darts from Stephan's hand.

"Chris," he called out loud. "I think Copper wants to go out for a walk."

Copper was lying next to the doorway of the drawing room. At the mention of his name, the golden-red dog pricked up his ears.

"Alright," she answered, wondering what her brother was up to.

"That's alright, Christiana, I'll let him out. It seems my turn is over," Stephan replied eyeing Ram curiously.

"Oh, I think Chris had better go with him," Ram insisted. "Remember how the wolves sometimes come around in the snow? He might take off with them."

"Wolves?" Christiana looked at her eldest brother who was the image of his father.

"Yes, wolves. Better take that old walking stick." James had just walked in and quickly realized what was going on.

"Better yet, Stephan, perhaps, you could walk with her. A couple of years ago, the wolves could have had her, but she's grown to be a rather nice little sister, and we'd hate to lose her now." Alex's words echoed her own teasing after his rescue from the British.

264

Christiana blushed but Stephan grinned. "I suppose I wouldn't mind. I imagine nice little sisters are rather rare."

On her way to get her cloak, Christiana caught a glimpse of Uncle Zephaniah who was lighting his pipe. He winked at her through a puff of smoke.

At the door, the couple stepped out on the porch. Large flakes of snow were finally drifting silently to the ground from the low hanging clouds that continued to blot out the sun. The minute Copper was out of the door, he ran through the snow, dashing here and there, snatching at the flakes landing on his nose. Christiana laughed as the animal cavorted through the cold white fluff like a frisky puppy.

As she and Stephan moved along the lane that led out of the village, she finally said, "I like your Uncle Zephaniah very much, Stephan."

"He likes you too. Thanks for inviting us. Losing Calhane was a hard blow. I appreciate your family making him feel so welcome. You're very lucky, Christiana, to have such a family."

"Hmmm, I know," she responded. "I must say, they think quite a lot of you too."

"They do?"

"Obviously. You're the only young man my brothers have ever allowed me to go walking with, unchaperoned. Ever since you first came last year, Father's been taking your side and Mother has agreed with him, not to mention Gran who scolded me from the very beginning for being rude to you." With that, Christiana had to grin.

The couple walked slowly, chatting about Kentucky and the people in Dunston and about Jean-Marc and Rachel's wedding plans. They were oblivious to the chill in the air. The snow created a pearl-like mist that softened the shadows through the trees. It was a time of serenity and quiet— a time for them to be by themselves.

Christiana halted beside the trunk of a bare sugar maple. Looking back, she realized just how far they had walked.

"I suppose we'd better start back. Everyone will begin to wonder about us."

"Christa—"

The sound of his voice made her look up at him. His blue eyes studied her upturned face. "What is it, Stephan? Is something wrong?"

He shook his head slowly as he gently brushed away a snowflake from her pink cheek.

"Christa, I've really missed you," he finally said quietly.

"I've missed you too, Stephan." Her words were barely a whisper.

Suddenly it seemed as though time had stopped and they were moving in slow motion. Stephan drew her to him, closing his arms about her. The large crystalline snowflakes falling about them might just as well have been apple blossoms, for nothing could have penetrated the aura of spring-like warmth that surrounded them when his lips met hers in a long and tender caress.

Finally, he said softly, "I've been wanting to do that since the first moment I saw you last night."

The kiss had taken her breath away. She could only smile. A gentle wind now sighed through the trees like distant violins as they held each other close.

Their precious moment was suddenly interrupted by a sharp bark from Copper. Looking down, they saw him sitting at attention at their feet, cocking his head curiously. He barked again.

"Aw, have a heart, Copper," Stephan begged.

Christiana laughed. Stephan grinned at her ruefully. "Well, he'd better get used to it. I plan on kissing you quite frequently when we're married," he finally said.

"Married?" she exclaimed.

Searching the depths of her dark blue eyes, he said solemnly, "Yes, if you will . . . I know Kentucky is a long way from your family, but we can come back for visits, and they can come to see us—"

He went on without hesitating. "Christa, I finally have something I can offer you. Uncle Zephaniah has made me his partner in the farm. It's a great place. I know you'll love it. There's everything there anyone would ever want or need—except you."

"Oh, Stephan," she whispered.

"I know this seems sudden, but I've thought of little else for a long time, and it isn't easy to get to talk to you alone. You don't have to answer now, just think about it."

"I have," she smiled, "and for a very long time too."

"I can understand if you don't want to leave Duns—what?"

She smiled at him. "I've thought about it for a long time too," she repeated. "Before you came last night, I was so happy to be with my family, but there was still something missing. When you arrived, my happiness was complete. Yes, I will miss my family very much, but I don't think I could bear to be without you ever again. Yes, Stephan, I will marry you."

It took a moment for her words to sink in. When they did, he picked her up and swung around in a dizzying circle with a whoop of joy. Copper barked happily.

Setting her down again, his expression drew sober once more. "You really mean it?"

She nodded with a warm smile, "Yes, Stephan. I love you. And wherever you are, that's where I want to be."

The announcement caused a great excitement throughout the house with almost everyone congratulating them and wishing them the best for their future together. Only Christiana's father seemed a bit subdued by the news. This caused her some concern, and later as she and her mother were in the kitchen preparing to serve the mince pie and plum pudding, she drew up the courage to ask her mother about it.

"I know Father likes Stephan, but he doesn't seem happy about us being married. Why?"

Jessica laughed and hugged her. "Don't worry, darling. He thinks a lot of Stephan. Just give him a little time to get used to the idea. Most fathers are very protective of their daughters and are never really sure any man will ever be worthy of their hands. Your Grandfather McClaren was the same way about your father at first.

"It's especially hard because you're the only girl, youngest child at that. He finds it difficult to accept that you're not still his little Christa crawling up on his lap for a bedtime story . . . and, of course, the fact that Kentucky is so far away doesn't help."

Christiana began slicing one of the pies. She too wished Kentucky was not so far away; however, she had such a deep sense of rightness about her decision that went beyond her initial love for Stephan. She knew somehow that this would be the place where the two of them could live and love and work together, building a home and family and a relationship as deep and enduring as her parents' relationship. If Kentucky was that place, then Kentucky it must be.

On returning to the drawing room to announce dessert in the dining room, the two women discovered the men deep into a conversation about politics, not unusual between Macklin men.

Uncle Robbie was puffing thoughtfully on his pipe. "I fear this slavery issue will someday be the straw to break our fragile country's back. One cannot fight for the cause of freedom while depriving a group of people of their God-given right to be their own man."

Jessica spoke up quickly to dispel the gloom settling

over the group. "Now, Robbie, let's not be discussing such things on this wonderful Christmas day."

"Sorry, Jessie. It's just that the problem seems to be gettin' worse here in Virginia and the rest of the South with the expandin' plantations. We've managed our place all these years with hired free men. Others could too."

"Well, Mr. McClaren," Stephan interjected. "Perhaps you should all move out to Kentucky with us! Few of the small farmers there have need for slaves."

"Aye, if I were a wee bit younger, I'd consider it," Robbie agreed. "I hear that there's a vast amount of good open pasture land just right for raising horses."

That night, Christiana couldn't sleep—too many exciting things to think and dream about. Restlessly tossing and turning, she finally got up and walked over to the window. Through lacy frost patterns on the glass she could see that the snow had stopped. The clouds had cleared, revealing a brilliant moon that cast a sprinkle of glittering diamonds across the newly fallen snow. This magical quality of the fantastic dream world outside only enhanced her jubilant mood. Nothing could spoil her happiness now.

Dreamily surveying the shimmering wonderland before her, her attention wandered to the edge of the trees across the lane from her house.

"What was that?" she thought. "Oh, it must be my imagination." Yet for just an instant Christiana did think her eyes detected movement along the dark fringe of trees.

She told herself it was nothing. But suddenly she found herself shivering as an unexplainable sudden dread worked its icy fingers up her spine.

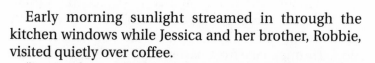

# 28

Early morning sunlight streamed in through the kitchen windows while Jessica and her brother, Robbie, visited quietly over coffee.

"Jessie, I hate to break up the party," he said in his thick Scottish burr, "but we've been here two days now, and we must get back to Cherry Hills while the weather's clear. I don't like to leave ol' Anderson in charge too long. He gets dictatorial after a while."

"I understand, Robbie," Jessica replied with her cup in her hands. "Hasn't it been a wonderful holiday! I just wish Mother and Papa could have been here to see all the children."

"Aye, they'd be very proud. They're a fine lot, Jessie, and it looks like the newest addition will fit in well."

Jessica blinked back an unexpected tear. "Yes, Stephan's a fine young man. I just wish Kentucky wasn't quite so far away. Oh, Robbie, they've grown up so fast. Our nest will soon be empty."

"That's the way of life, Jess. You'd not have it different. And look, they keep poppin' back to the nest for a visit now and again with chicks of their own."

They both chuckled as Luke ambled sleepily through

the door. The little dark-haired boy climbed onto Jessica's lap and hugged her neck.

"It just seems that it's happening so quickly."

"Don't ya fret about their short engagement now." Robbie's accent sounded more and more like their father everyday. "You know Christiana. She doesn't make such important decisions impetuously. She knows her own mind and heart, and in this case a week-long engagement isn't too short. Besides, as she said, it might be years before her whole family is together at one time again. They'll be fine, just fine."

"It was very sweet of you to give them a mare and stallion for a wedding present," Jessica added.

"Well, if the pasture land there's as good as they say, maybe someday they'll have horses to rival our own Virginia thoroughbreds!"

"Christa said you invited them to come with you today to make their choices." Turning her attention to Luke she continued, "Well, my precious little one, are you hungry for some breakfast? Your daddy and grandfather have already been up and away with your uncles on a hunting trip, so after breakfast, we're going to bake some applesauce cookies to surprise them when they get back."

The youngster whispered in her ear, and Jessica smiled. "Yes, if you eat all of your breakfast, you can help drop them in the pan."

Later that afternoon, the sun was dipping low above the western forested hills as Christiana and Stephan were returning from Cherry Hills Farm.

"If you consider Uncle Robbie's gift as part of my dowry, do you feel like you've made a good bargain?" she asked with a teasing lilt to her voice.

Stephan reined in the team in front of the stable. "Hmmm," he considered her words for a moment. "They are the finest horses I've ever seen." Then grinning slyly at her he added, "And you along with them? Just a minute." Leaning toward her, he stole a kiss then nodded. "Yeh, I think it's a pretty fair deal."

The mischievous twinkle in his eyes sobered as the couple sat together before getting down. "You're the fairest, most wonderful thing that has ever happened in my life," Stephan told her.

Just then Copper jumped up from the floorboard. His scruff was bristled, and he fairly flew out of the carriage. Stephan grumbled, "I'm going to have to have a long talk with him."

Christiana chuckled. "It's probably that old lynx that's been worrying him lately. I'll go see what he's up to; then I'll fix us a cup of tea while you take care of the team."

After helping her down from the carriage, Stephan watched his bride-to-be follow Copper's hastily made trail through the snow and around the house. Whistling as he worked, Stephan quickly rubbed down the horses and put fresh hay in their stall mangers. He'd been whistling a lot lately. "And why not," he thought. "Life is wonderful."

Stephan headed for the house, rubbing his hands together against the cold. That hot cup of tea was sounding better and better. Looking to the western sky, he noticed level blue-gray cloud banks layered against the pale, nearly colorless background just above the horizon. Such a sky hinted of more snow before morning.

Stephan hung his hat and heavy coat in the hallway and started for the kitchen when Jessica called from the drawing room.

"Stephan, you're back." Joining him in the hall, she asked, "How was your visit to Cherry Hills?"

"Fine. Mr. McClaren's a very generous man. The pair of horses he's given us are the best I've ever seen."

"Good," she smiled, "Where's Christa?"

"She's fixing some tea. She probably came in the back."

The kitchen was warm and fragrant with the aroma of a rich beef stew bubbling in the pot hanging in the fireplace.

Stephan looked around the room. "Where's Christiana?" he asked.

"With you we thought," Gran answered as she lifted baby April out of the baby-tender chair.

"She came around the back following Copper." Stephan glanced toward the back door.

"Copper?" Marianne had just walked in the room with little Luke right behind her. "Luke wanted to go out and play with Copper a few minutes ago, but I told him he was with you."

Stephan walked toward the back door. Opening the door he quickly scanned the garden. No one was there. Just then Luke tugged at Stephan. "Copper in!" he jabbered.

Stephan stepped back and picked him up. "You saw Copper?"

Luke nodded.

"Did you see your Aunt Christiana?"

The little boy shook his head no. "Copper in!" he repeated pointing outside.

"Where's Copper?" Stephan asked, wondering why the boy would be pointing outside.

In exasperation, the youngster placed his hands on either side of Stephan's face and looked him squarely in the eye. "Copper in! Man shut!"

"Luke—"

Marianne suspected a toddler's vivid imagination but Stephan quickly put the child down and stepped out on the back porch again. A muffled bark was coming from the direction of the spring house at the back of the garden.

"Copper's in the spring house!" he declared.

Racing across the large backyard, Stephan noticed tracks in the snow. They were paw prints mingled with a lady's small shoe dusted by the trailing hem of a cloak.

The spring house door was barred from the outside. Copper now began to bark furiously. The snow in front of the small stone building looked trampled and hard.

A sudden cold gripped Stephan's insides and then he saw it: a single track of large footprints—moccasin prints—deep in the snow leading into the surrounding forest. No other footprints appeared.

With a dim hope that Christiana was inside, Stephan quickly unlatched the door. The big dog leapt through the open door past him, wagging his tail.

Stephan stepped inside and closed his eyes in anguish. The threatening words of Raven's Claw echoed in his mind: "It's not over!" Suddenly he faced the nagging uncertainty he had felt when hearing about Raven's Claw's death. Over the past few months the menacing figure of his adopted brother still haunted his dreams. He could not forget that awful night in Mac's study and the look of terror on Christiana's face as she watched Raven's Claw, poised with a knife, challenging him. Although he'd never understood the hatred that had grown within Raven's Claw toward him, he had realized that night that the venomous threat was a promise meant to be kept. As much as he had wanted to believe it was over, he had never really been convinced.

"Stephan, what's wrong?" Jessica's voice shouted from behind him.

He turned to look into her face, suddenly pale with anxiety. How could he tell her?

Jessica searched his face. "Stephan?"

"Raven's Claw," he finally announced grimly. "He's got her."

"No!" Jessica gasped and stumbled back.

Stephan caught her arm to steady her. Squeezing her hand, he reassuringly vowed, "Don't worry. I'll find them. I'll bring her back."

With that, Stephan raced back to the house. After gathering his coat and hat, he hurried into Mac's study to retrieve the rifle over the mantle. He wasn't going to waste precious minutes going all the way to the Lowes' for his own. But the rack was empty. He remembered the hunting trip. There wasn't a weapon left in the house.

Then the dull glint of steel caught his eye. He spotted a bone-handled Shawnee knife on the mantle. It was the one Raven's Claw had thrown at Mariette. The appearance of this very knife in his nightmare flashed across his mind and made him pause a moment, but only a moment. There was no time to waste worrying about some bad dream. Grabbing the knife, he slipped it in his belt and headed toward the kitchen.

Jessica was busily placing the cap on a canteen filled with hot coffee. Marianne handed her a knapsack with a loaf of freshly baked bread. Jessica handed the two items to Stephan. "You may need a warming drink on your way back."

His face was set in stern determination. "Keep Copper here," he directed. "He'll only warn Raven's Claw I'm coming."

Jessica hugged him tightly.

"Be careful," she said aloud as the back door slammed shut.

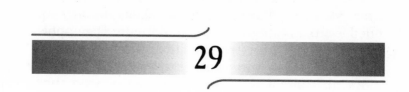

**29**

The snow-shrouded trees cast cold, deep blue shadows across the terrain as Stephan jogged along the clearly visible trail of tracks that wound deep into the forest. With cold fury, he could see by the distance between footprints that the White Shawnee was carrying Christiana and moving quickly, but not as quickly as he would if he were trying to escape completely. Stephan knew that Raven's Claw was luring him into a trap by using the one bait that would, without a doubt, bring Stephan to him on his own ground. His pace quickened as he thought of Christiana.

Stephan's breath was coming hard and his lungs were aching from the exertion and cold. Slowing his pace, he tried to push beyond his anger and focus on the situation with clearer reasoning and less volatile emotion. As cunning as Raven's Claw was, it would do neither Christiana nor himself any good to run recklessly into the trap. They couldn't be too far ahead. He had to keep a sharp wary eye open. He suddenly felt that every lesson he'd ever learned from Wolf Stalking and the Shawnee had been preparing him for this very moment. Against Raven's Claw, he would need every skill acquired from his Indian teachers.

Suddenly the tracks veered to the left although a natural break in the thicket ahead continued straight. Stopping a moment he searched a wide circle around him. Nothing was moving in the failing light. Not one bird song sounded in the hushed chill air. As the shadows began closing in beneath the trees, he had to fight back the growing anger that would only goad him into the mindless chase that Raven's Claw wanted. Still, he must catch up with them before dark or it would be next to impossible to follow the trail until dawn.

Ahead through the narrow clearing of the natural path, he could see the one-man trail resume again some hundred feet along. He started on the shorter path to intercept the tracks again wondering why Raven's Claw had veered from this trail. There was no sign the Indian had been this way unless . . . Suddenly something tugged at his foot. Instantly he dropped to his knees. A loud swoosh whizzed above his head as a large pine bough whipped across the path. Had he been running as before, he would have tripped the cord before realizing it.

It was an old trick of forest warfare. A flexible tree limb had been tied back just at eye level. When the trip cord was released, the bough would lash across the trail striking the victim in the face. While not deadly in itself, the blow could momentarily blind the person, making him easy prey for an enemy lying in wait.

Stephan crouched there a moment, waiting, his eyes darting from shadow to shadow. Not the hint of movement anywhere. This trap was meant only to punish or to taunt, not to kill. Not yet. Raven's Claw must have rigged the trap days ago before the latest snowfall. The thought that this had all been planned as Raven's Claw lurked about waiting for the right opportunity made him curse under his breath. Now, he would have to move with extreme care for he couldn't trust even the unblemished snow to be safe passage.

Swinging back, the man entered the narrower trail to follow the tracks through the thicket. Then through the gathering gloom, he detected a shadow moving low to the ground. Then another appeared, and another. Wolves! He was downwind, and they were moving away from him. Slowly proceeding along the tracks, he could see the animals criss-crossing the trail. It didn't take him long to realize they were following the scent.

The sight of a second set of smaller footprints caused him mixed feelings. Christiana was walking now so she must be alright. His temper flared because she was being rushed along roughly. The tracks showed her staggering here and there.

Soon the wolves slowed down and began to spread out in a circle. Stephan realized Raven's Claw wasn't far. As he picked up a sturdy limb lying near the trail, he saw them only forty yards away, moving along the edge of a low bank in a dry creek bed. He drew the Shawnee knife from his belt.

Apparently Raven's Claw had not yet noticed they were being stalked by the wolf pack. Christiana was walking in front of her captor. Even in the dimming light Stephan could tell she was near exhaustion when she stumbled and the Indian hurried her along.

There was no time for a stealthy approach. Shouting and waving the makeshift club, he charged forward. "Ayiii! Wolves! Ayiii!"

The wolves stopped, looked about quickly and broke from their circle to disappear into the trees.

Stephan's screams pierced the silence of the forest. Christiana whirled about to see a figure charging at them like a phantom in the night. In the same instant she saw the wolves.

Then Raven's Claw saw them too. He quickly drew his knife and pistol from his belt. Raising the gun, he fired at one of the disappearing wolves. When he spotted

Stephan, a cruel grin replaced the fear that had seconds before etched his scarred face. Raven's Claw stuffed the pistol in his belt and waited.

Christiana had been praying Stephan would find them. From the moment that Raven's Claw had jumped out from behind the spring house, clipping her on the chin and carrying her half-dazed into the forest, she had prayed he would find them quickly. But now, seeing Raven's Claw poised with his knife, she suddenly wished he had not.

Almost without thinking, Christiana grabbed the Indian's arm and reached for the knife. Instantly, he seized her wrist and slammed her back against the creek bank.

Raven's Claw turned just in time to see Stephan flying through the air toward him. Christiana's distraction had thrown the Indian off balance. His knife was turned away from his intended target, and the two men crashed into the snow-covered rocks of the creek bed.

Christiana watched in horror as Raven's Claw flipped Stephan over his head and scrambled to his feet to dive on top of him with his ready knife. Stephan clutched the wrist of the knife-wielding hand and smashed it against a rock so hard that the weapon flew into the snow. The two men scrambled to their feet, circling a moment. Stephan tossed his knife aside, refusing the advantage of being armed when his opponent was not. Raven's Claw immediately leapt forward and they began exchanging vicious blows.

Raven's Claw was a taller man by about four inches, and he outweighed Stephan by at least thirty pounds. However, his bitter jealousy could not match the fury he had unleashed within Stephan. The Indian had underestimated the power that could be generated by a loving protective instinct. Always confident of his superior physical strength, Raven's Claw had not counted on any inner resources giving Stephan such surprising power. Stephan finally struck a last jaw-cracking blow that sent Raven's Claw tumbling to the ground to stay.

Falling to his knees, Stephan roughly turned over his semiconscious adopted brother and wrenched his hands behind his back. Ripping the leather headband from his head, Stephan bound the man's hands.

When he finally stood up, Christiana rushed over to throw her arms about him, choking back sobs of relief.

"Are you alright? Did he hurt you?" he asked breathlessly.

"I'm alright now," she trembled. "Oh, Stephan, I was so frightened for you."

"It's over now," he soothed, pressing her head against his chest again. "Everything will be alright."

"He said he'd laid all kinds of traps for you," she continued, still clinging fearfully to him.

"I only ran into one. He must not have reached the others yet."

It was almost dark now. Stephan inhaled a deep breath of cool air. "We need to find some shelter for the night and build a fire. We'll probably have more snow before morning."

The temperature had begun to drop with the darkening curtain of night. "We passed a rock ledge overhang back along the creek," Christiana said through chattering teeth.

Stephan retrieved the knife he'd tossed aside and the pistol Raven's Claw had dropped from his belt and handed the pistol to her. "Here, hold onto this," he told her as he slipped the knife back in his belt. He then pulled the Indian to his feet.

The three people moved back along the creek to find the small alcove washed out along the bank. About four feet tall and six feet wide, it was recessed under a rocky ledge about three feet into the bank.

Stephan built a fire. Grateful for the warm coffee, he and Christiana shared the bread in his knapsack.

Using the lead shot from the small leather pouch as well as powder from the powder horn Raven's Claw had carried, Stephan loaded the pistol. He returned it to Christiana when he'd finished. "Keep an eye on him. If he makes a wrong move, use it. I'm going after some more wood. We'll need it before the night is over."

Raven's Claw was laying back against the earthen bank across the fire from her. In the flickering light she saw a face with strong features that could have been quite attractive. The ragged scar along his right cheekbone from Copper's attack did not detract as much as the meanness smoldering in his blue eyes and the grimly wicked smile that seemed to twist his features rather than enhance them.

The Indian watched Stephan walk away and the grim smile touched the corner of his mouth. "He should have finished me when he had the chance. Your father's prison cannot hold Raven's Claw." His arrogant manner was not only offensive but also intimidating.

"After Lieutenant Knox and Mr. Chenault's testimony about your responsibility in the death of the members of the inspection commission last year, you won't be in prison long." Her words came stronger and more confident than she truly felt inside.

He spat on the ground. "Bah! The White man's hanging rope causes me no fear."

"Perhaps not, but God's judgment afterwards ought to," she answered with certainty.

Just then, they heard a dull metallic snap and an agonized cry just a few yards away in the darkness.

She jumped up. "Stephan!"

The long silence was broken finally by a gasping reply. "Stay there."

"Stephan?" She searched the darkness just beyond the circle of the fire's light.

A low sinister chuckle rippled through the night air. She turned around furiously. "What have you done?"

"I think the great Yaro'ka-i has just found the bear trap I left for him."

She trembled and found herself taken aback by the rage this man aroused in her. She had never thought herself capable of such extreme loathing against anyone, and it was an unnerving discovery.

"Stephan? Stephan, I'm coming to help you."

"No! Stay there! Watch him! Just give me a little bit—"

His voice was strained with agony and she could hardly bear waiting there but she did. Before long she heard another moan of pain and a loud snap. "Good," she thought, "he's been able to pull himself free of the trap."

Slowly stepping away from the fire toward the sound of his voice, she watched Raven's Claw warily. Finally, Stephan appeared, supporting himself with a heavy limb used as a crutch and dragging one leg. Christiana hurried to him and helped him back to the fireside.

Raven's Claw waited without moving, content to see what damage his devious device had done.

As Stephan settled gingerly to the ground, Christiana could see a tear in his knee-high moccasin just above the ankle.

Wincing, he moved to find a more comfortable position. "Thanks to Blue Flower's double-skin leggings," he said, "it didn't cut as deep as it might have, but my leg's broken."

"Oh, Stephan." Christiana's heart reached out to him as she knelt beside him.

He pulled out his knife. "Cut the top down a bit so we can stop the bleeding," he directed her.

She handed him the Indian's pistol. With a frown, she examined his four bleeding puncture wounds and was thankful to see that the bone was not displaced.

The most immediate problem was to stop the bleeding. Since the area was already swelling she quickly tore the bottom ruffle off her petticoat and wrapped the

282

wound only enough to slow the bleeding. She then cut the straps from the knapsack. Using two straight branches broken into equal lengths, she bound the two splints on either side of the break.

"You're pretty good at that." Stephan grimaced from the pain when she tied the splints.

"When you grow up with four older brothers, someone is always breaking something. Gran Barton was a doctor's wife and has taught Mother and me a few things."

Retrieving the canteen from its resting place by the fire, she offered it to Stephan who took some warming sips and eased back against the bank. Christiana sat down beside him to watch him closely, praying that the bandage would stop the bleeding. All the while Raven's Claw leaned against the far bank with a sullen smirk on his face.

Soon Christiana noticed that the fire was dying down. "Stephan, we're going to need more wood soon," she whispered.

"I dropped several good pieces out there," he told her. "It's not far."

"Will you be alright?" she asked, eyeing Raven's Claw suspiciously.

Stephan forced a grin and nodded.

Christiana then set out to find the wood. As she began picking it up, she spotted the black outline of the trap silhouetted against the snowy background, its steel jaws snapped tight. She shuddered and turned her back on the hateful thing. She bent down to pick up one last piece of wood.

Then she heard a low growl. Her blood chilled when she looked up to see two golden-green eyes reflecting the faint glow from the fire. A wolf!

With agonizing care she stepped back slowly, resisting the temptation to turn and run. Painstakingly, she inched backwards. With each step back, the huge animal advanced stealthily toward her.

As she neared the fire, she spoke in a steady calm tone. "Stephan, the wolves—"

Instantly, the crack of a pistol shot echoed through the woods. The predator stopped and turned, running off to disappear in the shadows. Christiana ran back to the fire.

Then, just as Stephan clasped her hand, a movement across the fire drew their attention. Raven's Claw was crouched on one knee. He had managed to work his hands free of the leather strip. Stephan grabbed the knife and braced himself.

"You've used your shot, and you'll need that knife, for I think I'll leave you to the wolves," the Indian said with a sneer. "They've got the scent of your blood now. As soon as the fire dies, so will you."

Raven's Claw could imagine no death worse than being torn by wolves, and he found great pleasure that this should be Page's fate. With these chilling words, he quickly disappeared into the darkness.

A blood-curdling howl nearby reverberated through the cold darkness. Christiana huddled closer to Stephan. An answering howl sounded closer, and suddenly two ominous shadows flashed by. Christiana buried her face against Stephan's shoulder expecting to experience the horrible reality of sharp fangs at any moment. When it did not happen, she looked up. Stephan was watching the flames of the low burning fire.

"The fool," he said. "He would have been safe here with us. Strange . . . Old Wolf Stalking warned him—"

A loud cry suddenly pierced the darkness followed by a dreadful rumble of savage growls. In a moment it was over. Only silence filled the night forest outside their little shelter. Then this silence was punctuated by the mournful eerie howl of another wolf.

The sound raised the hair on the back of Christiana's neck. She realized that instead of escaping the wolf pack by retreating in the dark and leaving the young couple as

284

bait, Raven's Claw had actually drawn the hungry wolves away from them. Laying her head back against Stephan's shoulder, she closed her eyes in an attempt to forget everything that had just happened.

Resting his cheek against her soft dark hair, Stephan patted her shoulder comfortingly. He felt relieved yet saddened. Two lives—Wolf Stalking and Raven's Claw—had been unnecessarily wasted by bitter hatred and resentment.

The howl of the wolf had barely died away when the sound of gunfire suddenly shattered the darkness.

"Christa!"

"Chris!"

Christiana recognized her father and Ram's voices. Jumping to her feet, she started calling in answer. Finally she spotted the lights of several torches and the dark silhouettes of men on horseback.

"Over here, Father!" she yelled as she ran into the woods toward the lights. "Over here!"

The lights moved toward her and in a minute five riders had reined to a halt in a ring around her. Mac dismounted and hugged her tightly. Then the twins and Ram were beside them, all hugging her in turn. Uncle Zephaniah was there too. She led them to Stephan who had pulled himself up to stand on one leg and welcome the rescue party. Within a short time, the entire group was on its way home.

As Christiana rode behind Mac along the trail toward home, she asked, "Father, what about Raven's Claw?"

Mac turned slightly in the saddle and patted the arms that encircled his chest. "The wolves finished their work before we could scare them off. You'll have nothing to fear from him ever again."

# Epilogue

Rachel smiled as a joyful tear streaked down her cheek. She was reading a letter she had just received from Kentucky.

January 13, 1815

The only thing missing at the wedding was my dearest friend—you. I pray you'll forgive me, but there was no time to plan for anything other than a ceremony with the family in attendance.

I've been so blessed all my life, Rachel, and I'm so happy now. I can't help wondering why the Lord has been so good to me. I pray the same happiness for you and Jean-Marc, dear friends.

Stephan's leg is much better, and soon he'll be able to get about without a cane. He is so wonderful. He said that maybe our departure for Kentucky was delayed by his broken leg so Mother and Father would have a chance to get used to the idea of us being married. I think it helped them not to miss everyone so much after having had a house full of people.

I do miss Mother and Father and Gran, but they've promised to come for a visit in the spring. It really is lovely here, even in the dead of winter. I can hardly wait to see it come spring.

When we first arrived, we spotted a large nest in one of the tallest trees along the ridge at the eastern edge of the farm. It's an eagle's nest, Stephan says. It's almost as if the Lord has placed it there to assure us that this is where we belong.

The farm is larger than I imagined, and the house needs a little work—a woman's touch. It's been ten years since Stephan's aunt passed away.

Please try to come visit after your wedding. I'll be there in spirit, if not in person. Give everyone our love.

Sincerely, Christiana

P.S. Copper sends his love too.

"She's amazing," Rachel commented after reading the letter to Jean-Marc. "She sounds as though they've never had any trouble. But they have had their share of difficult times."

"Yet they've never let those times obscure the good."

Jean-Marc was studying a newly purchased painting by a budding artist reflecting the style of the great C. W. Peale. It was a dramatic scene of a thunderstorm threatening a frontier hunting party. In the lead was a buckskin clad character with strong features pointing toward the sky. Conspicuous against the darkness of the thunderclouds was a magnificent bald eagle fearlessly facing the storm's fury. In one shadowy corner cringed a raven seeking shelter under the low hanging boughs of a fir tree.

The moment the young Frenchman saw the painting, he immediately thought of Stephan Page and the Macklins. Now, he drew Rachel's attention to the painting. "Just as the dark areas of this painting emphasize the light, together they create an inspiring picture." Taking her hand in his, he continued, "The Macklins seem to come through their difficult times stronger. I'm sure it's because they stay together, upholding each other."

Rachel was captivated by her fiancé's voice as he set the canvas aside and leaned closer to say, "Just as we, mon cheri, will face the good and the bad together, always. But I think there will be more good than bad. In this country it could be no other way!"